P9-DIA-118

RH

The
Guest
House

Center Point
Large Print

**This Large Print Book carries the
Seal of Approval of N.A.V.H.**

The
Guest
House

Erika Marks

CENTER POINT LARGE PRINT
THORNDIKE, MAINE

This Center Point Large Print edition
is published in the year 2013 by arrangement with
NAL Signet, a member of Penguin Group (USA) LLC,
a Penguin Random House Company.

This is a work of fiction. Names, characters, places,
and incidents either are the product of the author's
imagination or are used fictitiously, and any
resemblance to actual persons, living or dead,
business establishments, events, or locales
is entirely coincidental.

The text of this Large Print edition is unabridged.
In other aspects, this book may vary
from the original edition.
Printed in the United States of America
on permanent paper.
Set in 16-point Times New Roman type.

ISBN: 978-1-61173-938-1

Library of Congress Cataloging-in-Publication Data

Marks, Erika.
The guest house / Erika Marks. — Center Point Large Print edition.
pages ; cm
ISBN 978-1-61173-938-1 (library binding : alk. paper)
1. Large type books. I. Title.
PS3613.A754525G83 2013b
813′.6—dc23

2013026180

To my parents, my sister, and my brother,
for time together,
and the stories we will never tire of telling.

The
Guest
House

Harrisport, Massachusetts
July 1966

*R*oad hog!" Edie Worthington yelled into a fresh cloud of exhaust that a speeding Mercedes Gullwing had left in its wake.

She stopped her ferocious pedaling long enough to shove back the sweaty red tendril that had been plaguing her the entire way back from the sandwich shop. If she'd had a pocketknife, she'd have pulled her bicycle over into the sandy shoulder and chopped off every last infuriating lock right then and there.

She gripped her handlebars and glared down at the bulging lunch bag in her basket, thinking that what she really wanted to do was line up every damn tuna sandwich in the middle of the road and ride over each one slowly, back and forth, until they were waffled with tire tracks and flat as pancakes.

Did those boys think she'd joined her father's building crew so she could spend the entire time fetching their damn lunch and picking up their bent nails like some kind of steel-toed maid? Her father had warned her it wouldn't be easy being the only girl on a five-man crew, but she'd insisted that she wanted to be a builder. It had been a dream since she was six years old. While every other little girl in Harrisport had been dressing baby dolls and pouring pretend tea, she'd been fighting the boys for a turn with Lincoln Logs. But how was she supposed to learn anything if all they ever let her do was organize drill bits?

It hadn't helped, of course, that this job was one of the biggest they'd ever had: building the guest house for Garrison Moss and his prickly wife, Lois. The Mosses were wash-ashores from North Carolina who'd partnered with a firm in Boston and found themselves smitten with the Cape after their first visit five years earlier. They had one son named Tucker, a few years older than she was; Edie had seen him in town the summer before and sized him up from afar, as she did with all summer people, especially those who paid for their Cokes with twenty-dollar bills.

Another car sped by; she reached up and pulled hard on the brim of her straw hat to secure it. Now the turn to the private dirt road was in sight. Birch Drive. Finally. She'd get off the main road and be bathed in shade, left to ride in peace and quiet for the remainder of her trip.

And maybe, just maybe, she wouldn't deliver pancakes when she got there.

Part One

1

Harrisport, Massachusetts
July 2012

*I*t was like opening a summer house after a long, dark winter.

That was how Lexi always thought of the start of peak season in Harrisport. Sure, it was a whole town and not a single dwelling, but in her mind, the rituals were the same. In fact, if you sat at the best booth in Dock's, the one that had the clearest view of the village, like she was doing now while she waited for Kim to arrive, you could watch the transformation in its entirety. Almost overnight, Main Street would blink awake. The nine interminably plodding months that comprised fall, winter, and spring would practically vanish with the snap of a shade. Shop windows that rarely saw more than a few holiday decorations between Labor Day and July first would be stripped bare and dressed in a matter of hours. Overhangs unfurled like petals; sandwich boards came out and clapped into position on the sidewalk. Ladders went up and shopkeepers climbed them, ready to soap off winter's grime and scan the horizon like newly appointed captains at the bows of their ships.

But it wasn't just the store owners who jumped to attention. Preparing for the rush of summer people, or "wash-ashores," as they were called on Cape Cod, was the responsibility of every local resident of Harrisport. Babysitter or fire chief, mail carrier or bar back, your world became a lot busier and (hopefully) a lot more flush when peak season arrived, because once the summer families returned to their cottages, the punch lists and the parties would follow. There were celebrations to cater, linen and silk to dry-clean. Repairs and renovations, planting and weeding. Roofs that had failed to endure particularly harsh winters, pipes and wiring that were finally showing their age. By July, contractors and landscapers would arrive at Pip's to get their morning coffee a little earlier, and stroll into Dock's for their after-work beers a little later. Traffic would increase through town, thicken and slow. Roy's Bread Basket would sell out of their pecan toffee rolls before nine on a weekday, and if you wanted a table at the Osprey House you'd better have made your reservation a week earlier.

Fourth of July arrived like a car horn, a clear and startling burst of sound signaling that it was time to get out of the way; summer had begun.

Two years away from it, two winters, two summers, and Lexi marveled at how little had changed. When she'd returned from her graduate program in photography at the Royal Academy of

Arts in London the week before, she'd expected to find alterations, stitches that had surely come apart in the town's seams. But sitting here now, sipping her margarita in a plastic cactus-stemmed glass that might have been as old as she was, catching recognizable whiffs of fried clams and sunbaked Naugahyde as she watched familiar faces file through the tavern's open door, she wasn't so sure.

But what had she expected? Two years away was a drop in the bucket after thirty-two of them. She could have been gone from Harrisport for fifty years and come back to find her hometown the same: her mother and older brother, Owen, still running their father's construction business in town; her best friend, Kim, still owner of the natural-food store.

Every bit of it, exactly the same.

"Sorry I'm late." Kim Donnelly slid into the booth, swinging her beach bag–size purse across her lap and landing it on the bench beside her. "Jay couldn't find Miles's uniform. Miles freaks out if he doesn't have his lucky socks." She took a moment to shift the straps of her sleeveless shirt before she saw the electric green margarita in front of her. Her face lit up. "Please tell me that's what I think that is."

"You really have to ask?" Lexi directed her narrowed gaze at the bar. "I actually had to tell the new bartender how to make it. What happened to Kenny?"

"He moved to Phoenix," said Kim, pushing back her blond hair and scooping up her drink. "And Johnny's not new; he's been here over a year."

"A year? And he doesn't know how to make a mint margarita? Shame on him. Shame on *you*." The women raised their drinks and clinked them. "To summer," said Lexi.

"To summer," Kim repeated. She took a long sip, moaning with pleasure. "God, I've missed that taste." She smiled at Lexi across the booth. "I can't believe you remembered our drink."

"Of course I remembered. I was gone two years, not twenty."

"Trust me; some days it felt more like twenty."

Lexi reached for her best friend's hand and gave it a loving squeeze. For years, too many to count, they had been meeting at the dockside restaurant, sinking into the same booths, resting their elbows on the same gnarled tabletops and chipping away at the dents in the thick shellac with their thumb-nails, falling into the same routines with the rest of their neighbors, all of them bound to the cycles of the seasons, as linked as the tides to the moon.

"Look at us. . . ." Kim glanced around at the busy tables and sighed. "It's like we're all a bunch of kids trying to smoke the rest of our cigarettes before our parents come home."

Lexi had to agree. For all the anticipation and excitement of summer, there was a palpable melancholy too. As grateful as everyone was for

16

the infusion of outsiders and their money, a part of each resident couldn't help resenting the loss of their quiet, their privacy. But it was always a trade. Everyone knew that and accepted it.

For Lexi, that trade had never been a begrudging one. Once upon a time, her anticipation of peak season was colored only in shades of euphoria. The first week of July once meant more than just the arrival of crowds and longer lines for gas and everything else. For Lexi, it had meant the return of Hudson Moss, the return of a joy she'd kept tidily closed up all winter, just like the great Moss cottage itself, sealed up safe from the coldest, quietest months, just waiting for summer's cue to throw open the sashes of her own heart, to be the object of Hudson's affections once again. Yet no matter how excited he had appeared, no matter how deeply he'd kissed her or how long he'd made love to her, Lexi could never fully shake the feeling that for him, life in Harrisport would never be real—only a holiday life; that his real world had existed in the nine months between September and June—months that for her had been utterly purposeless without him. And just when the vines of her trust had finally grown thick and sturdy around her heart, he'd yank them out again like weeds.

A silver Porsche sped past the window; Lexi followed its path reflexively.

Kim smiled. "You still look, don't you?"

"Old habits." Lexi reached for her drink to cover the flush of guilt that climbed her cheeks. Eleven years after the last time Hudson Moss's prized sports car had cruised the streets of Harrisport, and she was like one of Pavlov's dogs whenever a similar car cut through her field of vision.

"I do it too," admitted Kim. "It's like I still expect them to be here every summer. You heard about the house, right?"

Lexi frowned quizzically.

"They're finally putting it on the market," explained Kim. "Thank God. That poor thing was rotting like a piece of fruit."

The Mosses, sell their prized house? Lexi struggled to accept the news. For years, long before she'd ever fallen in love with Hudson Moss and been allowed entrance into his family's vaulted rooms, she'd coveted the Mosses' shingle-style cottage from afar. It had been in the Moss family for generations—Lexi's mother and father had even helped to build a guest house on the property when they were young (and fallen in love in the process). It was unimaginable that another family would roost there.

Lexi felt Kim studying her. "You look upset," said Kim.

Lexi shrugged. "I'm not upset. I'm just . . . surprised."

"Why? You know how Florence hated it here.

I'm shocked she waited this long after Tucker died to unload it."

Lexi did know; of course she did. Throughout her relationship with Hudson, Lexi had witnessed plenty of chilly, sour looks from his mother—most of them during those sticky summer days, the suspicious stares that had made Lexi wipe self-consciously at her neck, sure there must have been some damning love bite there that Hudson had left during their frantic lovemaking in the guest house, maybe a missed button on her blouse, or a telling patch of knotted hair where he'd tangled his fingers.

Lexi shook her head, letting the memories go. "I just can't believe no one in the family wants it, that's all."

"Like who? Hudson hasn't been back since . . ." Kim paused, regret pooling in her eyes as she met Lexi's gaze and knew there was no need to clarify. "There is Cooper, I guess."

Cooper. Lexi nodded absently, the mention abruptly steering her thoughts to the last time she'd laid eyes on Hudson's younger brother. Eleven years ago, the same night Hudson had broken off their engagement in the guest house, Cooper had appeared in the doorway like a beacon, a shining light to lead her to safety when she'd been plunged into darkness and more than willing to step off the edge of the world. He'd kept her company while she'd bawled her eyes out, while she'd drained a whole bottle of champagne. He'd driven her home in his father's car, driven her up and down the coast for hours because she'd told him she couldn't bear to go home alone.

And then, when they'd finally run out of road and he'd delivered her to her apartment, Cooper had kissed her, a bold and passionate kiss that she hadn't expected. And in the years since, when Lexi had remembered that night, she'd felt a sense of confliction. She'd wanted Cooper to kiss her; there was no denying it. Somehow, in the midst of her heartbreak, her wounds still fresh, she'd felt a startling attraction to Hudson's eighteen-year-old brother. Even now the memory warmed her skin with a strange mix of embarrassment and recalled desire. No wonder she'd been too ashamed to ever admit the kiss to Kim. She'd been turned on by her ex-boyfriend's teenage brother. It was criminal.

"He's a writer now."

Lexi looked up, snapped out of her musings.

"Cooper," clarified Kim. "Lynn carries his books in the store. Mysteries. He has some series about a detective who lives in a camper on the beach with his dog. She was telling me about the most recent one. *Sundown*, I think she said it was called. Apparently it was a big seller for her last summer."

A writer. It made sense, Lexi thought as she

reached for her drink. While Hudson had been the gregarious one, quick to entertain and command a room, Cooper had been studious and quiet, content to hang back in the wings and observe, which was why his kiss—and the intensity of it—had shocked her.

"Okay, enough stalling." Kim leaned forward, arms folded, eyes narrowed firmly. "Spill."

Lexi smiled into her margarita. "There's nothing to tell."

"Oh, come on. What about that professor? Anton?"

"Alden," corrected Lexi. "It wasn't serious."

"You said it was."

"I *thought* it was."

"Has he at least *called?*"

Lexi licked salt off her lip. "I told him not to."

"Why would you do that?"

"Because there's no point," said Lexi. "He's there; I'm here."

"Because you *left*."

"Of course I left. It was a two-year program, Kimmie. We both knew it couldn't go anywhere."

Kim frowned, unconvinced. "Both of you—or you?" When Lexi refused to answer, Kim tried again. "Then what about that bartender at the pub you always went to, the one in the picture you e-mailed me?"

Lexi shook her head. "I only went there a few times."

21

Kim blew out an exasperated breath. "You were in London for two years and you didn't meet anyone?"

"I met plenty of people."

"Men," said Kim.

Lexi's smart phone hummed on the table between them; she picked it up.

Kim grinned. "It's the professor, isn't it?"

Lexi didn't recognize the number (area code 919—where was that?), but with her drained savings account, she didn't have the luxury of sending a possible job offer to voice mail.

"I should take this," she said, already shimmying out of the booth.

"I'll get us an order of clam strips," Kim said.

Lexi nodded approvingly, then answered the call as she navigated among the crowded tables. "Hello?"

A male voice said, "Can I speak to Alexandra Wright?"

A job offer, it had to be. Only people who didn't know her well called her that—and the voice had come on too quickly to be a telemarketer. "This is she."

"Alexandra, this is Cooper Moss."

Lexi frowned, not hearing clearly over the roar of customers as she passed the bar. "I'm sorry—who?" she said, pushing through the front door and emerging into the soft evening air.

"Cooper," the man said again. "Cooper Moss."

Lexi stopped at the edge of the steps, catching the name finally.

"Hudson's younger brother," he added after a moment. "You don't remember me, do you?"

Her breath caught, the recollection of his kiss still fresh in her mind, filling her with an irrational embarrassment, as if he'd been eavesdropping on her recent conversation with Kim.

"Is this a bad time?" he asked, his Southern accent noticeable now.

Lexi turned and blinked at the tavern, seeing Kim in the window, talking to the waitress.

"No," she said, finding her bearings at last. "No, it's fine. Of course I remember you, Cooper. What can I do for you?"

"I don't know if you heard—I don't know why you would have—but I'm coming back to Harrisport to see about the house. My mother wants to put it on the market. I'm trying to convince her to wait, but she's determined.

"The reason I'm calling is that I'm finally having the property listed on the historic register. Jim says my dad never did that."

Lexi thought of all the times her mother had chastised the Moss family for their negligence, their home being the sole holdout of all the massive summer cottages along the shoreline to seek nomination—an oversight the Moss family had chalked up to forgetfulness, but Lexi's father, Hank, had always insisted it was just another way for Tucker Moss and his clan to assert their influence, and their entitlement, over the residents of Harrisport.

"I have someone here in Raleigh handling the research for the application," Cooper continued, "but I need someone to photograph the property. The woman at the town office said you do architectural photography."

"I do, yes."

"I'm in Boston right now," said Cooper, "but I'm planning to be on the Cape later tonight. Do you think you could come by the house tomorrow morning and we could talk specifics? Is eight too early?"

Lexi stared at the sidewalk, stunned into silence by the offer, her mind racing at the implications of it, the layers of impossibility. Going back to the Moss house. Seeing Cooper again, and what if Hudson was there too? But it was a job, a good job; how could she say no?

Cooper cleared his throat gently. "If you have plans, I understand. I know it's short notice, and you're probably already booked for the season. . . ."

Lexi heard a knock and glanced up to see Kim at the window, looking exasperated and waving her back inside.

Lexi turned away. "No," she said. "Eight's fine."

"Great. I'll look forward to it."

She hung up, chastising herself for her indecision as she slipped her phone into the back pocket of her jeans and headed for the steps. What was she so nervous about? It was eleven years ago, for God's sake. A lifetime, surely a blip on the radar of Cooper's memory. If he remembered their kiss at all, he was probably hoping she wouldn't bring it up, which she wouldn't. Absolutely not. The subjects of that night and Hudson would be off-limits.

It was a job, right? No different from any other.

She reached the tavern door and tugged it open, her heart finally slowing its frantic beat, the familiar smell of freshly fried clam strips still sizzling in their paper baskets filling her lungs.

Edie Wright stepped up as close as she could to the fish market's counter and squinted down into the blurry spread of price tags that pierced the carpet of crushed ice.

Sixty-four and she still refused to get reading glasses. It wasn't vanity. God, no. A vain woman didn't wear men's jeans and swing a hammer at eighteen while her classmates preened in culottes and sling-backs. It was simple stubbornness; that was all. A refusal to acknowledge the onset of age and the annoying accessories that came with it. The aches and pains, the bolts of stiffness in hands that once could cut down a pile of two-by-sixes in thirty minutes—those clues were proof enough of time's relentless march. Losing Hank to a heart attack three years earlier had been the cruelest clue of all. A wife always knew she could lose her husband, but Edie had never really believed the two of them wouldn't leave this earth together.

"You could just *ask,* you know." Faye Webb appeared behind the counter, chuckling as she secured the matching bobby pins that flanked her round face.

Edie righted herself, lips pursed. "And you could make the damn numbers bigger, *you know.*" The women shared a tired laugh; then Edie waved her hand at the case, exasperated. "Oh, the hell with it," she said. "Just give me two pounds of shrimp. Lexi's got some fancy dish planned for dinner."

"Bet they worked her hard over there."

"Oh, you know how she is. No one has to tell her to work hard. It's telling her to let up that she needs to hear."

"Seems everybody's coming home to roost lately," Faye mused as she scooped up a fistful of shrimp. "You heard the news about the Moss place, I'm sure."

Edie looked up at the name. She blinked a moment at Faye, long enough that the woman offered an explanation as she dropped the shrimp on the scale. "Apparently Her Majesty wants to be done with the place for good now that Tucker's gone. She's sending one of the boys up here to check it out before they put it on the market."

God, please don't let it be Hudson. The plea

26

came reflexively. Edie lowered her eyes, as if her friend might detect her unfounded dread.

"When did you hear about this?" Edie asked, smoothing down the short graying red hairs at the base of her neck and forcing a casual tone to her voice that she most certainly didn't feel.

"Yesterday, at the post office—it's a little over two; that okay?"

Edie nodded dully, not even looking at the scale. Faye was an old friend, one of the few left of the old guard in Harrisport who remembered the days when the Moss family had swooped in and out of their town like a flock of exotic birds every summer. But for most of the residents, this news would be good for little more than a few minutes of gossip at Pip's counter. After all, it had been years since the Moss family had held court at their seaside kingdom on Birch Drive. That was practically a lifetime, the way summer families turned over along the shore nowadays—a footnote.

She wondered what her daughter would think to learn the news. Would Lexi care? Probably not.

What was she so worried about, anyway? It wasn't as if the Mosses were moving back to Harrisport. Faye had claimed they were returning for a quick visit to sell the house, to be done with it.

Lexi might never even know they'd come and gone.

• • •

The frozen custard stand was already busy with the early evening crowd when Owen Wright swung his truck into the gravel lot at seven ten and waved to his sixteen-year-old daughter where she waited for him on one of the stand's weathered benches. Meg was hard to miss in her blinding electric-pink T-shirt and matching visor, the unfortunate uniform implemented by the stand's owners—an outfit that would surely have resulted in life-ending humiliation for the fashion-obsessed girls his daughter went to school with in New York City.

"Busy day?" he asked when she'd climbed into the passenger seat and buckled up, her loose red ponytail swinging around.

"Crazy." She fell back against the seat. "A Little League team showed up at four, and of course *every kid* wanted a Pirate Ship Split, and *every kid* wanted substitutions. And then Andy started freaking out because Sydney was putting the hats on upside down—like the kids even *cared*. I mean, seriously!"

Owen grinned as he steered them out of the parking lot. He loved his daughter's work reports, loved every mundane second. The summer weeks she spent with him were a treasure, each day a piece of gold, and he pocketed every minute. He knew that scooping ice cream six days a week couldn't compare to the excitement of her life with

Heather in Manhattan, but he wouldn't apologize for that. After all, Meg had spent the first fourteen years of her life in Harrisport; coming back for the summer may not have been exotic, but it was familiar, and Meg seemed to genuinely enjoy reconnecting with the places—and people—from her childhood. If her enthusiasm was false, Owen was ashamed to say he was grateful to her for it.

"Daaad . . ." Meg's stern voice drew him out of his reverie. He glanced to where her narrow eyes pointed and saw the offending Tupperware on the end of the dash. "You didn't eat your salad."

"I know, I know," he admitted. "I was just so busy."

"Too busy to eat an already made salad? That's so lame."

"I'll have it tomorrow."

"After it's been sitting all day in the sun? Gross. You will not." She wrinkled her mouth. She always reminded him of Lexi when she did that; Owen's grin widened. "It isn't funny, Dad."

He nodded, forcing his amusement down. "I know."

"You'll never live to see my wedding at the rate you're going."

"Oh, so you *are* getting married now?" Just the other day, she'd assured him she'd be a proud old maid, a declaration that had left him at turns relieved and guilty.

"I never said I wasn't getting married," Meg clarified. "I just said I wasn't sure."

"Hey, before I forget . . ." Owen glanced at her. "Your mom left me a message this afternoon. She said she tried your cell twice and you didn't answer."

Meg pulled at a hangnail on her pinkie. "I'll call her back later. My phone's almost dead."

"Why don't you call her now," he said, gesturing to his cell in the cup holder.

"I'd better not. We might lose the signal."

"I never lose a signal around here."

"No, really, I can wait till we get to Grandma's. I'm sure it's nothing."

She was making excuses, Owen thought, and he wondered why. Before his divorce, he'd never been a suspicious person. Now it seemed he saw secrets everywhere. He turned his attention back to the road and let the worry go. Most likely Meg just didn't feel up to a call with her mother. As much as Heather and she got along, Meg would often claim exhaustion after one of her mother's phone check-ins. Some days Heather's text messaging was interminable; Owen could hear the alerts chiming out insistently.

Of course, his real worry was that Heather had found some reason to require Meg to return home early, some urgent commitment she couldn't be excused from, no matter what court orders said. The previous summer had seen a similar battle, when Heather had informed him that Meg needed to get back to the city a week earlier than planned to start field hockey practice. Never mind that Meg wasn't even fond of the sport, or that it had meant leaving the custard stand shorthanded at the last minute.

"So what's this about George's opening in LA?" he asked.

Meg spun to face him. "Mom told you about that?"

"She left it in the message."

"What did she say?"

Owen glanced at Meg, thinking she looked stricken. "Just that it was over Thanksgiving and she wanted you to go. Is something wrong?"

"No, nothing's wrong." Meg turned back to face the road, reaching out to turn on the radio. "I don't have to go, you know."

"Do you *want* to go?"

She shrugged, pressing at the radio buttons too fast to actually hear her selections. Try as Owen did to pretend otherwise, the mention of his ex-wife's boyfriend still squeezed the air out of his lungs.

"You know, it's okay if you do," he said gently.

Meg smiled but didn't answer, and Owen didn't press, just let the sound of an old Dire Straits song fill the car. They drove on in silence, and even though Owen knew there might be lots of reasons why Meg had fallen so quiet, most of which had nothing to do with him, it was still hard not to calculate the time they spent in each other's company not talking. Before the divorce, he'd never worried too much if they had gone whole days without a real conversation. Now the shared minutes were precious, as quantifiable as any limited thing. As of today, he had exactly twenty-eight days left with his daughter before she'd pack up and return to New York City.

Twenty-eight days.

In a few weeks, he'd get that figure down to hours. Then minutes.

And all he could think, for the thousandth time, was that none of this had been his idea.

2

*R*egardless of the differences between mother and daughter—and there were plenty—when Lexi and Edie shared a kitchen, they were a seamless team, matched to perfection. Lexi, compulsively tidy and organized, always handled the prep work, while her mother, wildly messy and too impatient to be bothered with exact measurements, let alone recipes, took orders at the stove. Tonight's menu was an ambitious one—orange-curry shrimp and roasted root vegetables—but Lexi was determined to make it a special meal, knowing it was the first family dinner since she'd returned from London, now that Meg was home for the summer. Team Wright was back in Harrisport; a celebration was in order.

At her chopping board, Lexi heard the telltale hiss of boiling liquid and glanced up to see the rice bubbling over while her mother stared out the kitchen window.

"Mom, the pot."

"Oops. Shoot." Edie reached over for the knob and lowered the heat, stirring the foaming mixture back down to a manageable height. "I was just noticing Jeff Oberman's van in the Doughertys' driveway. I hope they don't mean to have him take down that maple. I'll chain myself to it if they do. Honest to God."

And she would too, Lexi thought with a smile, pulling a standing grater down from the cabinet. It was no wonder their mother had burned so many of their meals growing up; a kitchen window with a perfect view of the street? What self-respecting busybody could resist such a temptation?

"Traffic's already getting bad."

"I've noticed," Lexi said, sliding an orange up and down the bladed grooves, the oily sweetness of the zest quickly filling the air.

"I swear the Fourth never used to come this fast when you were kids."

"It didn't." Lexi set down the orange to take a sip of the white wine she'd been nursing while she worked. "Winter was endless and summer was a blur."

Edie glanced at Lexi and grinned. "Maybe it could be again."

"What is that supposed to mean?"

Edie shrugged. "I'm just saying maybe you won't rush into a new job right away. Maybe take some time for yourself first, find someone to spend time with . . . someone *special*."

Lexi groaned. "You're worse than Kim."

"God, I would hope so. I'm your mother; I'm supposed to be."

"I just got back. Let me at least move out of my mother's house first, okay?"

Edie sighed, shaking her head. "You always do that."

"Do what?"

"Make excuses for why you can't get serious about someone."

"And just who am I going to get serious about around here? I know everyone in this town, remember?"

"It's summer," Edie argued. "Half the people walking by this window are new faces."

Summer faces, Lexi wanted to clarify. *Summer people.* She'd been down that bumpy, dead-end road before; her mother knew that better than anyone.

"Speaking of familiar faces . . ." Edie sighed. "I don't know if you heard—"

"About the Moss cottage?" Lexi asked. "Yeah, I know."

"You do?"

"Cooper called me."

"Cooper?" Edie blinked at her, startled. "Why in the world would he call *you?*"

"Because they're finally listing the house on the National Register and he wants to hire me to photograph it for the nomination form," Lexi said matter-of-factly, hoping she could avoid her mother's concern if she kept her answers short. No such luck; she glanced up from her grating and found her mother staring at her.

Lexi frowned. "Don't look at me like that. I thought you'd be thrilled they're finally listing it."

"I am." Edie shrugged. "I'm just surprised you'd want to go back there, that's all."

"It's a great opportunity to expand my portfolio," said Lexi, scooping up the fragrant pile of zest and dropping it into a small bowl. "Not to mention it's good money."

"When did all this happen?" Edie demanded.

"This afternoon—you're not stirring the sauce."

Edie frowned as she picked up her spoon and swept it impatiently around the pan. "Were you going to tell me?"

"You're acting like I took a job with the FBI."

"I think I'd prefer that."

Lexi gave her mother a level look. "I know that

house like the back of my hand. Who better to photograph it?"

"Oh, I don't know. Maybe someone who didn't have her heart broken inside it?"

"Eleven years ago."

"Your brother will have a fit," Edie warned.

"It's none of Owen's business what job I take."

"He'll make it his business."

Lexi stared at her simmering garlic, knowing her mother was right. As much as she had appreciated Owen's loyalty, Lexi had grown tired of her brother's inability to let go of his grudge. She'd moved on—why couldn't he?

"You should really tell him," said Edie. "Before he hears it from someone else."

As if on cue, Owen's truck rumbled up the driveway, sliding into view of both women through the kitchen's screen door. Meg came into the house in front of her father, a pie box in her arms, which she delivered to Edie with a hug.

Edie pointed Owen to the fridge. "There's beer or wine, Owe. Help yourself. What do you want to drink, Meggie?"

Meg slipped between her aunt and grandmother, inspecting the pan. "I'll have some wine."

"You will not," Owen said, looking startled.

"Mom lets me have wine when we have people over," Meg informed him gently. "All the girls at my school drink wine, Dad. It's not a big deal."

36

"I passed the Bells' place today, Owe," said Edie. "The dormers are looking fabulous."

"They're getting there," Owen said. "You hear back from Lou on that bathroom reno you quoted him?"

"Not yet," Edie reported, handing a basket of bread to Meg for the table. "I may have to start Operation Nag if I don't hear soon."

Owen pulled a beer from the fridge. "How about you, Lex? Any leads on work?"

Lexi stirred her dish, feeling her mother's pointed gaze beside her. She shot her a silencing look before she answered, "Nothing firm yet." After all, what was the point in telling her brother now? She hadn't even met with Cooper, for God's sake. For all she knew, he might change his mind when he heard her rates—though Lexi doubted it. Money was never an issue for the Moss family. Still, she had no interest in stirring a pot she had yet to put on the stove.

"You could always work at the bike shop, Aunt Lex," Meg said cheerfully as she set the table. "Caroline's older brother works there. She said they're really short-staffed this summer."

Owen frowned. Caroline Michaud worked the frozen custard shack three days a week and had returned this summer, according to Meg and much to Owen's distress, with an ankle tattoo and an affinity for clove cigarettes. God only knew what her brother was into. Owen had seen those guys at the bike shop—hell, he'd *been* one of those guys once—caring only about kegs on the beach or scoping the shoreline for the season's new crop of bikini-wearing summer visitors.

As much as he missed having Meg with him in Harrisport, a part of him was relieved that she didn't have to contend with boys like that year-round.

Dinner ended the way it always had in the Wright house—with a clatter of dishes and a few hurried good-byes. Growing up, she and Owen had always had somewhere to run off to: a party, a date, a friend waiting. Now as she climbed the stairs shortly before ten, Lexi realized she had nowhere to be. Her brother, her niece, even her mother had rushed from the table with a destination. For Lexi, the night was an empty page.

Going up, she smiled at the patchwork of framed family photos that covered the wall, stopping briefly at her senior picture. It was always so hard to look at that photograph, knowing it had been taken just six months before she would meet Hudson Moss—harder still to analyze her confident and carefree eighteen-year-old face and not feel longing, the desire to step back in time and stop the girl she was from falling headlong toward heartbreak. And now she had agreed to go back to the house where it had all started.

She thought about her mother urging her to seek out a relationship this summer, how she'd bristled when Lexi had claimed—rightly so!—that there was no one here in Harrisport to date whom she hadn't already dated. It wasn't an excuse; it was the truth. Or Kim looking discouraged when Lexi hadn't come back from London with sordid stories of great love affairs. She'd been neck-high in photography critiques for twenty-four months— who had time to get involved in something serious?

In her room, she sat down and opened her laptop. She had always been drawn to architectural photography, seeing the curves and edges of a building's construction much in the same way a portrait photographer might capture the lines of the human form. It was a natural desire; growing up around her parents' building business, she had been raised to appreciate architecture in all its iterations, from the sweetly scented skeletons of new lumber frames to the weary and parched bones of an old property, but it was the details she loved most: the parts of a room that most people passed by without seeing, the beauty and grace in a simple drawer pull or a built-in cabinet; the textures of historic fabric, the roughness of hand-hewn beams; worn hardware, cabinet pulls and latches; the puzzle pieces of dovetails; mortises and tenons. If she'd had more time, she would have dug through boxes to find some of her older work, but these shots would do, she decided, as she scrolled through several of the digital portfolios she'd compiled during her graduate program. She hoped Cooper would find the samples acceptable.

Excitement charged through her. After all the summers she'd spent in the Moss house, all the times she'd marveled at its interiors and wanted to capture every inch on film, now she'd finally have her chance. If only her family could have been half as excited for her—but what had Lexi expected? The roots of their battle reached far and grew deep. Lexi doubted anything could uproot her family's distaste for the Mosses now.

Like all kids who grew up in Harrisport, Lexi knew about the Moss house long before she'd ever seen it. Even if you'd never set foot on its lush and rolling back lawn (and why would you unless you'd been hired to mow it?), even if you'd never walked through its kitchen and caught a whiff of fresh-glazed pastries, you knew it was the house where the lavish display of fireworks blew up the sky every Fourth of July, rivaling Provincetown's show year after year. The fact that Lexi's parents had been hired to build a guest house on the property in the sixties led friends to believe that Lexi had a superior knowledge of the inner workings of the summer family from North Carolina, but the truth was that growing up, Lexi couldn't have cared less about the Mosses or their fireworks. She'd gleaned early on the rules of engagement when it came to summer families, and she had no interest in playing a game she couldn't win.

It hadn't helped, of course, that for as long as she could remember, every time the subject of the Moss family came up around her father, his expression would darken and, without fail, the usually fair and forgiving Hank Wright would purge a shocking serving of vitriol.

"Maybe he and Tucker Moss got into some big fight," Kim had suggested once when they were young. "Maybe they beat the tar out of each other that summer they built the guest house."

"It's possible," Lexi had replied, though she'd never known her father to lose his temper that way. Still, it had seemed a likely theory, for what else could possibly have happened to leave such a sour taste in his mouth so many years later?

The summer after her senior year, Lexi became determined to find out.

"Why does Dad hate the Mosses so much?"

She'd joined her mother at the sink to work on the dinner dishes and just come right out with it, startling Edie with the question almost as much as she'd startled herself.

"He doesn't hate them," Edie had insisted, keeping her eyes fixed on the basin of dirty dishes. "You read too much into things. You know how impatient your father gets with summer people. He'd say the same thing about the Douglases or the Flemings."

But Lexi didn't believe it. An hour later, when the house had grown quiet, she'd borrowed her father's truck and driven to the off-white cape Owen and Heather had been renting just outside the village.

Lexi had smelled the charcoal as soon as she'd pulled into the driveway. Lilacs grew against the garage, swollen with lavender blossoms, but she'd pushed past them without stopping for a sniff, intent on finding her brother in the backyard, where he stood over the grill, monitoring a pair of sizzling steaks.

He looked up and smiled. "Hey, Lex, what's going on? Hungry?"

She took a seat in one of the rickety lawn chairs and sat forward, arms crossed, wanting to get right to it. "Did something happen with Dad and the Mosses?"

Owen looked at her through the chimney of cooking smoke that climbed toward the star-sprinkled sky. "Why would you ask that?" he said.

Lexi held his gaze, just in case he meant to derail her as her mother had done. "Mom won't tell me, but I know something happened, so what was it?"

Owen frowned down at the grill.

Lexi bit at the inside of her cheek. "Dad and

42

Tucker Moss got into it over something, didn't they?"

"You could say that." Owen hooked the long-handled spatula on the edge of the grill and came over to take the other chair, sitting forward like she was. "It was over Mom, actually. She and Moss were together once."

Lexi sat back, startled at the admission. "What do you mean, *once?*" she asked. "You mean like once upon a time? Or like, *just* once?"

"I mean they were together that summer."

"But Mom always said that was the summer she and Dad fell in love."

"It was," said Owen.

"So what happened?"

"I don't know, Lex. Just that Tucker Moss broke her heart before she started seeing Dad. It's not exactly a popular topic of conversation."

The steaks popped. Owen climbed to his feet and returned to the grill.

"That's why Dad refused to try for their roof replacement job a few years ago," he said. "It would have been huge money—and it's not like we didn't need it—but he wouldn't even put in a bid."

Lexi stared at the grass. "They should have told me," she said numbly. "I should have been told."

"Why? What difference does it make now?"

All the difference in the world. Don't you understand?

43

Heather came out of the house then, carrying a glass of wine. "How much longer on the steaks?"

Lexi rose, her legs shaky. "I should go."

"Lex, wait." Owen moved toward her. "Don't go yet. We should keep talking about this."

But there was nothing more to talk about, Lexi decided as she walked back to the truck and climbed in, feeling the knot inside her stomach cinch. It was terrible news. The very worst. For she'd done something awful, something she couldn't undo. Something she wasn't sure she wanted to even if she could, and this truth of her mother's unfortunate romance had simply come too late.

Lexi had already fallen hopelessly and irreversibly in love with Hudson Moss.

3

*M*orning rolled across the harbor, slow as sap behind a heavy fog, the mist still so thick when light finally dawned that it was nearly impossible to see the water from the shore. Lexi took the long way through town. She loved the early hours, when the sidewalks weren't yet crowded and the storefronts were still shuttered, the farmers' market vendors just setting up. No matter how many times Lexi passed the rows of squat, dormered capes that flanked the village, she never tired of their rambling charm, the climbing roses that spilled down trellises like overfrosted cakes, the wreaths of dried wisteria vines that hung from doors and gateposts.

It was easy to see what drew people to her hometown summer after summer. Lexi was no more immune to the beauty of the Cape than anyone who'd just arrived to it for the first time.

Even with the added travel, Lexi reached the entrance to Birch Drive at ten to eight, impossibly punctual, as she'd been her whole life. Melancholy trickled into her thoughts as she steered down the road. Had she somehow expected the landscape to appear changed since the last time she'd driven through it? How could it? Trees that had been there a hundred times longer than she had didn't look any different rising up on either side of the washboard dirt, their canopy of leafy branches providing the same dappled shade it had provided for decades of summer mornings. It was only when she passed the gatehouse and noted the evidence of decay that had faded its weathered shingles that Lexi saw the passage of time that had lapsed between this visit and her last, and with the proof came the memories. She'd collected mail with Hudson there, left notes for him there, even sought shelter there in a downpour while he'd changed a flat on his father's sports car.

But it wasn't until she'd turned down the last stretch of dirt and the driveway began to widen that Lexi found herself truly pulled back in time. It was the smell, she decided as she parked and climbed out of her car. A fruity sweetness to the air that she always swore she could never detect anywhere else on the Cape, a magical blend of tide and the gardenia blossoms that Florence Moss had insisted on carting up from North Carolina and planting summer after summer, even though the poor things rarely survived the coastal winters. Lexi scanned the side of the house and saw a pair of bushes in bloom, their flowers a flawless white against the dingy grayed shingles, and she smiled. How ironic, she thought. It seemed Florence's flowers had finally taken to the property, ultimately far more so than Florence.

Her gaze rose to the house, lifting slowly as if she weren't sure she wanted to take it in all at once. Not that it was even possible to see it all in one view; that was how massive it was. Still, her eyes managed to capture enough that she felt an unexpected charge of disappointment as she scanned the enormous gables, the curving eyebrow dormers, the chimneys that rose up like two stone skyscrapers, then down to the porch that stretched nearly the full length of the house, as wide and danceable as a ballroom. It saddened her, more so than she would have imagined, to find the cottage so weathered-looking. But it was more than the drooping facade, the parched cedar shingles, the deep green trim that was peeling and faded, the untended lawn. In all the years she'd visited this spot of earth, she'd never known it to be so quiet. It seemed unnatural, as if some law of the universe would require motion on the property at all times: an idling car, a burst of music, the cacophony of screen doors thrown open in unison, the thump of bare feet rushing out, dragging towels and scraping the steps with the metal ends of beach umbrellas.

And voices! Cries of victory or defeat over a badminton game. Then, when the sun slid down a satin sky and the lawn burned pink and violet, the tangle of party tones blended with the chorus of a string quartet. Bow ties and champagne toasts. Slipped shoulder straps. Heels abandoned in a patch of sea grass. Magic. From her very first visit, despite her every intention to resist its seduction, Lexi had been spellbound. Just like those gardenias, night or day, life had seemed forever in bloom here. Until, of course, the moment it wilted.

"Alexandra?"

She turned and saw Cooper Moss coming toward her in jeans and a white-collared shirt with the sleeves rolled up to his elbows. She had wondered whether she'd recognize him, whether her memory of him had held up. It had. His hair, though still cut close to his scalp, had darkened from sun-bleached blond to sueded brown. His limbs, still long and lean, moved with the grace and confidence of age.

He extended his hand and she took it, finding his grip warm and tight. "It's good to see you," he said. "I really appreciate your coming down on such short notice."

"Of course," Lexi said. "I'm just glad it's finally getting on the registry."

"Me too. I couldn't believe it when I heard my father never made that happen. It's sad, really," Cooper said, squinting up at the cottage. "All those years everyone took such good care of her. Registering her now, when she looks as limp as an old boutonniere, seems almost cruel." He swept his gaze back to Lexi and smiled. "The lady at the town office told me you've just come back from grad school—London, was it?"

"Yes, the Royal Academy. And someone told me you're a writer."

Someone. Lexi felt foolish saying it that way. Like she'd heard it on the playground.

"I am." He grinned, deep dimples sinking into his cheeks. "All those years of coming to the dinner table with my face buried in a book and driving my mother nuts finally paid off."

Lexi smiled, searching his gaze for evidence of what he remembered from the last time they'd seen each other, but he gave no clues to any discomfort or regret, just a warm and steady interest. She chastised herself for thinking he'd given their kiss a second thought. All the kisses that had surely decorated his memory in the years since that night. Who was she kidding to imagine theirs had stood the test of time?

Relief settled over her, burying a flicker of disappointment she chose to ignore.

Cooper gestured to the house. "Why don't we get started?"

Of all the times Lexi had entered the cottage, she could count on one hand the times she *hadn't* come through the kitchen. At first she'd been so sure her direction to the service door was to minimize her presence on the property; then in time she'd come to think it was more because Hudson was always ravenous, but eventually Lexi came to see that the real reason was Florence. Hudson and Cooper's rigid mother was notorious for her decree that all guests under the age of twenty-four—who, in her opinion, had a preternatural inclination for slamming doors—use the service entrance exclusively.

"After you." At the door, Cooper stepped back to let her enter first. All at once, the familiar smell of old wood baking in a relentless summer sun filled her lungs. She took in the space, the empty stretches of stainless steel, the wall of tall cabinets, the breakfast booth built into the window. Sunlight trickled in. If memory served her, by eleven the linoleum would be burnished gold, and nearly as hot underfoot as beach sand.

"I wish I had something to offer you," Cooper

said as they walked by the counter. "I got in too late to go to the store. I don't even have any coffee."

"That's fine; I've had plenty." Lexi followed him past the nook of the butler's pantry, the dry, musty scent of old shelf paper tickling her throat, reminding her of stolen moments with Hudson there. His lust had been reckless and immediate, as unpredictable as heat lightning. She never knew when he'd pull her behind a door, or press her against a wall or a shaggy-barked tree. It had excited her beyond words.

Stepping now through the doorway and into the great room at last, Lexi took in a sharp breath. She had wondered whether the enormous space might lose some of its majesty without any furnishings, without its plush Oriental carpets, its fat leather couches, its standing lamps. It hadn't. Her eyes lifted to the vaulted ceiling, resting a while at the peak where the massive beams intersected before her gaze drifted to the room's huge stone fireplace. Behind them, a stretch of windows with stained-glass bays in their upper sashes offered an impressive view of the lawn and the water beyond it.

"How soon are you putting it on the market?" Lexi asked.

"That depends," said Cooper. "I'm hoping we can take our time. I'd like one more summer here."

Lexi glanced around the empty room. "You're *staying* here?"

He smiled. "It's not as grim as it sounds. Everything still works. And a few of the guest bedrooms have mattresses. And just between you and me," he confessed as he walked over to the fireplace, "I'm overdue to deliver a manuscript to my editor. I thought this might be the perfect place to hunker down and just get it done." He ran his palm over the edge of the mantel, a flawless piece of oak that had been wedged into the stones.

Lexi joined him at the other end of the fireplace, her hands lured to the mantel as his had been. Was Hudson as determined as their mother to see it sold? Lexi couldn't help wondering whether he was, not to mention why Cooper still hadn't mentioned his older brother. She hoped his silence on the subject meant Hudson had no part in this plan and, more important, no intention of visiting.

"Just so you know, I charge by the hour," she said. "It's a big house. I would probably need a week to photograph it properly."

"Of course. Whatever it takes. I don't lock it up. You can come and go as you please."

She nodded, wondering for a moment how it would feel to enjoy unlimited access in a place she'd once seen as a fortress. "I brought my laptop so you could see some of my work," she said.

"That's not necessary. You came highly recommended. Besides . . . I've seen your work before." Cooper lifted his eyes to hers, a deep brown, pooling with warmth. "Hud used to hang your photographs in his room at college."

Lexi smiled, unexpectedly pleased at the information. She'd only ever visited Hudson a handful of times at Duke, and always hoped to find evidence of herself in his college world, a universe she feared she was exempt from.

"Hudson was the reason I took up photography in the first place," she admitted. "He gave me my very first real camera."

Cooper smiled. "I know. I remember."

Lexi reached for her earring, twisting the silver teardrop between her fingers.

They smiled at each other, the past crackling briefly between them, until a thick burst of salt-scented air came through the screens and carried it away.

It had been a photograph that caused her path to cross with Hudson's in the first place. She'd been waiting for Kim to find a reference book in the library and was killing time by wandering through a photography exhibit one of the local artists had donated for the summer. It was a series of black-and-white portraits, the subjects all ages, the settings always sparse. In the two months it had been up, Lexi had viewed it over a dozen times, hoping to glean clues to how the photographer had worked his magic with lighting and composition.

She was studying one of her favorites, a portrait of an old woman on a porch swing, when Hudson had approached her; she'd been so entranced that she hadn't even realized he was there until he'd said, "Are any of these yours?"

She'd been so startled, first by the sound of his voice, then by the suggestion that she might have actually taken one of these brilliant works of art, that she'd needed a long moment before she could answer. "No," she said at last. "I wish, but *no*."

"I bet you could have taken any one of these," he said, his drawl more noticeable to her as he gestured to the rows on either side of them.

Lexi shook her head, turning her gaze back to the portrait.

"It's not as easy as it looks," she said, pointing to the woman's jawline. "I bet the photographer spent hours getting the light on this side of her face to look that beautiful."

"It's beautiful, all right."

She'd turned to find he was staring at her, not the picture. A surge of heat rushed down her limbs.

She had recognized him immediately. Every girl in Harrisport knew about Hudson Moss, knew how handsome he was, how charming. High season always brought lots of attractive guys from away. "Boys of summer," she and Kim had called them. Just like the Don Henley song that still lived in Dock's jukebox. They were fun to look at and fantasize about, but Lexi knew better than to think she might have a chance with one—her brother, Owen, had made sure of that.

"Is this what you want to do?" Hudson asked her. "Take pictures like these?"

"I'd love to," she admitted. "But you need a real camera and lots of equipment."

"Like what?"

"Special lenses, light meters."

She waited for him to suggest she get herself some, to assume that she had the means that he did to make her dreams happen, but he didn't. He just smiled and said, "I bet you'd be real good at it if you ever did."

She laughed. "How would you know?"

He shrugged. "I don't," he said. "It just seems like someone who loves something would be good at it."

"Why? Are you good at the things you love?" she asked.

"I don't know. I'm still waiting to find out, I guess." He pulled his hand out of his pocket and held it out to her. "I'm Hudson."

"Lexi," she said, meeting his eyes as she slid her fingers into his.

"It's real nice to meet you, Lexi."

As she'd walked the length of the corridor with Hudson Moss for the next few minutes, slowing with him at each photograph, Lexi had assured herself that there was no harm in polite conversation, in a brief and simple exchange. Where could it go?

But even as she walked home, his parting request to take her out sometime tucked in her memory like an unwrapped gift, Lexi knew there was nothing simple or brief about what had transpired between her and Hudson Moss in that library hallway. Passing the Salty Shelf Bookstore, she glanced over and saw her reflection floating like a cloud in front of the display of beach reads, the flush of desire and hope already fixed on her cheeks like a sunburn.

Five days later, Lexi, pulled a strappy tie-dyed silk dress off the rack at Klein's on Main Street and slipped it on in the dressing room. When she shoved the curtain back and emerged, Kim whistled.

Lexi shook her head firmly. "I look like I'm trying too hard."

"Well, of course you're trying," said Kim. "Why else are we here looking at some dress that costs more than dinner at Osprey?"

Lexi tugged at the tag to read the price and sighed.

"Your folks will flip when they find out," Kim said. "So will Owen."

"They won't find out."

"But what about when Hudson picks you up at the house?"

"He's not picking me up at the house," said Lexi. "I'm meeting him in front of the library. No one will know."

Kim grinned. "Unless, of course, you fall madly in love and have his little Moss babies and then *everyone* will know."

Lexi stepped back into the dressing room and yanked the curtain closed. "It's just dinner," she said.

"Yeah, right," whispered Kim through the curtain. "You don't buy a new dress for *just dinner*."

What could Lexi say to that? Her best friend knew her better than anyone, knew that for all of Lexi's insistence that she couldn't care less about the Moss family or their oldest son, she'd been utterly dazzled by Hudson Moss and his startling blue-gray eyes and his Southern accent in less time than it took to load a dishwasher. She'd imagined herself somehow immune, special.

She wasn't.

Lexi returned the dress to the rack, as if not buying it might keep her from caring so much about one date. A flash of fear struck her as they stepped back out onto the sidewalk, as though she'd lied on a job application and been subsequently hired, as though at any moment she might be found out to be a fraud. There was still time to quit, to confess. But the bigger part of her wanted to see if she could succeed in her imagined charade, though she wasn't sure who she might be trying to fool.

"I bet he takes you to Weatherly's," said Kim with a wink. "And if you don't order the most expensive thing on the menu, I'll never forgive you."

But he didn't take her to Weatherly's. When Hudson Moss picked her up in front of the library, insisting on climbing out to open and close the passenger door for her, he drove them past the two blocks of expensive restaurants and out of the village.

"Where are we going?" Lexi asked.

He smiled. "A friend's house."

She scanned the view as he turned them off the main road and down a private drive. When he swung the car between two high stone walls and steered them toward a massive house that rose up at the end of the driveway, her stomach lurched.

She knew the house well. It was one of the newer ones on the shore, an overbuilt monstrosity put up to replace a once-stunning shingle-style cottage that had been left unattended in the wake of an estate battle. Her mother had wept openly when the board had approved the original cottage's demolition and quickly denounced the new design as an architectural horror to anyone who would listen.

Lexi stared up at it, guilt filling her. "What are we doing here?" she asked.

"Whatever we want," said Hudson, taking her by the hand and leading her up the wide curved steps to the front entrance. "The Foxes are out of town for another week. Their son and I are good friends. Seth gives me the new code every summer." Hudson plucked a key from the leaves of a potted fern and slipped it into one of the oversized double doors. Inside, the shriek of an alarm sounded; Hudson reached to the keypad on the wall and deftly tapped in a code. He flicked on lights as they made their way through the house, one chandelier after another bursting above them.

He led her downstairs into a series of rooms decorated in a Tuscan style, complete with stone archways and murals of vineyard views. She watched as he slipped behind the bar and pulled a bottle from the shelf.

"Isn't this place amazing?" he asked as he filled two tumblers with an obscene amount of rum.

Lexi couldn't answer. She'd caught her reflection in the mirror behind him. Swells of outrage rose in her throat. She'd fussed over her outfit for two hours for *this?*

She marched toward the stairs.

"Hey—hold up!" Hudson called behind her.

But Lexi wasn't about to wait, a fact that was clear to Hudson as he followed her up the stairs to find her on her way to the front.

"What's wrong?" he asked, catching up to her just before she'd reached the entrance.

"This is your idea of a date?" she said. "Bringing me to this hideous house and getting me drunk?"

"What? No! Heck, I thought you'd be impressed."

"Impressed that you bring me to an empty house because you don't want to be caught in public with me?"

"Is that what you think?"

"What else can I think?"

For a long moment, Hudson looked wounded and remorseful, like a chastised boy; then he straightened and said purposefully, "Okay, then." He reached past her for the door, threw it open and stepped back out onto the front porch. "Let's go back to town," he said. "You pick the restaurant. Better yet, we'll go straight back to the house and sit right at the table with my folks so they can meet you. Come on."

Lexi remained on the steps, frozen. She'd vowed she wouldn't invest any part of herself in tonight, in needing him to prove something to her, and here she was, making demands. She knew what she'd stepped into by accepting his invitation and yet minutes into their evening, she was crying foul. And worse, he was calling her bluff. Lexi wasn't sure which scared her more: if he didn't take her to his house or if he did. Being faced with Tucker and Florence Moss wasn't her idea of a good time.

Hudson let out a deep breath and slowly came back up the steps to face her. "I didn't take you out because I wanted you all to myself," he confessed softly. "I was worried if we went out, you'd see all these friends of yours and I'd lose you to 'em."

She searched his face, his pale eyes, trying to decide if he were telling the truth.

He squinted up at the house and smiled sheepishly. "You think it's hideous, huh?"

She felt her own lips pulled into a small grin. "Ugly as sin."

In the quiet, the breeze fingering his blond waves, he looked rakish and just tender enough that she couldn't imagine leaving. Out of the confusing knot of emotions that twisted in her stomach—guilt, hurt, shame—desire untangled itself and rushed to the top, victorious. This was her choice to make, wasn't it?

"I'm an idiot. Tell me what to do to fix it," Hudson said, stepping closer to her.

She looked beyond him to where the sea hid beneath the rise of the lawn, abandon coursing through her like liquor. "You really want to impress me?"

He nodded.

Then, without a word, she dashed past him and pushed through the grass for the beach.

They stopped their race at the edge of the surf and looked out at the water. Lexi swallowed, trying to slow her heartbeat even though she knew their chase wasn't to blame. A moment ago she'd had her chance to flee, to circumvent the certain drama that would unfold if she stayed and saw this night through, but she'd chosen instead to take it with both hands, to hold on to its reins no matter how hard it might try to buck her off.

And it would.

She turned to face Hudson. He smiled down at her, his breathing quick too from their sprint, his eyes flashing playfully.

"You mean this?" he said, nodding to the water. "You want me to get in and do laps to impress you, that it?"

She shrugged, the idea foolish to her now. There must have been girls in North Carolina: college girls with skin that never freckled from the sun, girls who never smelled like the sea, who never had to shake sand out of their shoes or their sheets. Girls who didn't ask anything of him. Why in the world would he indulge her demands?

To her shock, he began to undress. First his shirt, then his shoes, then his socks. She'd been sure he'd stop before removing his pants but he'd kept on without hesitation, flinging his clothes beside him until he stood in just a pair of boxers, his body smooth and shining in the fading light. Without a word, he stepped into the curling surf, wincing as he moved farther in, his arms fisted out at his sides as if he were walking a tightrope. Lexi watched him until he was waist-deep, at which point he leaned forward and dove into the oncoming wave.

She sucked in a sharp breath, waiting for him to emerge, which he did, a few seconds later, and with a loud, victorious hoot.

He climbed out of the water and returned to her, smelling of cold and seaweed and a hundred other familiar smells that drew away all doubt.

"You didn't think I'd do it, did you?" he asked, winded.

She blinked up at him. "No," she managed. "God, no."

He smiled triumphantly. "Good."

She would find he was full of surprises. The best one arrived at the end of their first summer together, on a rainy August afternoon that she and Hudson had spent holed up in the guest house, much to Florence Moss's displeasure.

"Close your eyes," he said.

"Why?" Lexi asked, flutters of excitement already dancing in her stomach.

"Just close them."

Up until the moment Hudson revealed the Hasselblad film camera on the table, Lexi had been sure she could never love anyone or anything as much as she loved Hudson Moss. A Hasselblad! Before that day, the closest Lexi had come to holding a real camera was standing in line for school pictures. She'd taken a class the summer before—Intro to Photography—at the college but even those cameras weren't much better than her parents' ancient Instamatic.

She may not have ever used a Hasselblad but she knew how much they cost and her throat went dry.

"I could never afford this," she said, her hands shaking as she turned the camera, gently and reverentially, like the egg of a rare bird.

"I know; that's why it's a gift," Hudson said, then added with a wicked grin, "I have only one condition: You have to promise me you'll take lots of dirty self-portraits with it. Preferably nudes."

She smiled, leaning in to his chest, gratitude and pleasure charging through her. She wanted to rush home at once, to gather her parents and her brother together, to set the gift in front of them and declare: See, see! Not every Wright woman is cursed to heartbreak at the hands of a Moss man.

4

It was always apparent from the shingled front of Tides Natural Foods what season it was. On the first day the thermometer rose above seventy degrees, a pair of umbrella café tables would appear outside, where customers would enjoy mugs of French roast and crumble-topped cranberry muffins. Hanging pots of begonias flanked the doorway. Two water bowls were always stationed—and continually refilled—in a shady nook beside the front door for canine guests. The window display would lure indulgent summer visitors with playful setups of organic wines and gourmet trail mixes for beach and bike excursions, shade-grown coffees, and herbal sunscreens.

Lexi always loved that first inhale when she'd step inside the store, a cool, smoky blend of fresh herbs and nutty grains. As much as the interior and the inventory had changed in the ten years that Kim had owned the store, the smell never had. Van Morrison's "Tupelo Honey" played low. Lexi slipped past a shaggy-haired young man in a blue Tides T-shirt stocking the dairy case and found Kim behind the store's café counter.

"The place looks great," Lexi said, sliding onto one of the counter's stools and running her hands over the porcelain-tiled surface—Owen's handiwork four years earlier.

"Okay, so out with it," declared Kim, setting down a cup of coffee in front of Lexi. "What's he like now?"

"Who?"

"Who do you think? Cooper."

Lexi picked up her mug and blew across the top, the memory of Cooper's dimpled smile forcing its way to the front of her thoughts. "He's exactly what you'd expect. Well-mannered. Well-spoken. Cordial."

"Oh, please. Who cares about all that crap? Is he hot?"

"Kim . . ."

"He must be," Kim said with a teasing grin. "You're turning bright red."

"I am not," Lexi defended sharply. God, was she? She downed a fast sip of coffee.

"It just seems strange that Hudson wouldn't come too. Maybe Laurel didn't let him," Kim suggested. "She always felt so threatened by you."

Had she? Lexi had once hoped so, desperately.

Kim sponged the counter. "So you don't think it's weird?"

"What?"

"There we were, talking about Cooper Moss, and out of the blue, he calls you? You know what this is, don't you?"

"A coincidence."

"A *sign*."

For Kim, every coincidence was a sign, a cosmic signal that could—and usually would—change a person's life.

"A sign of what, *exactly?*" Lexi asked warily.

"I don't know." Kim smiled, looking utterly pleased as she tossed her sponge into the small prep sink behind her and dried her hands on her hips. "I guess we'll find out."

• • •

The first time Lexi heard of Laurel Babcock was when she was sipping the foamy head off a dark beer.

It had been late spring. She was visiting Hudson at his dorm, one of three visits she'd get in the four years he was at Duke, and he'd taken her downtown for burgers. A friend of his, Timmy Watson, an angular med student with flame-red curls, had been their chauffeur.

"Oh, you know Pearl Pizza, Hud," Timmy had insisted during one of their debates on the best local food. "The place with the purple booths. The one around the corner from Laurel's apartment."

Laurel. The name had been thrown out like a comment about the weather, inconsequential, neither prefaced nor lingered upon, and yet Lexi had seized on it, the way only a woman might. Something in Hudson's eyes, something fleeting yet unmistakable—a flash of panic, a blink of interest?—had given the comment roots, and those roots burrowed deep into the soil of Lexi's thoughts for the rest of the visit. That night, she and Hudson made love. Even then, she'd chewed on that name like a piece of tough meat that simply wouldn't soften enough to be swallowed.

Laurel.

The next morning, as they'd spooned sugar into weak coffee at a table in the cafeteria, she'd demanded an answer.

"Who's Laurel?"

"Who?"

"Laurel," she said again. "Timmy said her name last night."

He began sawing into an overcooked omelet. "What are you talking about?"

For a moment, Lexi had felt a deep sense of regret and embarrassment, as if she'd been heard talking in her sleep. Her voice came out soft and small, a voice she didn't recognize and immediately disliked.

"Last night," she said. "Timmy mentioned a girl. Laurel. I wondered who she was."

Hudson had just stared at her. His expression had been so full of condemnation that Lexi had wanted to run from the cafeteria then and there, but instead she'd reached for her coffee and taken long sips, hoping the moment and her foolish inquisition would dissolve in the quiet.

"She's just some girl Timmy knows," Hudson said, stabbing a triangle of egg with his fork and dragging it through a puddle of ketchup. "Some girl whose party we went to once."

Some girl. The relief had been as soft as a down comforter, and Lexi had snuggled under it. Never minding the doubt that began to gnaw and scratch at the surface of her heart like a mouse.

"Is there someone else?"

The question had come out, as all unfortunate

questions do, on the phone a month later. Lexi had been folded into the window seat in her room on a snowy February night, bundled in a blanket and watching her reflection in the frosted glass as she'd held the receiver tightly, her heart racing in the quiet as she waited for Hudson's answer.

He'd crumpled. "It's not what I want," he'd said. "*She's* not what I want."

Laurel. It had to be Laurel.

"What then?" Lexi had asked, that awful soft voice returning.

"My parents. Her parents. We've practically grown up together."

"So have we," Lexi said back.

"No, I mean from the time we were kids."

We're still *kids,* she wanted to say, but tears blocked her voice. But he wasn't a kid, and this proved it. Did he see her as a kid just because she'd chosen to stay on the Cape to attend community college and live at home until she could afford a place of her own? Outrage and hurt wound within her. Of course he did. Wasn't it obvious?

Lexi swallowed. "Is she at Duke too?"

"Not right now. She's abroad this year. Spain."

Abroad. No wonder Lexi had never met her. Convenient.

Her mind began to spin, imagining scenes between Hudson and this Laurel who was supposed to be just "some girl," the history they must have shared, the one that had been set in stone long before Lexi had stepped into Hudson's world. She'd imagined her love for him like a handprint in soft cement, always permanent once dried. All this time there'd been someone else, another print.

Nausea turned her stomach, making her skin hot. She pressed her cheek against the frost-flecked glass to cool it and closed her eyes.

"Do you love her?" she whispered.

"I don't want her the way I want you, Lex."

"Come see me," she pleaded, emboldened by his confession, choosing to ignore that he hadn't answered her question. "Come for spring break. We'll go to the Vineyard. I'll get us one of those cottages in Menemsha and we won't come out until they make us."

He laughed at that, as if she might be kidding. Or worse, as if the idea were a preposterous one.

"I can't. You know I'm going with Timmy to Aspen."

"You can choose what you want," she said. "It's your life."

"But I *do* want to go to Aspen, Lex."

"I'm not talking about Aspen," she said.

Four months later—four months of falling asleep on a damp pillow and thin meals and phone watching—Hudson had arrived on the Cape with the words Lexi had been dreaming of.

"I ended it," he said. "I told her I want to be with you."

And just like that, Lexi had melted back into him. Like egg whites folded into cake batter. She'd yielded every part of herself to make him sweeter, to make him complete. Never imagining a person could change his mind, that even dried cement could be split apart.

5

*M*eg Wright pulled out a handful of Nilla wafers from the box and spread them out on the table in front of her. From the time she was little, she'd always eaten them the same way: always in pairs, flat sides together. Arranging them so was oddly comforting, the ritual almost as calming as the taste of the cookies themselves.

She didn't know why she'd been feeling so nervous lately. No, she did. George and her mom were getting married. The big gallery show in LA her mom wanted her to attend? That was actually going to be the ceremony. Her dad would freak. She knew he would. God, he still nearly choked just saying her mother's boyfriend's name—this news of their engagement (and planned wedding!) would send him into full-blown cardiac arrest. Or worse, he might just curl up like a pill bug and not say a word. Meg wasn't sure which response scared her more.

It had been hard enough staying with him that first summer after the divorce. He'd moped around. He'd cooked mushroom omelets in the middle of the night. Half the time Meg got the feeling he expected her to make him feel better, and the other half he fished for information about what her mother was doing in New York, and whom she was doing it with. Meg had hated lying to him, but she'd hated even more seeing his expression when she'd told him the truth.

It wasn't as if she didn't have her own things to be pissed off about! It wasn't as if she was crazy about George, but she didn't hate him. The truth was—and she would never have said this to her father—George was actually pretty cool. He didn't freak out if she wanted a glass of wine or if she brought a guy home after school. He treated her like an adult, while her father—Meg stared woefully at the Nilla wafers in her hand—still bought her the same cookies she'd been eating since she was five.

She loved her father more than anything, but sometimes he held on so tight she couldn't breathe.

Meg heard the sound of the truck rumbling up the driveway, then the slam of the driver's door. Owen came inside a few moments later, carrying a pizza.

"Sorry I'm late," he said, setting the box down on the table.

Meg frowned at it. "I thought you said we were getting dinner from that new noodle place?"

"Since when don't you like Russo's mushroom pizza?" Owen asked, sliding into the seat across from her.

"It's not that I don't like it," she said with a small shrug, wondering why she even bothered to bring it up. "I just thought we could try something, you know, *different*."

He flipped open the pizza box, releasing a fragrant burst of warm, spicy air. Seeing the glistening lumps of sausage on one half, Meg gave her father a disapproving look.

"I swear I told them no meat," Owen defended quickly.

Meg served herself a slice. "And you wonder why I worry about leaving you and your rapidly increasing cholesterol levels here alone."

"I'm not alone. Did you ever call your mom back?"

"Don't change the subject."

"Honey, I'm not alone. I have you and your aunt and your grandma. . . ."

"You're alone *here*. And you get mopey."

"I don't get mopey," he argued.

"*Dad*. You get ridiculously mopey."

"Hey, I don't want to talk about me," he said, dropping a slice onto his plate. "What about you?

You still haven't told me about this last semester, about your friends, what you've all been doing down there in the big city. Come on; enlighten your old man."

Meg's heart thundered at the question; she was unsure of how to answer. After his tailspin over her wine comment, the truth was out of the question. Just the week before she'd come here, Wiley and Emma had opened Wiley's parents' liquor cabinet after school and made them all Cosmos. Meg had downed three and then sneaked Ty Anderson back into her room at midnight, where he'd stayed until five the next morning.

She reached absently for the last two Nilla wafers beside her plate and sandwiched them. "There's nothing to tell," she said. "We do the same things as we did last year. Go to the movies a lot. Go shopping. You know. The usual."

Her phone chimed on the counter. Owen glanced at it, frowning. "What's your mom want now?"

Did it never occur to her father that it might be someone else trying to reach her? "I'm sure it's nothing," Meg said, glancing longingly at the phone, wondering what Ty had written back to her earlier text.

"Mom said you're looking at Barnard."

"*She* is," Meg said, aware of how despondent her answer had sounded. The truth was that lately, and unbeknownst to either one of her parents,

Meg had been scanning the Web sites of colleges much farther away, University of New Mexico and UCLA.

"You still want to take a day to see Tufts this summer, don't you?" Owen asked, and his expression was so bright and hopeful that Meg didn't have the heart to tell him she'd let her mother talk her out of applying to Tufts last month.

"You bet," she said instead.

"And maybe we could go to the aquarium. See the penguins." He reached for another slice. "God, you haven't been there since you were in middle school."

Meg nodded agreeably. "Sounds great, Dad."

The first time Owen saw George Schneider—which was at the art council's fifty-dollars-a-head reception at the Osprey House—his immediate thought was that the visiting artist looked nothing like Heather had described him.

In the weeks leading up to the big event, Heather had been buzzing about the arrival of the painter she'd worked tirelessly to bring up from New York, the man whom the art council, of which Heather was vice president, had commissioned to create the mural in the library's newly built wing. She'd said he was forty-five; he looked easily five years younger. She'd suggested he was heavy; he wasn't, a fact made glaringly apparent by the snug knit shirt and tailored pants he'd arrived in. "You should know that George is terribly reclusive," Heather had explained, prepping Owen on the drive over to the reception as if George Schneider were the Dalai Lama. Another lie: the man was as gregarious as a game-show host, greeting Harrisport residents like old friends, particularly the women, Owen noticed on more than one occasion—an observation that had been met with an irrational degree of outrage from his wife. "George isn't like that," Heather had claimed on the ride home. "And how would you know? You hardly spent two minutes with him. I was counting on you to be my escort, and you spent the whole time holed up with Keith Poole talking business!"

A clever tactic, Owen had thought bitterly in the days after Heather had announced her love for Schneider: turning the tables so that Owen would think he'd failed her on some level that night. As if his antisocial behavior were an offense equal to her infidelity.

Owen had lost a wife so Harrisport could gain a mural. Was it any wonder he never visited the library anymore?

Now climbing the stairs after shutting down the house for the night, Owen paused to glance at his daughter's door at the very end of the hall. He was lucky; he knew that. Plenty of teenage girls spent their summers goofing around on the beach, mixing with boys who were too old and too reckless, wanting to grow up too fast. Despite the high-end, puffed-up city life Heather had relocated their daughter to, Meg had retained her small-town ways, and he was grateful for it. So long as he could keep the Caroline Michauds at bay, Meg would be fine.

6

*I*n the still darkness, Cooper Moss shifted on the mattress, hot in nothing but a pair of boxers. The dormer sashes were as high as they'd go, but no breeze came through the screens. He'd found a fan in the garage, one of the old tanks he remembered as a kid that had lived atop dressers all summer long, and he was relieved to find it still worked, even if the blades were as loud as a propeller plane.

Staring up at the sloped ceiling and drawing in deep breaths of moist, warm pine, he could have been twelve years old again. The endless nights he'd lain awake under these eaves, listening to Hudson and his friends outside on the lawn, recently stumbled back from the beach, or holed up in one of the guest bedrooms, their laughter sailing down the hall with the faint smell of pot smoke that Hudson had told him was just candle wax, and for the longest time Cooper had believed him.

But he wasn't twelve; wasn't even close. His thirtieth birthday was two months away, and the house was silent, empty. No one to walk in on in the bathroom, no one to snake past on the stairs. No laughter, no fights. It was obscene, he thought. This much space for one person. As much as he loved the old house, he wasn't sure his coming here to postpone its sale was in its best interest.

Of course, what Cooper was *really* doing in Harrisport was stalling. He had five months to come up with a first draft of a new book for his editor or be in breach of his contract. It wasn't an unmanageable timetable—he'd written two drafts of his first novel in that time, but that manuscript had been inspired, a piece of his heart. He might have said the same about the books that had come after it. But after three Tide McGill mysteries, he was growing tired of his editor's favorite beach-bum detective. He longed to write new characters, new settings. He hoped he'd find fresh ideas in coming back to Harrisport, but in the single day he'd been here, it seemed all he'd conjured were familiar pieces of his youth.

Like Alexandra Wright.

It had been great seeing her again. Cooper would admit he'd worried she might have had a change of heart once she'd arrived. He would have understood if she had, if the old house was too haunted for her to bear, but she'd seemed confident, not at all hesitant to step inside when he'd held the door open for her. He'd wondered whether she'd have remembered his part in that final evening in the guest house after Hudson had broken off their engagement, the kiss he, Cooper, had stolen when he'd taken her home. He *hoped* she might have remembered but he doubted it. She'd been so crushed by the heartbreak of Hudson's dismissal—not to mention thoroughly drunk—Cooper suspected she barely remembered him there at all, let alone his ill-timed kiss.

The truth was, Cooper had never paid much attention to her those first few summers—but why would he have? When he was thirteen, girls and all the drama they seemed determined to stew in could never compete with the lure of books and the ocean. Alexandra Wright had been just a breezy, barefoot girl his brother couldn't keep his hands off of. Then came the night Cooper found her at the guest house, a loose dory that had needed mooring before it floated out to sea.

It had been unusually stormy that last summer, raining in long stretches, relentless sheets that had filled the house with a terrible damp, sour and mildewed, like someone fanning out an old book every time a room was opened. Strangely, unfittingly, the bad weather had ceased when Laurel had come that final week in August, the arrival of Hudson's new fiancée brightening more than the sky. Their mother's blue eyes—up until then perpetually narrowed with displeasure—had relaxed the instant Laurel took her seat at their dinner table. But even at eighteen, Cooper could see Hudson didn't want Laurel Babcock the way he'd wanted Alexandra Wright; he could see how infrequently his brother's hands strayed toward Laurel, hands that had sought out Alexandra like vines.

The years had been kind to her. She was still beautiful, maybe more so, her body more lush with age, her confidence firmly settled. But there was no question she wasn't the same carefree young woman he remembered, the one who'd dared Hudson to meet her on the roof to watch the fireworks that one Fourth of July. She'd become guarded, careful. And yet, looking upon her today in the great room, Cooper had felt a startling rush of compassion and desire, as fierce as the one he'd felt sitting with her in his father's Porsche that August night.

Truthfully that night had been the first tear in his relationship with Hudson. He was so angry that his older brother could have dismissed her so cruelly, so disgusted that Hudson could have led her along when he'd never had any intention of marrying her. Cooper had overheard the discussions between his father and Hudson in the weeks before, the details of Hudson's proposal to Laurel Babcock planned out as strategically as a company merger. Alexandra had been blindsided.

How the confessions had poured out of her that

night. Cooper had tried to capture every word, as if he'd known he might be the guardian of her sorrow for a very long time. There were pieces of that night in novels he'd written—pieces of her too.

Yet for all the intimacy of that one evening, as clear and fixed as it was in *his* memory, she'd not shown an ounce of recognition—or discomfort— in his company today. She'd looked at him with a pleasant detachment.

No, Cooper thought with a rueful smile, if she did remember the kiss he'd boldly—and badly— delivered, it bore little significance to her.

He turned toward the window, reaching back to lace his hands under his head. What would Hudson think to know he'd seen Alexandra again? Would he care? Probably not. Cooper couldn't understand then—and still didn't—how his older brother could turn off feelings like a gas range, twist from a rolling boil to a simmer, then out entirely.

"You're too honest, for one thing," Hudson had informed him when Cooper was sixteen. "You don't have it in you to be smooth, and frankly you have to be if you want to make the most of it." When Cooper had pressed Hudson for an explanation of what "it" was, his older brother had grinned broadly and said only, "You'll see." In time, Cooper had.

There had been many women he'd wanted over

the years, but few he'd wanted with that deep, youthful hunger, that reckless breed of lust that could drive him around a track at full speed. Alexandra Wright had been one of those few. Now she was here. And so was he.

Almost asleep, Cooper heard the crash of a door. He bolted upright and fished around in the dark for his shorts, tugging them on as he began down the hall.

Vandals, he thought. Probably just town kids messing around. He should have figured. All the summers they'd come back to find the remnants of winter visitors, local teenagers so crazed from cabin fever that they'd stormed the house, camping out on the porch, or the bolder ones finding their way in through a second-floor window, only to be evicted when the caretaker came around for his weekly checkups on the property. Small as Harrisport was, there was no way everyone in town had caught the news of his return.

He was grateful for the rush of air against his sticky skin as he walked down the corridor to the stairs, in no hurry and feeling no fear. He could have called the police, could have even picked up his smart phone just in case, but he didn't see the point. This was how he knew he was old, he thought as he marched easily down the steps; he was more concerned about the kids he'd find than in their finding him.

He came down the servants' stairwell and felt the wall for the light. Throwing the switch, he bathed the room in a flickering yellow and sucked in a startled breath to find his father's college roommate standing at the counter with a hand clenched at his breast pocket.

"Uncle Jim?"

James Masterson released himself and laughed. "I'm just glad I got this on solid ground," he said in his familiar drawl, patting the bag of groceries beside him. "Five seconds earlier and we'd be mopping up my old friend Bushmills with a towel."

Cooper grinned. "Then squeezing that towel into a pair of glasses, right?"

"Yes sir," said Jim, tugging out the bottle. "This is hundred-dollar whiskey."

Jim gestured to Cooper's lack of a shirt, then pointed to the ceiling and chuckled. "I sure hope I didn't get you in the middle of something."

"There's no one here but me."

"For now, anyway." Jim brandished the bottle. "Join me?"

"Sure. I'll see if I can find us a couple of glasses."

Cooper crossed to the butler's pantry and jerked on the overhead's chain, squinting against the bare bulb's harsh light. He surveyed the scattering of leftover glasses and dishware in the cabinets, a pale collection compared to the deep, tidy rows of goblets and china he recalled from his youth.

"Sorry for scaring you, son," Jim called. "Your brother was supposed to tell you I was coming up."

"Hud and I don't talk much," Cooper answered, his fingers drifting wistfully over the mismatched lineup, finally landing on a pair of juice glasses.

"So Florence tells me."

Cooper tugged the light off and exited the pantry to discover that Jim had already taken a seat at the breakfast table.

"How in the world did you find this place?" Cooper asked, pulling out a chair for himself and setting the glasses down. "It's hard enough in daylight."

"Oh, I've been here before," Jim said, pouring them each a generous serving and handing one to Cooper. "Your daddy brought me here for a month the summer after our senior year at Duke. It was to be our last big hurrah before joining the ranks. Cheers."

"Cheers." Cooper clinked his glass against Jim's and they each took slow sips. Cooper watched the older man a moment as he swallowed his whiskey, thinking he hadn't aged. Jim Masterson still managed that same crooked smile, the same boyish mop of curly hair, almost all white now— the only evidence to indicate his years.

Jim set down his glass and sighed. "Okay, here's

the bad news: Your mother doesn't want to wait till September to put it up for sale."

Cooper nodded. "I figured she'd say that. So much for my summer plans."

"Now hold on." Jim raised his palm. "I wouldn't pack up just yet. Between you and me, it's not going to happen as fast as Florence thinks. I can tell you right now we're weeks away from getting this listed. Have you seen the guest house yet? The last report from the care-taker said it suffered water damage over the winter. We'll have to see to that repair—and who knows what else," Jim added, glancing warily around the room.

"You know how she gets, Uncle Jim," Cooper said, sitting back. "She'll be on the next plane with a team of Realtors if you tell her that."

"She's welcome to try. But I know more about the market than she does, and I know this house won't sell for nearly what it's worth, looking like this. But enough about her . . ." Jim sat forward, tapped the table affirmatively with his glass, and said, "When do I get to read the next Tide McGill mystery?"

"I'm not sure." Cooper rolled his glass in his palm. "I've been thinking maybe Tide needs to take a vacation for a little while. Maybe let someone else's story fill the pages."

"Any ideas?"

"None I'm particularly excited about." Cooper

studied his last sip before downing it. "I'm hoping something here will inspire me."

"Or some*one*." Jim winked. "I bet there are a few old flames here you might like to start a fire with again, am I right?"

"Hardly." Cooper pushed his glass at Jim for one more pour, his last, he decided as he watched Jim fill it to the top. Hot or not, he'd sleep well now. "No, I think you have me confused with Hud."

"Your brother did do some damage in this town, didn't he?" agreed Jim. "I was more like you. Too nice for my own good, frankly."

Cooper smiled. "Oh, I'm sure you made your mark on a few hearts."

"Pencil marks. Easily erased, I assure you."

"I never really knew any girls in Harrisport," Cooper said. "Most of the people we ever knew here were summer people like us. They came when we came and left when we left. I *did* ask Alexandra Wright to photograph the house for the historic registry application. You probably never knew the Wrights. They're a local family. Builders."

"Oh, I knew 'em." Jim grinned, his gaze drifting wistfully toward the window. "Your daddy was in love with Edie Wright a long time ago. Though she was Worthington then."

Cooper frowned. "You must be thinking of Hud and Alexandra."

"No, I'm thinking of your daddy and Edie," Jim said firmly, glancing up to see Cooper's dubious expression.

"Dad never told me about that."

"He didn't tell a lot of people. Heck, I probably shouldn't have, either," said Jim, winking as he corked the bottle, "so let's just forget I did and call it a night."

"Oh, no sir." Cooper tugged the bottle from Jim's hand and set it back on the table. "This is a writer you're talking to. You don't just drop a bomb like that on a writer and call it quits."

Jim chuckled as he rose. "Sorry, son. This old man's up way past his bedtime."

"Fine," said Cooper, rising too. "But be warned: I'm not letting you off the hook. There's a story there, and I plan to hear it."

Harrisport, Massachusetts
July 1966

*T*ucker Moss steered the red convertible with one arm draped across the back of the plump leather seat. Up ahead, the long stretch of sun-speckled pavement would turn abruptly to rutted dirt and he'd have to draw his hand down to the gearshift, but for now, he could relax and let the sea air tumble through the car's interior.

He loved these winding roads, loved the way the roadster took them. Never mind that in a few months this road would be impassable without a plow. He'd be back in Charlotte and stuck to a desk at the firm by the time snow fell wet and heavy here. But on this thick and humid day, winter was a thousand years away. There was only the moist, salty smell of the air, and the hot sun slicing through the trees, gloriously blinding. For just a while, he might have been anyone, free to do anything he wanted.

"Ten bucks says your old man calls me Joe again," Jim Masterson shouted across the convertible's front seat, his North Carolina accent nearly lost in the roar of the wind.

Tucker smiled at his college roommate and

shouted back in his own similar drawl, "And ten bucks says you don't correct him. *Again*."

"Hey, I don't want to be rude," Jim defended, pushing his glasses higher with the pad of his thumb. "He *is* your father."

As if he'd ever let me forget it, Tucker thought. This wasn't the first time he'd envied Jim Masterson his life: a father who was as agreeable to a son who wanted to follow in his legal footsteps as to one who wanted to run off and join the circus. No wonder Jim was always such an optimist. It was easy to hope for the best when you never knew what the worst might be.

"Hey, watch out."

Jim pointed to a girl on a bicycle who appeared at the edge of the approaching curve, dressed in dungarees rolled to midcalf and a checkered shirt, a fat red braid swinging under her straw hat. She navigated the bike along the soft shoulder one-handed, her other hand flattened on the top of her hat.

Tucker slowed, afraid of startling her, but despite his best intentions, she glanced back and promptly lost her balance. She teetered for what seemed an eternity, her feet shooting out as the bicycle thumped toward the ditch.

"Oh, crap," whispered Jim.

Tucker watched helplessly as she spilled into the culvert. He steered the roadster to the shoulder, shoved it into park, and dashed out to help. By the time he arrived, the girl had already climbed to her feet, her straw hat crooked, knees and palms covered with dirt and sand. Her bicycle lay on its side, its back wheel still spinning. He reached into the ditch to stand it up, but she stepped in front of him. "I can get it myself," she said, glaring. Her eyes were piercing under the dappled shade of her bent brim, a startling shade of pewter. It was hard to be sure how old she was. She could have been fourteen or forty, given the hard frown line that ran down the center of her forehead, or the way her small, pale lips were set.

"I'm just trying to help," Tucker said.

"It's a little late for that," she snapped back, straightening her brim. "I wouldn't have crashed if you'd just kept driving, you goddamn maniac."

Jim hooted. "Listen to this one!"

"You wouldn't have crashed," Tucker said gently, "if you'd had both hands on the handlebars."

"What do you know?" The girl righted her bike and climbed back on, color seeping up her freckled cheeks.

Tucker saw a brown bag in the dirt and retrieved it, brushing sand off its bottom, then handing it to her. "I hope that wasn't your lunch."

"It wasn't." She took the bag from him and tossed it roughly into her basket.

"Why don't you let me give you a ride," he

offered. "My name's Tucker, and this is my good friend Jim—"

"I don't need a ride," she said, moving her bike past him.

"No, really." Tucker was determined now, the desire to remedy his offense irrationally urgent. "I don't mind. I can come back for your bike. I live right up the—"

"I know who you are." She stopped and turned back to him. Their eyes locked. "And the way you drive, I think I'm much safer on my bike."

The young woman continued on, pushing her bike through the sand.

Tucker considered her a moment longer as she marched beside her bike, her red braid sweeping furiously across her back, reminding him of the swishing tail of a vexed horse. He had the sudden and ridiculous urge to tug the knot from its end and unweave it between his fingers, wondering what shade of red it would be all spread out in his hands.

Instead he climbed back into his car and returned them to the road.

"Never let it be said Tucker Moss doesn't know how to sweep a girl right off her feet," Jim teased when they'd picked up speed.

Tucker said nothing, just shifted his eyes to his rearview mirror so that he could watch the young woman slip out of view, undone that she could know something about him and that he could know nothing about her.

• • •

"Heck, Moss, I thought you said y'all lived in a cottage!" Jim Masterson exclaimed as they rounded the final turn and the massive, multi-gabled house came into view.

"This *is* what they call a cottage around here," Tucker said, steering the sports car down the driveway and pulling in beside the carriage house.

"What's with all the trucks?" Jim asked as they made their way through the cluster of vehicles that filled the turnaround, the sounds of construction growing louder.

"Dad's building a guest house." Tucker led Jim to the side entrance and pushed through the screen door into the kitchen.

Doreen Packard looked up from the far end of the long counter. The stout, red-cheeked woman with a bowl of silver-black hair and thick glasses broke into a broad smile of tiny square teeth. For five years, the Packards had managed the Moss cottage: Dorrie its kitchen, her husband, Louis, nearly every other inch of the grounds. Their twin daughters, now living off the Cape, had each served as waitress, sous chef, and chambermaid every summer of their teens.

"Your father's fit to be tied," Dorrie said, one plump hand on her hip. "You were supposed to be here for breakfast."

"I know; I'm sorry." Tucker stopped to give the woman a kiss on her upturned cheek.

Doreen surveyed his guest. "You must be James."

"Yes, ma'am."

"I suppose you boys would like something to eat?"

Tucker smiled. "You're the best, Miss Dorrie."

"I know I am; now scram," she ordered, gently shoving him out of the way. Tucker grabbed a pair of nectarines from a bowl of fruit on the banquette and handed one to Jim, buffing his on his sleeve and biting into the sweet flesh as they walked through the dining room and into the great hall.

"This house is unreal," said Jim, his eyes huge as he looked around. "Why do you ever leave?"

"Winter." Tucker led Jim past the enormous stone fireplace to the end of the room, where a bank of windows looked out onto the grass, and beyond it the dunes. Jim pointed to a group of builders who sat in the shade of the pines that trimmed the lawn, eating their lunches.

Almost at once Tucker spotted the girl on the road mixed among the men. She'd taken off her straw hat, her bright red hair shining like a siren in the cluster of bent heads.

"Hey," said Jim, seeing her too. "Isn't that the . . . ?"

"There you boys are!" Garrison Moss marched into the room smoking a cigarette, hand outstretched. Tucker offered his reluctantly, then stepped aside for Jim's turn. "You're looking skinny, Joe," Garrison said sternly. "Aren't they feeding y'all down there?"

Jim flashed Tucker a quick told-ya-so look. "Oh, they are, sir. Too well, honestly."

"I hear you'll be starting with your daddy's firm this fall too."

"Yes, sir. I'm looking forward to it."

"As well you should be." Garrison gave Tucker a pointed nod.

Dorrie leaned in the doorway. "Lunch is ready when you are, boys."

"Great, I'm starved." Tucker took the opportunity to escape, relief flooding his face as he moved to the door and nodded for Jim to follow.

"You boys get unpacked and settle in," said Garrison. "Son, take Joe down to the beach and show him our little slice of heaven. Dinner's at six. Dress like gentlemen, and don't be late."

"Take your pick," Tucker said, gesturing to the four guest rooms that flanked the corridor.

Jim, not surprisingly, bolted for the one seaside.

"Boy, is this the life!" he declared, flinging his bag onto the creaky twin mattress and circling the low-ceilinged, beadboard-paneled room like a goldfish trying out a new tank. "All this space for just the three of y'all?"

"It's never just the three of us," said Tucker. "You'll see for yourself soon enough. My mother can't stand less than forty people here at any given time."

"Where *is* your mother?"

"Probably shopping somewhere." Tucker walked to the dormer window and drew back the curtain, absently searching the lawn and the activity surrounding the new foundation on the edge of it.

Jim picked up a corked glass bottle filled with tiny shells and studied it. "Florence must love it here."

"Actually, she hates it," Tucker admitted. "She came once last summer, got bit by a tick, and didn't leave the house for the rest of the week."

Jim chuckled. "And you figured the only way you'd get her back was to promise her a proposal, huh?"

"Something like that," Tucker muttered, the plan to ask his college girlfriend to marry him not exactly his, any more than it had been his idea to ask Florence Stoddard out on a date in the first place two years earlier. But with her father being the Stoddard in the Moss and Stoddard law firm, the match had been orchestrated as effortlessly as any of the firm's settlements.

Jim flopped onto the bed, hard enough to make the frame shiver, a wicked grin sliding across his face. "So how long before I get to meet this Helen goddess you promised me?" he asked.

"Slow down, Jimbo. We only just got here."

"Easy for you to say." Jim rose up on his

elbows, his chin thrust out with playful indignation. "You've been talkin' her up to me for three months!"

Tucker smiled, guilty as charged. "Soon," he promised.

"All right, then." Jim tore open his bag and yanked out his swim trunks, snapping them in the air like a flag at the start of a race. "Then let's see this beach!"

7

he real pisser about divorce was the lack of closure. It didn't matter that you had the court order, the piece of paper, the signature. What had amazed Owen Wright—and still did—was how little all that paperwork did for one's heart. Instead of having the chance to really hash it out with Heather in a way that he might have understood, she'd leaped immediately under the safe canopy of documentation and legalese and stayed there indefinitely, virtually untouchable and wholly unaccountable. Try as he did to make peace with the process, no amount of sessions with lawyers, no amount of testimony or counseling could force a person to accept the end of his marriage if he hadn't been the one to choose it.

If anything, the process was worse. Coating it in formalities only made the pain that much more acute, as if he might get so wrapped up in the logistics that he would forget to be angry, to be hurt, to be sad. And adding insult to injury was the decree that he was supposed to cloak those emotions for the sake of Meg, not because he didn't want to spare her any pain—God, he did; of course he did!—but because it was the fair thing to do, the adult thing to do—a claim that boiled Owen's blood. Fair? *Adult?* What about the adult thing of not cheating on one's spouse? What about working through problems instead of throwing in the towel at the first opportunity? Heather had been neither adult nor fair in their marriage, yet he was supposed to be both in the demise of it? The hell with that.

But he'd done it, bitten his tongue every time he'd felt the urge to bad-mouth her in front of Meg, to speak openly about the betrayal. And likewise, Meg had steered clear of blame around him. Once in a while she'd sprinkle their conversation with condemnation of her mother's behavior, comments spoken under her breath, never loud enough that Owen believed they were intended to be heard or used as a jumping board to a more full dialogue. He wasn't the one who had put their daughter in this terrible situation—that had been Heather's doing—and yet he was expected to bear the weight of its fallout honorably. What a crock.

It hadn't helped that he knew very few other men who'd gone through a divorce. Sure, there was the support group that met every Thursday night in the basement of the Congregational Church (he'd gone there for a few weeks at his family's urging, sucked down weak coffee, mostly stared at the floor, then missed a meeting and never gone back), but outside of that smoke-filled, drop-ceilinged room, he felt freakish, a failure. Regardless of what friends claimed over and over—that he, Owen, wasn't the first (or the last) man to be cheated on—Owen felt certain no other man's pain could be anywhere near as intense as his own. And no amount of muffins or cigarettes or folding chairs set up in a circle would convince him otherwise.

It still ached and it still stung and he'd come to believe it always would. Yet whenever Heather called, whenever he heard the ding of his phone and glanced down to the caller screen and saw her number there (like he was doing right now), his first instinct was to take the call, and to take it as quickly as possible. Shameful as it was, a part of him still wanted to hear from her, still wanted to believe there was a chance she'd come to her senses and changed her mind.

He took a fortifying swig of coffee and answered.

"Did Meg lose her phone? She hasn't responded to any of my texts."

Heather offered no greeting, just got straight to the point, as she always did.

"She said she did."

"Well, she didn't."

"Fine, I'll make sure she does."

"Is she there now?"

Owen glanced at the ceiling. "She's upstairs getting ready for work."

"Did you get my message about LA?"

He reached out to straighten a picture of him and Meg on the fridge. "I got it."

"I want her to come with us, Owen."

Us. The pronoun that used to refer to him and her. He frowned. "I have to think about it."

"What's to think about?" Heather demanded. "I'll be with her. It's not like I'm sending her out there alone."

"It's not that," he said. "It's Thanksgiving. She comes here for Thanksgiving."

"I thought we could switch for Christmas this year. Owen, she really wants this trip."

Did she really? When he'd asked Meg, she'd seemed ambivalent.

Owen leaned back against the counter and dragged a hand down his face. The truth was, he loved the idea of having Meg back for Christmas. Loved it more than he hated George's insufferable art opening. It meant she could visit for twice as long. Really, aside from the reason for the switch, it was great news.

"Okay, fine," he said. "We'll work it out when the date gets closer."

"Of course." Heather's voice rose agreeably. "We've got plenty of time."

You *do,* Owen wanted to say as he hung up. *You've got our daughter almost all year round.*

jeff says this party at aidan's is gonna be sick. sure u cant sneak back for 1 nite?

i wish! don't have 2 much fun w/out me

wanna skype 2nite?

if i can

lets do like last time

my dads home! no way

chicken

perv

"What's so funny?"

Meg looked up from her smart phone to find her father glancing inquisitively at her, realizing too late that she'd been smiling as she read through Ty's text messages. She forced her amusement down and changed the screen.

"It's nothing," she said. "Just some joke someone posted on Facebook."

Owen frowned at the road. "You should be careful with that," he said. "What you put on there gets saved for all eternity, you know."

Meg turned to the window so he couldn't see her roll her eyes as she answered patiently, "Yes, Dad. I know."

"I read about stuff that kids put on there—and ten years from now, when they go to get a job, that stuff's still there—"

"I know, Dad."

"—and you think you deleted something and the next thing you know—"

"Dad," Meg cut him off gently, "I know, okay? It's not like I'm going into politics."

He smiled. "You don't know that."

"Yeah, I do."

Owen pulled them into Scoop's parking lot. "I was thinking we could go into Boston tomorrow like we talked about."

His face was lit up with hope; Meg dreaded telling him: "I can't. Aunt Lexi's taking me to the beach. I told her she didn't have to now that she was working down at that house, but she said it was fine."

Owen blinked at her. "What house?"

"That huge place on the water," said Meg. "The one Grandma and Grandpa worked on once. She's taking pictures down there. You didn't know?"

8

*A*s Cape history told it, the invasion of the "wash-ashores" started in the late 1800s. From the beginning, it was the Cape's simplicity, its natural charms that held appeal for the wealthy city dwellers who came to claim the land. Early architects were instructed to build with the landscape in mind, to construct big but undecorated homes. Those who moved there did so to get away from the hustle of cosmopolitan life, to escape it—and the locals built as they were told. But it was that exchange that set in motion a legacy of strained relations. Men who had made perfectly acceptable livings as farmers and fishermen became Realtors and builders to suit the demand. The division in the sand was drawn early on.

Now, as Lexi stood in the middle of the Mosses' great lawn and looked around, she could feel the awe and excitement—and maybe even a bit of the ambivalence—of those who came before her. She'd found Cooper's Jeep gone and a new car in the driveway when she'd arrived, nervous for a moment that it might have belonged to Hudson, but the South Carolina plates calmed her fears. When no one came out to greet her, she wondered whether the car belonged to a girlfriend of Cooper's, thinking maybe his guest was holed up in one of the upstairs rooms waiting for Cooper to return with breakfast: a box of toffee rolls from Roy's, or one of the Edgewater's famous lobster omelets sent out in a flecked cardboard container.

She steered her thoughts to more important matters and set up her equipment on the porch. The sun had yet to push through the morning mist, but when it did, the heat would arrive with it, and she'd want the shade of a deep roof.

By eleven, after two productive hours and not a glimpse of another person on the property, Lexi was back on the porch changing her lenses when she heard the creak of the screen and spun around, startled. In the doorway stood Cooper, barefoot, wearing swim trunks and holding a beach towel in one hand. "I'm sorry," he said, moving toward her. "I didn't mean to scare you."

"You didn't," she said. "I just thought you were . . . I didn't see the Jeep."

"I let Jim take it to get food."

"Jim?"

"My father's best friend. He arrived last night to help me coordinate repairs to the property."

"Oh." Lexi nodded; so much for her theory about a lover. "Then you've hired someone to do the work?"

"Not yet. I've got a guy coming over this afternoon to take a look at the guest house," Cooper said, gesturing to the small cottage at the edge of the lawn that was partially visible behind a curtain of skinny pines. "It's in rough shape, as you might have guessed from the outside."

Lexi wanted to tell Cooper that her mother and her brother could do the work, wanted to offer up their services on the spot, but she didn't. There were only so many times she was willing to kick the hornet's nest.

Cooper squinted up at the sky. "I think the sun's supposed to get here eventually."

"I don't mind. I prefer to shoot exteriors when

it's overcast. The light's even and I don't have to worry about harsh shadows or glare."

"Good to know." He smiled. "I wish I could say the same for writing."

"No luck yet with a new story?"

"Unfortunately, no," said Cooper, slinging the towel over his shoulder. "I'm hoping a hard swim might shake loose some ideas."

A hard swim. Lexi took in a quick survey of his body, a flush of warmth heating her skin.

He stepped closer. "I would have thought you'd be one of the holdouts," he said.

"Excuse me?"

He nodded to her camera. "That's digital, right?"

"I avoided the technology for as long as I could," she admitted with a sigh. "It's just easier. The only downside is getting people to believe the photographs haven't been manipulated. I can spend an hour getting the light just right and clients look at it and assume I spent ten seconds changing the levels on my computer."

"That must be frustrating."

She shrugged. "Not really. Frankly, I enjoy the challenge. I still treat the camera as if it were a traditional camera; I still bracket my shots as if I won't have the chance to fix my mistakes or ramp it up in Photoshop. Honestly, the only thing I *really* miss is my darkroom."

"No space?"

She smiled. "No money. It's too expensive to maintain. Most of the photographers I know say the same thing. I still have my old film camera but I rarely use it now."

Cooper looked wistfully at the camera in her hand. "I dated a photography student once who practically lived in the school's darkroom." He raised his eyes to meet Lexi's, a slow smile pulling at his mouth. "I'm sure I'm not the first guy to leave college thinking darkrooms are sexy as hell. Something about that dim red light."

Lexi turned back to her gear, his confession unquestionably provocative. It didn't help that he stood there in nothing but a pair of shorts, a uniform she might have seen him wearing for weeks at a time when they were younger. But now, his body older, surer, the exposure of skin seemed to charge the air with suggestion. Surely he felt it too?

"I should let you get back to work," Cooper said, moving to the steps.

Lexi nodded, faced again with the uncomfortable feeling that she'd imagined something erotic in a moment that had been utterly innocent.

"Good luck shaking loose those ideas," she offered.

"Thanks," he said. "And good luck with your light. Or lack of it." He began down the lawn; she watched him go, thinking of his words—a lack of light—then wishing suddenly, desperately, for a flash of hot sunshine, no matter what it did for her shot.

"Alexandra?"

Cooper had stopped and turned back to face her. She met his gaze.

"If there's anything you need," he said, "anything I can do to make the job easier for you, let me know, all right?"

She considered him a moment, then said, "There is one thing."

"Name it."

She smiled. "Call me Lexi. No one calls me Alexandra unless they're really mad at me."

"Duly noted," he said, walking backward down the lawn. "Lexi it is."

Edie Wright pushed through the door of the village market and sighed at the blast of cold air against her damp skin. It had already been a stressful morning and she'd yet to arrive at the office. Several of her crew had called in to ask about their next project. They needed work and apologized for calling, but things had grown dire. Edie didn't need to be told. It had been weeks since their last job, and as much as the women wanted to stay loyal to her, Edie knew that if push came to shove, they'd have to accept other work. In high season, that meant being behind the counter at the Crab Trap or waiting tables at Russo's. Edie couldn't bear it. Here it was, peak building season, when every male crew from Provincetown to Sandwich was booked solid, and she couldn't even get so much as a half-bath renovation job. More than forty-five years since she'd fought for a place on her father's crew, and still she struggled to make the people of the Cape see her female builders as every bit as capable as her son's male crews.

She could ask the Bridges, she thought as she wandered down the frozen aisle. She knew Karen had been talking about redoing their kitchen cabinets; she knew too that Karen and Bob's retirement had reduced their budget. She'd offer them a price they couldn't refuse.

"Edie Worthington?"

She turned, startled by the sound of her maiden name. No one had called her that in over forty years.

A lanky, white-haired man waved to her as he approached. She squinted at him.

"You don't remember me, do you?" he asked cheerfully.

Edie looked hard at the man, sure she heard a Southern accent but still no closer to placing him. "No," she said carefully. "I'm sorry; I don't."

"James Masterson. *Jim.*" His lips spread in a puckish smile. "Tucker Moss's college roommate. We met a long, long time ago. I'm not surprised you don't remember—I'm deeply wounded," he added, clapping a hand dramatically over his heart, "but I'm not surprised."

James Masterson? Memories flashed back like lightning. Cokes on the beach. A plate of pastries. Feet scrambling to get across a roof.

"You had glasses," she said, her voice quiet with amazement that she would recall that.

"So you *do* remember me," Jim said, obviously pleased. "Yes, I did. But thanks to the wonders of LASIK surgery, I don't anymore. You see, I went the backward route with my eyesight. Started out life blind as a bat, and now I'm going to finish it out with twenty/twenty." He hesitated, his amusement turning wistful. "It's good to see you, Edie."

She blinked at him, still in shock. "It's been . . . God, it's been years."

"Young lady, it's been *centuries*."

"Not quite," she said. "Decades, maybe."

"You'd never know it to look at you. You look exactly the same."

Edie smiled. "What brings you to Harrisport, James?"

"The house. Florence wants to put it on the market as soon as possible. I offered to come up and help manage the sale."

"I heard," said Edie. "About Cooper coming to see to the cottage, I mean."

"Then you knew about Tuck," Jim said, his voice dropping.

"Yes, I had heard that too."

109

"And I just learned about your Hank, Edie. I'm so sorry."

"Thank you, James."

The air between them fell silent. Edie looked up at him. "Are you in town for long?" she asked.

"It all depends on how much work we have to do to get the house in shape for sale, how difficult it is to get a crew to help. The guest house had a hard winter."

Edie could swear Jim's eyes flashed knowingly at the mention of the spot where they'd first met, but maybe it was only her imagination. Either way, her mind turned sharply from memories to the present. The saleswoman in her bolted from slumber. It was too perfect an opportunity not to at least try.

"You know, James," she said, "I'm still in the construction business. My son runs most of the bigger jobs, but I have a crew of my own I've trained over the years. They're quite good, and available if you're looking."

Jim nodded thoughtfully. "I should have known you'd never put down that hammer of yours."

"I hope you'll keep us in mind," she said, giving her cart a gentle push to signal her intention to leave. "Wright Construction. Our office is on Bridge Street, across from the library."

The tangy sweetness of Jim's famous pulled-pork barbecue slid under Cooper's door at six, and just as he might have done at fifteen, starving after a day at the beach, Cooper rose to find its source. It was amazing to him what just the scent of home-cooked food could do to a space. As he walked downstairs, the cottage felt lived-in for the first time since he'd come back. He'd been searching for the moment, the event that would spark his true sense of return to the place of his childhood; Jim had delivered it.

Cooper came into the kitchen and found Jim at the counter, sleeves rolled up past his elbows and nursing a gin and tonic.

"Smells great."

"Good," said Jim. "I saw there's a little wicker number on the porch, if you'd care to dine al fresco."

Cooper gathered settings and a chilled bottle of chenin blanc and carried the load outside, finding the sky a startling lavender and the air filled with the whistle of crickets. Jim arrived a few minutes later with their plates and they took their seats.

"I saw your photographer today," said Jim. "She's a lovely girl."

Cooper smiled. "Yes, she is."

"Looks nothing like her mother, though," Jim added, shaking open a napkin over his lap.

"You remember her mother that well, huh?"

"I do, indeed. In fact, I spotted her this morning at the store."

"No kidding?" Cooper reached for the wine and filled their glasses.

"We talked for a bit, caught up, if that's the term for it," said Jim, reaching for his fork. "Which reminds me, did that contractor ever come by to look at the guest house?" Cooper nodded; Jim's eyes narrowed expectantly. "And?"

"It needs a ton of work," Cooper reported. "Unfortunately, he says he can't start until the fall. He doesn't think anyone else around here will be able to either. It's peak building season."

Jim slowed his chewing, considering the answer. "That's interesting timing," he mused. "As luck would have it, Edie said she has a crew looking for work right now. I happened to mention we might be needing help on the guest house, and she offered her services. I could give her a call tomorrow. Wouldn't hurt to get her over here just to take a look. I'm sure she'd find it amusing, even if she didn't take the job."

Cooper drew up his glass. "Why would she find it amusing?"

"You don't know?" Jim smiled, shifting his gaze reflexively to the lawn, the view of the guest house shrouded slightly by dusk's dimming curtain. "She and her late husband helped build it."

"You're kidding. I never knew that."

"Ah, yet more secrets I'm spilling."

"Speaking of which . . ." Cooper picked up the

bottle and added more wine to his glass, then some to Jim's. "Now you can tell me the rest of that fat night crawler of a story you dangled and yanked out of the water the other night."

"And what story was that?"

Cooper gave Jim a weary look; Jim chuckled. "Oh, *that* one," he said. "I should warn you, son: It's long."

Cooper gestured to their full plates with his glass. "Good thing we just got started then."

Harrisport, Massachusetts
July 1966

*T*he sun shone without interruption for four straight days. Tucker took advan-tage of their good fortune and showed Jim every inch of the Cape, leaving plenty of time for lazy after-noons on the beach and games of badminton before dinner.

The construction crew had taken advantage of the sun too, making the most of perfect building weather to frame up the guest house in record time.

Tucker considered their progress from the window of his father's study on Thursday morning, his gaze drawn again to the movements of the red-haired girl he'd tried to help upon his arrival. While the men scaled the scaffolding to sheet the roof, she'd been relegated to the edge of the lawn with a stack of short boards, an assignment that Tucker could discern by her fierce expression was not an agreeable one.

"I wasn't aware you had such an interest in construction, son."

Tucker turned to meet his father's reproachful gaze; Garrison had arrived in the doorway and now came into the room, pointing his son to the upholstered chair in front of his desk. "Have a seat."

"Yes, sir." Tucker sat, rubbing his palms expectantly along the carved mahogany of the chair's arms. He waited while his father shuffled through a pile of papers, frowning down at them as if they held some tremendous mathematical equation that had stumped brilliant minds for years.

"So . . ." Garrison began absently, still surveying his documents. "Your roommate seems to be enjoying himself."

"Yes, sir."

"He have a girl down there?"

"No, sir."

"Why not?" Now Garrison raised his eyes, which were narrowed with consideration.

Tucker shrugged. "Says he wants to take his time."

"What for? I guarantee you that boy won't have a spare minute when he starts working for his father. Now's the time to get all that squared away."

Squared away. Tucker hated the way his father could make finding love sound like something to check off your life's to-do list, like laundry or a license renewal.

"Speaking of such matters . . ." Garrison snapped open a silver case, slid out a cigarette, and tapped the end against the metal edge. "Your mother just informed me the jeweler called. The ring's ready to be picked up. I promised her you'd go get it as soon as we're done here."

"Now?" Tucker said, oddly panicked at the announcement. "But Florence won't be here for another month."

Garrison lit his cigarette. "You know how your mother gets."

Tucker nodded. He hadn't even seen this ring—not that it mattered. It was understood he'd use it to propose to Florence when she arrived with her father in August. Tucker wondered what other arrangements had been made on his behalf regarding his future fiancée.

"Oh, and Horace wants you boys in Boston first thing next week," said Garrison, waving away a cloud of smoke. "I assured him your grades were top-notch, but he feels strongly that ya'll will benefit from a refresher before you take the bar."

Next week? Tucker swallowed his disappointment and forced an agreeable nod. He rose and left his father already engaged in a lively phone call with one of the partners by the time he'd closed the door behind him. Upstairs, Jim slept on; Tucker left him a note explaining his absence and slipped out through the kitchen.

As soon as he reached the bottom of the steps and looked out at the driveway, Tucker saw that the red-haired girl had stationed herself in the crescent of space he would need to pull out the roadster. A fierce charge of excitement or dread—maybe both—ran through him, knowing he'd have to approach her and ask her to move her work. She had her back to him as he came closer, her thin frame hunched over a board, biting her lip as she pounded at the point of a nail to drive it out the other side.

"Hi," he said tentatively, not wanting to startle her, especially not while she was wielding—swinging!—a hammer.

She paused briefly, shot a quick assessing look at him over her shoulder, and returned to her work.

Tucker took another step forward. "Look, I really hate to ask you to move all this, but, you see, I have to pull out. So if you might could—"

"It's fine," she said, lowering her hammer and already shuffling loose boards into a pile.

"At least let me help." This time Tucker didn't wait for her answer before he started gathering the rest of the boards and carrying them to the edge of the lawn.

He handed her the hammer, wondering what had become of her hat.

"What is it you're doing here, if you don't mind my asking?" he said. "See, I thought builders were supposed to put nails *into* boards, not hammer 'em out."

"They are." The girl blew a lazy tendril out of

her face. "But some *idiot* put up a partition wrong, so all the boards had to come down, and I'm taking the nails out so we can use them again. The boards, not the nails," she clarified.

Tucker smiled. "Yeah, I figured that."

She squinted up at him, considering him in a way that Tucker couldn't quite make out.

He slid his hands into his pockets. "I really am sorry about your bike."

"Hey, Edie!" someone called out from behind them. Tucker turned to see a tall, dark-haired man with his hands cupped around his mouth. "Kyle needs more spade bits!"

"Tell him to hold his goddamn horses!" the girl shot back at him.

Edie. It suited her, Tucker thought.

"Must be hard working with all these guys," he said.

Edie swung her braid testily over her shoulder.

"Are you the only girl?" he asked.

"Do you see any others?"

Tucker glanced up to find the same dark-haired man scowling at him from behind a stretch of studs. "That must be your brother, then. He's giving me one of those big-brother glares."

"Hank's not my brother," she said.

"Boyfriend, huh?"

"No," she snapped, but her glance back to Hank made Tucker suspect he wasn't the first person to wonder. "What's it to you, anyway?"

119

Tucker frowned, exasperated. "Look, did I do something to offend you?" he asked carefully. "I mean, besides the whole business with your bike. Because I swear, you're at me like I ran over your favorite pair of shoes."

Edie Worthington considered him a moment; Tucker watched a shift in her expression, softness glinting in her gray eyes. "Well, I don't see how you could have, since I don't *have* a favorite pair of shoes."

"Oh." He saw the smallest hint of a smile creep up her lips. "Then that couldn't have been it. Maybe a favorite *hat?* I did notice yours has gone missing."

Now her grin wouldn't be kept down. She sighed, her whole body, once rigid as a nail, relaxed. "It's not you," she admitted. "I'm just mad as hell because every time I ask Hank to let me do something real, he puts me to work doing *this* crap." She gestured to the pile of boards. "And I'm not even the one who screwed it up in the first place!"

"Maybe he worries about you," Tucker suggested.

Edie flashed another glare in Hank's direction. "That's not it. He's even more a drill sergeant than usual because my dad's running a job in Eastham. And Hank can't stand the idea of a girl being a better carpenter than he is."

"Are you?"

Edie frowned. "Not yet—but I could be," she added firmly. "If he gave me a damn chance. He thinks he knows what's best for me and he doesn't."

"Yeah," Tucker said quietly. "I know the feeling."

"Ede, the spade bits! Come on, already!"

They both turned at Hank's call, Edie's cheeks suddenly soaked in scarlet. Tucker steeled himself for another of her cuss-filled shouts, but instead she just turned back to him and rolled her eyes. "I have to go," she said, "before I get court-martialed."

Tucker smiled. "You're always welcome to come down to the beach to cool off after work, you know."

Edie squinted up at him skeptically.

"I'm serious," he said. "It must be awful hot out here all day. I'm sweating like a dog right now and I'm not even doing anything." Which wasn't entirely true; he was talking with her—could that have been the source of his heat?

"We're not allowed on the beach," Edie said.

"Says who?"

She shrugged. "Everyone knows that."

"Well, I don't, and it's my beach as much as anyone's. I say bring your suit tomorrow. Heck, tell everybody on the crew to bring one."

"What would your father say?"

"Never mind my father; I don't," Tucker said as

he began to walk backward toward the roadster, the lie feeling as refreshing and thrilling as a cold drink.

All the next day, Tucker had the strangest sense of killing time. Even while he and Jim battled it out over badminton and took a drive to Orleans for a late lunch, Tucker couldn't shake a sense of impending excitement. When four thirty drew near and Jim suggested Tucker join him for a before-dinner swim, Tucker changed into his trunks but said he'd follow later, wanting to be in sight when the crew—and Edie Worthington in particular—began to put up their tools.

It had been a hot day—not as grim and humid a heat as he would have endured in Charlotte if he'd been there, but it was thick enough that a quick dip would have been welcome. At the first sign of cleanup, Tucker pushed out the side door and crossed the driveway to where Edie and the others were packing up.

"So where's your suit?" he asked brightly.

She looked up and blinked at him. "You were serious?"

"Of course I was." Tucker shrugged. "Never mind, you don't need one to get your feet wet."

He watched her eyes shift back to the rest of the crew; Tucker spotted head carpenter Hank looking their way as he deftly wound an extension cord between his elbow and wrist. Tucker offered him a cheery wave; Hank didn't send one back.

"So what do you say?" Tucker asked.

Edie smiled, giving the group one last look before she answered. "Just give me a minute to say good-bye."

Edie was almost to the guest house when she saw the Mustang slide down the driveway and swing into an open spot beside Hank's truck. She knew the hot-pink Mustang—everyone in Harrisport with eyes in their head knew it—but what Edie *didn't* know was what business its owner, twenty-year-old Missy Murphy, the daughter of Harrisport's most-loved restaurateur, Teddy Murphy, had at the Moss job site.

In the few minutes it took for Missy to slip from the driver's side, looking as fresh and untouched as a newly milled board, and carrying a picnic basket between her hands as tightly as a bride her bouquet, Edie stepped up beside Sonny, who was cleaning buckets, and demanded, "What's Missy Murphy doing here?"

"Give you one guess," Sonny said, his gaze fixed on the shapely blonde as if she'd come to deliver him a thousand dollars. Edie frowned, stymied by the useless answer, and tried to solve the mystery herself while Missy approached, deciding, with a prickle of agitation, that what Sonny had meant was that Missy had obviously come to make a play for Tucker Moss.

Missy approached Edie with the sort of detached half smile that someone would give a clerk at a department store, looking to see a shoe in their size. As she neared, Edie scanned the older girl's outfit, deciding Missy looked ridiculous and cheap in her lilac gingham tank top and sailor shorts. Who arrived at a job site showing off her stomach like it was a newly painted wall?

"I'm looking for Hank." Missy pushed a piece of gum between her glossed lips. "Is he here?"

Edie blinked at Missy, shocked at the question. Had she asked for *Hank?*

"He's inside," Sonny answered before Edie could, pointing to the guest house. Missy shifted the basket in her hands; the salty smell of chowder filled the air.

"Thanks," Missy said, her gratitude directed solely at Sonny before she turned and marched toward the guest house, her honey-blond hair bouncing over her shoulders.

Edie looked back at Sonny and frowned. "Might want to use one of those buckets to catch your drool," she said.

"Very funny," snapped Sonny, his eyes still fixed on Missy's careful steps down the lawn. "That sneaky son of a . . ."

"Who?" demanded Edie.

"Who do you think?" Sonny snorted. "Hank. He's been wanting to ask her out for weeks."

Weeks? No, thought Edie. Surely Sonny was

wrong. How was it that Edie hadn't known any of this? She spent eight hours a day with Hank Wright, knew what he ate for lunch, what he wore, what part of his jaw he always missed when he shaved.

She stifled a sense of outrage, then another flush of hurt, though she wasn't sure why she should feel left out or care who Hank Wright dreamed about when he wasn't ordering her around.

"Lucky stiff," said Sonny, returning to cleaning his buckets.

Edie sniffed. "I've had Murphy's chowder and it's not great," she said.

Sonny chuckled. "I'm not talking about the *food,* Ede."

"You're sure no one will care?" Edie asked as she followed Tucker through the grass, a tangy breeze hitting her face the minute they crested the dune.

"See for yourself." He pointed down the beach to where Jim Masterson was waving madly to them on top of a striped towel. "Look; you've even got a welcoming committee."

Edie smiled, loving the feel of hot, velvety sand under her arches. She'd abandoned her boots on the lawn, socks too, and rolled up her overalls in preparation for the surf.

"Ahoy, mates!" Jim leaped to his feet, assuming a mock salute, then a bow as they arrived.

Tucker made the introductions. "Edie Worthington, James Masterson."

"But everyone calls me Jim—among other things," Jim said, grinning as he thrust out a hand. "Nice to meet you officially, ma'am."

"You too." Edie offered Jim a rueful look. "I wasn't exactly in the best of moods when you first saw me."

"Who could blame you?" Jim exclaimed. "He's a menace on the road, Edie. And hardly a Southern gentleman. Now, me, I'd have *carried* you home."

"Don't mind Jim," Tucker said. "He's a terrible flirt."

"And he means it too," said Jim. "I'm truly lousy at it. Ask anyone."

Edie laughed, thinking again how glad she was that she'd taken Tucker up on his offer, wondering for a fleeting moment whether Hank saw her leave—or if he was too busy with Missy Murphy. Not that she gave a crap what—or who—he saw. He could choke on that goddamn oversalted chowder for all she cared.

"I'm afraid I've drained the well," said Jim, gesturing to the bucket of ice beside the towel. "I was just on my way up to see what my chances were for restocking. That housekeeper of y'all's is ferocious. I didn't dare take an apple out of the fruit bowl."

"Oh, Miss Dorrie's a sweetheart," said Tucker. "Her bark's worse than her bite."

Edie knew they meant Doreen Packard; Doreen and her mother were close friends. For years Edie's mother had shared Doreen's tales of summers serving the Moss family. Edie had never paid much attention to the stories; she suddenly wished she had.

Fortified by Tucker's assurances, Jim departed for the top of the beach, leaving Tucker and Edie standing alone.

Tucker nodded to the water. "You want to give it a feel?"

"Sure." Edie followed Tucker down to the edge of the surf. The frigid water stung her ankles.

"I bet you swim in this, don't you?" he asked.

"Sometimes," she admitted. "Don't you?"

"Not me. Jim's been in a few times, but my skin's still not thick enough."

"Are you serious? How many summers have you been coming here now?"

"Too many to admit, I know," he said. "I do love it here, though. It's different from our coastline. You must be on the beach every chance you get. I would be if I lived here year-round."

"I love the beach," she said, "but I love other places more."

"Really?" He smiled at her. "Maybe sometime you can show me one of 'em."

She met his eyes. "Maybe."

Tucker dug his heel into the wet sand, watched the small divot fill with water.

"I was thinking if you weren't busy," he said, "maybe you'd like to come with me and Jim to Provincetown tomorrow."

"What for?"

"I don't know. Just go for a drive. Walk around the town. Get some lunch." He caught her gaze again and searched her eyes. "What do you think?"

Edie turned back to the water, not sure. He made it sound so simple, but what if someone saw them; what if word got back to Hank that she'd been driving around with Tucker Moss? Hank would never let her live it down. And why was she suddenly feeling guilty for something she hadn't even done? God knew Hank was seeing to his own matters, stockpiling his own secrets.

Consternation rose in her throat.

Besides, P-town was safe. It was unlikely they'd see anyone she knew, anyone who knew her or her family.

And she did enjoy Tucker Moss's company.

"All right," she said brightly, feeling a swell of excitement rush out with her answer, prickling her skin just as the frigid water had done moments before. "I'll come."

9

The town beach was already packed by the time Lexi and Meg carried their cooler and canvas bags onto it at eleven. Meg tented her hands over her eyes and scanned the length of the shore like a first mate, pointing delightedly when she'd found them a free square of sand. Two years away and Lexi swore the beach had shrunk. Even before she'd left for London, she never remembered it being this crowded before noon. Growing up, she and Kim could always count on a handful of "secret spots" to lay down their towels and bake themselves an unhealthy shade of copper. Now her secret spots were common knowledge—and fair game.

Feeling the familiar giddiness of ocean air and silky sand underfoot, they deposited their belongings and laid out their towels, climbing out of their cover-ups and sitting down, burrowing their rumps into the sand.

"Whoa," exclaimed Lexi, startled to see the tiny electric-pink two-piece that appeared when Meg's oversize T-shirt and jeans shorts came off. "Has your dad seen you in that?"

"No," said Meg, looking suddenly stricken as she fussed with her straps. "And you can't tell him. He would freak. He thinks I wear that ratty old one-piece from swim team. Why do you think I like coming to the beach with you instead?"

Lexi smiled, reminded of her own days of covert swim fashions. It was a rite of passage for every teenage girl on the water to reach that age when you'd leave your parents' house as covered up as a rosebush in winter, only to fling off the tarp of your clothes the minute your toes hit the sand.

Before Hudson came along and turned Lexi inside out, Kim had always been the daring one between them when it came to beachwear, every summer modeling a new two-piece, while Lexi had worn her same navy one-piece until it was pilled in the seat and muddy gray. But when Hudson had suggested she'd look hot in a bikini, Lexi had bought one that very same day, relishing her body and its effect on her new boyfriend as if she'd never bothered to notice before.

Owen had been unkind.

"Moss dresses you up like a stripper," he accused, seeing her in her new suit when she'd come home from the beach.

"He doesn't dress me up like anything," Lexi had defended. "I dress myself."

Of course, it had been a lie. Hudson Moss might as well have filled her drawers and closets himself; every piece of clothing Lexi looked at or even bought was with his opinion in mind. For five years, most every decision she made was the same.

A pair of young men ambled by, stealing glances at Meg.

"So tell me all the good stuff," said Lexi, fishing out a pair of Cokes from their cooler.

"Well . . ." Meg grinned sheepishly. "There's this guy. . . ."

"And . . . ?"

"And he's so awesome."

"Okay, come on. Let's see pictures," Lexi urged, pointing to Meg's bag.

Meg withdrew her smart phone and scrolled gleefully through her albums until she found one and held it out. "His name's Ty."

Lexi nodded approvingly. "He's cute."

"He's *so* cute. His dad's this big-time documentary producer. Ty makes these little films and sends them to me. I could show you one."

"I'd love that."

Meg gave a grateful smile. "You're so much cooler than my dad, Aunt Lex."

"Aunts get to be cool," said Lexi. "Dads get to be dads."

"Yeah, but mine doesn't even try." Meg groaned, scooping up a handful of sand and trickling it over her painted toes. "Did you see his face when I asked for a glass of wine?"

"He's overprotective," said Lexi. "He always has been."

"Is that why he got all pissed off when I told him you were working at that house taking pictures?"

Lexi turned to Meg. "You told him that?"

"I didn't mean to get you into trouble, Aunt Lex. I didn't know he wasn't supposed to know."

Lexi put her arm around Meg and gave her a reassuring hug. "It's okay, sweetie. You didn't get me into trouble. Your dad just holds grudges sometimes; that's all."

"About what?"

Lexi hesitated, trying to decide the best way to answer; part of her wanted to speak truthfully, but another part wanted to be more charitable. As frustrated as she was with Owen, it was important that Meg know her father's heart was always in the right place—even when it was somewhere he didn't belong.

"Your dad worries, that's all. Your granddad was the same way. I think a lot of men are."

Meg sighed. "I just wish it didn't have to be this hard; that's all."

"Which part?" asked Lexi.

Meg looked up at her, the self-confident teen suddenly a wary child, her light eyes bright with such concern that Lexi wanted to wrap her arms around her again and not let go this time.

"You know," Meg said with a sad smile. "All of it."

Stopped at the light just three blocks from the office, Edie clapped her hands on either side of her head and pressed the misbehaving strands down, keeping the pressure there for several seconds before letting go. She glared at her reflection in the rearview mirror, seeing the short spikes snap up, undaunted. She looked like a goddamn thistle blossom. All that was missing was a circling bee.

She'd thought it would be easier chopping it all off—and most days it was—but she'd slept fitfully the night before and her hair revealed it. Hank had been heartbroken when she'd cut it. Honest to God, she couldn't believe his face when she'd come in the door from Denise's shop. She might have rearranged his nail drawers, or lost his favorite hand plane.

"You never said a word," he'd managed, his voice a strange mix of wonder and deep hurt. "It's so . . ."

"Short," she had finished for him. "And I love it. I should have done it years ago."

"You might have told me you meant to cut it."

"It's just hair, Hank."

"So you'll grow it back."

"I will not," she'd said firmly. "Do you mean to leave me now? Is that the whole purpose of our being together—my damn hair?"

God, where had *that* come from? Edie had wondered even as she'd said it. The man had a right to be surprised, maybe even sad. After all, she'd worn her red hair down her back as long as he'd known her.

She'd watched him, not sure whether he meant to snap back at her, not about to blame him if he did.

"I'm too old for it," she'd said. "I really am."

"Wait." He'd given her a wry look then. "Are we still talking about your hair?"

Edie gave in to a sheepish smile, remembering the scene as she steered the truck into the parking lot of the white shingled building that bore WRIGHT CONSTRUCTION on its front, and along the ell addition that jutted out from its back, storage space that Hank had added in the seventies when their lumber distributor had gone under. A curious flutter of energy propelled her out of the pickup—maybe it was the memory, thinking of their married life—and stayed with her as she walked briskly to the front door.

Coming inside, she found Owen on the phone, his eyes shifting warily to her as he said, "She just came in. Hold on." He held out the cordless, his fingers clamped over the receiver. "It's some guy named Jim Masterson. Wants to talk to you about the Moss guest house."

"Oh." Edie reached for the phone, wishing now that she hadn't indulged in such a swift pace. Her breath seemed to come in short spurts, and a fine layer of sweat had arrived along her hairline. She pressed the phone to her ear. "Hello, James."

"Edie, I've been thinking about your offer to restore the guest house."

"I'm glad to hear it." Relief and trepidation rushed up in her. She'd hoped he'd call, hoped he wouldn't. "And?" she pressed.

"Cooper had a man come by and look at it yesterday."

"Who?"

"A gentleman by the name of Holloway."

"No-show Bo." Edie snorted. "He's no gentleman, but never mind. What did he say?"

"He said it's bad but that he can't possibly start until fall."

"Well, thank God for that. You don't want him, James. He's a menace."

"That's a strong word, Edie."

"I have stronger."

"Yes, I know." Jim chuckled. "I remember."

She glanced over her shoulder to find Owen studying her and looking concerned. She cleared her throat. "James, you let me get a look today and we'll have a quote to you by tomorrow morning."

"That soon?"

She *had* mentioned she was desperate, hadn't she? "That soon," she confirmed.

"Then by all means. How's three o'clock?"

"I'll see you then."

She hung up and walked the receiver back to Owen's desk.

"Who was that?" he asked.

"He just told you. James Masterson." She

walked back to her own desk and began riffling through a pile of papers, hoping to avoid the subject if she appeared busy.

Owen rose from his chair and followed her across the room. "I mean what does he have to do with the Moss place?"

"He's an old friend of the family," Edie said, feigning interest in a supply list.

"You were expecting his call."

"Was I?"

"That's what he said."

"Oh. Then I guess I was." Edie dropped into her chair, her skin warming. She felt trapped, like a child caught in a lie. Who was the parent here, dammit?

"So what did he want?"

"He wants to hire a crew to repair the guest house," Edie said, "and I told him I'd pull together a quote."

"Using whose crew?"

"Whose do you think?"

"Mom, be reasonable," said Owen. "The women aren't experienced enough to handle a job like that."

"How would you know?" she demanded.

"Let me talk to Anderson again. I'm sure I can get him to give you that glazing job my guys couldn't take last week."

"I don't need my son's seconds," she huffed.

Owen folded his arms. "Now you're just being difficult."

Yes she was, dammit. But so was he!

She scooted to the edge of her desk, trying to impart an authority she most certainly didn't feel at that moment. She might have known he'd react this way. And wasn't she the world's biggest hypocrite! How quickly she'd worried about Lexi taking a job at the cottage, and now she was begrudging her son's concern for her doing the same.

Edie took a breath and regarded her son, startled at how much he suddenly reminded her of Hank. Maybe it was the stiff posture, the mop of dark hair. Or maybe it was the deeply knotted brow.

She slumped forward on her elbows, losing steam. "Owen, my crew has gone weeks without work, and frankly if I don't find them something soon, I'll lose them."

"Both of you now," Owen said, shaking his head. "Both of you back down there."

"We're not 'back down there,'" Edie clarified gently. "We're working. It's entirely different."

Owen let his hands drop to his sides, unconvinced.

"Sure it is." He sighed. "Like apples and apples."

Cooper swung the Jeep into the tidy square of gravel that hugged the front of the white shingled building and pulled into a parking spot. It was a far cry from the place Jim had described to him over dinner the night before, but then, Jim had warned him the building had been fixed up. Now a visibly booming coffee shop, it seemed the only remnants of its previous purpose—besides the his-and-hers entrances—was the sign above the double doors, the faded block letters a dramatic contrast to the rest of the crisply restored building: GRANGE HALL.

Cooper crossed through the parking lot and decided to walk the perimeter of the building before stepping inside, wanting to glean as much as he could of the place where his father and Edie Worthington had spent a summer afternoon getting to know each other better. This was new territory for him. In his earlier novels, research had been minimal. Now he had a story to tell that wasn't his own.

Jim had been right to prepare him; it was a long story, indeed. But what a story! He'd be a fool not to at least pursue it; three days at the house, and he hadn't come up with a single idea that excited him.

A young couple came out one of the doors, carrying coffees, heads bent in conversation, the nearness of their bodies as they crossed to their car indicating that theirs was a fresh romance. Cooper's thoughts shifted to Alexandra, recalling her behind her camera, or the few times he'd looked up from his computer to see her crossing the lawn the day before, reminded each time of the summer days he'd hoped to catch a glimpse of her, just to feel that immediate and strange rush of lust tear through him like a fever. A woman's body had been a source of mystery and confusion then, a destination he'd craved and not known why.

He smiled now, thinking of the clumsy kiss he'd given her the night he'd driven her home. He'd felt bold and reckless behind the wheel of his father's precious car, wanting to repair the hurt his older brother had caused, wanting to comfort her, and wanting her too. How many times over the years had he replayed that kiss, hoping to remember it more clearly, but in his hunger, specifics had been lost. Her eyes had been glossy as he'd neared, the taste of her leftover tears ending up on his tongue. And who had pulled away first? She had, of course. He was the kid brother of the love of her life—the love who had just taken it all away.

For a long time Cooper had hoped he might have a chance to do that kiss over—more than a kiss; he'd imagined making love to his brother's fiancée—but then life had taken him and his heart to other places: lovers he'd been sure were the one, erotic and insatiable women who had steered him far from his teenage summer lusts. Now he was back in Harrisport, and that forgotten wish to have another chance with Alexandra—*Lexi*—was returning too.

He saw a well-shaded teak bench nestled invitingly at the back of the building. He'd get himself a cup of coffee and claim it.

Enough daydreaming. It was time to write.

Harrisport, Massachusetts
July 1966

*T*ucker should have suspected something was wrong when Jim didn't appear at breakfast. In their four years at Duke, he'd never known his roommate to miss out on a plate of biscuits and white gravy.

"I'm calling it Lobster's Revenge," Jim announced from his bed when Tucker stepped into the guest room and found his best friend's face as gray as a clam flat. "The little guys curse your intestines for eatin' 'em."

"Oh, Jimbo . . ." Tucker shook his head. "What a lousy break."

"Don't pretend you're not just a little bit thrilled. You'll have her all to yourself now."

Tucker frowned. "I'm not going," he said. "I can't leave you here alone."

"What did you plan to do? Sit by my bed all day like a nurse? No offense, but I don't want a sponge bath from you."

"None taken," said Tucker with a chuckle. "Lucky for you, Miss Dorrie makes a mean get-well soup."

Jim groaned. "I'll bet."

Tucker gave his friend's shoulder a gentle pat

as he rose. "I'll have her fix you something."

"Just make sure it didn't come up in a net or a trap," Jim said. "They're all in on this. It's a seafood conspiracy; mark my words." Jim paused, his teasing smile wilting. "You tell Edie about Florence yet?" he asked gently.

The question sobered Tucker too. He shrugged lamely.

"I don't blame you one bit, you know," said Jim. "She's a real firecracker."

Who could set my whole world aflame, thought Tucker.

"It's just a ride up the coast, Jimbo."

"Sure it is." Jim nodded, but Tucker could see his best friend knew the excuse was as weak as his stomach.

They'd agreed to meet by the town clock at eleven. Tucker had offered to pick Edie up at her house, but she had declined, suggesting a neutral location instead, a place neither in his world nor hers, as if the point of origin for their trip might somehow lessen any sense of wrongdoing. While she waited, Edie did her best to turn away from the busy foot traffic that lined the sidewalk on the other side of the street, just in case any familiar faces might catch a glimpse of Adam Worthington's daughter, though she suspected few would recognize her out of her usual dungarees and dressed now in a sleeveless floral shift and woven flats. She worried she had made a mistake wearing something so fancy; she didn't want Tucker Moss to think she was taking his invitation too seriously. She worried she'd come too early; she worried she'd come too late. With every minute that passed, a new concern arrived with it.

Then, as soon as she saw the flash of red come around the corner, her heart soared with relief. But there was only Tucker—where was Jim?

"Food poisoning," Tucker explained as he came around to open the door for her. "He wanted me to tell you he's sorry he couldn't come."

"How awful for him," said Edie. "You didn't have to leave him on my account."

"I tried to stay. He practically kicked me out."

Edie nodded, thinking what she suspected Tucker had already considered: Without Jim there, their plans took on an undeniable significance, an unspoken weight. Just the two of them made this a date, didn't it?

If the equation concerned Tucker, he didn't show it. Edie let his smile settle the nervous flutters in her own stomach as he pulled the car away from the sidewalk. She glimpsed a basket on the floor of the backseat. Tucker smiled. "Since it was such a nice day, I had Miss Dorrie pack us a picnic. I hope you're hungry."

She was—starving.

"P-town's a half hour away. We could find somewhere closer," she suggested.

"Sure. Where did you have in mind?"

"You still want to see one of my favorite places?"

He smiled. "More than anything."

She smiled too. "Then take a right at the light."

Edie leaned back into the smooth leather seat and felt her whole body relax as the convertible sent them speeding down the road.

The Grange Hall had been abandoned for only seven years, but with the harsh seaside climate, it looked more like seventy. Double doors balanced its unadorned facade like attentive eyes.

A pair of No Trespassing signs hung, crooked, off a nearby tree.

"What is this place?" Tucker asked, pulling them gently into a shady spot beneath a massive oak.

"It's the old Grange Hall," Edie explained. "They used to have meetings and dances here."

"What's with the two doors?"

"One for men, one for women."

Tucker laughed. "You're kiddin'."

"Nope," said Edie. "It's a wreck now. No one uses it. I think the town hopes every winter it'll just collapse in on itself and they won't have to figure out what to do with it."

Tucker squinted to read the faded stenciled letters that curled above the peeling double doors, a rusted but formidable-looking padlock gripping each one shut. "Seems a shame," he said.

"It is," said Edie. "I keep asking my dad to fix it up, but he could never afford to do it."

"Someone should," said Tucker firmly. They made a trail through the tall weedy grass. "You come here a lot?"

"More often than the folks who put up those No Trespassing signs would like," she admitted as they rounded the building. They climbed a pair of granite blocks to the back door, and Tucker watched in amazement as she turned the knob and, with a small shudder, the door gave way.

"Why bother with that big ol' lock in the front if they keep the back open?" he asked.

"You'd be surprised how few people come around and look."

Tucker followed her inside, the hot, musty smell of mildewed wood choking. He pressed his knuckles under his nose and winced. "You really like this place?"

"I love it," she announced, clearly unoffended by the stench. "I love to come in here and imagine how I'd fix it up. How I'd make it a house." Tucker watched, entranced, as she flitted around the open space, gesturing wildly as she mapped out the floor plan of her fantasy. "I'd put a kitchen here and a little breakfast booth right here; then I'd put up maybe a half wall over here for a—" She stopped, catching his admiring gaze. "What?" she asked.

He shrugged. "You're not like anyone I know, that's what. You're amazing."

145

"And you're full of it," she said, resuming her planning while Tucker continued to take her in. For fifteen more minutes, he followed her around the space, lost in her imagined home, so transported he no longer minded the sour smell. All he wanted to do was be near her, to be part of her waking dream.

While Tucker went back to the car for the picnic basket, Edie found them a soft patch of grass and they unpacked everything on a taupe spread, one corner of which bore an embroidered M. "Hope you like egg salad," said Tucker, handing Edie a wrapped sandwich.

She peeled back the waxed paper eagerly, but a pang of guilt came with her first bite, as she thought of her mother's good friend working to make the sandwich for her, knowing her mother would have a fit if she found out. Edie took a small dose of comfort thinking that Doreen didn't know the recipient of her hard work. Surely Tucker hadn't used her name in his request.

She looked up and found him smiling at her expectantly.

"How is it?" he asked.

"Delicious."

"And there's plenty more too," he said, pointing to the basket. "Brownies and fruit salad."

The guilt returned; Edie swallowed.

"So besides hammering nails out of boards and

getting run off the road by bad drivers," Tucker began, "what else do you like to do for fun, Edie Worthington?"

She smiled. "I just showed you."

"Ah. So you break into abandoned buildings regularly, do you?"

"Every chance I can," she said. "What about you?"

"Oh, I try not to break into too many if I can help it." She tilted her head knowingly; he grinned. "Nah. I pretty much follow Jim around. He's sure to find fun."

"And you're not?"

Tucker shook his head. "It eludes me most of the time, I'm afraid."

"I thought college was supposed to be fun," said Edie.

"Me too."

"So what did you study?" she asked.

"Law."

"Good for you. Now what?"

"Now . . ." Tucker paused to take in a deep breath, as if he needed fortification to answer. "Now I pray I pass the bar and join my father's law firm. It's agony."

"Oh, yeah, I'll bet," Edie teased. "It must be horrible to know you don't have to worry about getting some big job right out of college."

"As a matter of fact, it is." Tucker frowned up at the Grange; Edie watched him, seeing now that his trepidation was genuine.

He turned to her. "Can you keep a secret?"

She nodded.

"I'd sooner sell Cokes out of my trunk than be a lawyer at my father's firm," he said in a conspiratorial whisper. "At *any* firm."

"Then why did you go to law school?"

"I didn't have a choice. I mean, I guess I did, but . . ." Tucker sighed. "I'm his son, his only child. If I don't join the firm and keep the Moss name on that letterhead, who will?"

"But why is that your responsibility?"

"Lately I've been thinking of making a break for it," he said. "Waiting until everyone's there—my father, the partners, everyone—and just announcing that I'm not doing it. That if anyone wants to find me, I'll be on Fiji, selling coconuts on the beach." He looked at Edie and found her gaze skeptical. "You don't think I can do it, huh?"

She smiled, sighed. "I only wish I had your problem," she said. "My father wants to see Hank take the reins of the business. He doesn't think I could handle it."

"Hank or your dad?"

She gave Tucker a woeful look. "Both."

"Well, then." Tucker drew up his knees and hooked his arms around them. "Looks like we're both going to have to fight to get what we want, doesn't it?"

"Damn straight," Edie said firmly. "I plan to have a crew of my own one day. All women. All of us good enough to make the men envious. So if my dad and Hank think I'm going to sit back and needlepoint pillow covers, they're out of their goddamn minds."

Tucker chuckled.

"What's so funny?"

"You," he said. "Do you always cuss this much?"

"Cuss?"

"You know, swear."

"I know what it means," said Edie, reaching across him for the fruit salad and plucking a fat strawberry off the top. "What's the big deal? Everybody swears."

"I don't," he said.

"Why not?"

"It's disrespectful."

"To who?"

"To God, for starters. Everyone knows that."

She rolled her eyes and bit into the berry.

"Heck, I don't know why I'm bothering explaining it to you," Tucker said, grinning as he watched a thread of juice cling to her bottom lip. "Everyone knows y'all are a bunch of heathens up here."

"We are not," Edie defended. "We have religion."

He snickered. "Oh, right. *Baseball*. And maybe if you start prayin'," he teased, "your beloved Sox will actually win the series in your lifetime."

"Very funny." Edie considered him a long moment. "You're not what I expected."

Tucker leaned back on his elbows. "What did you expect?"

"You don't want to know."

"No, really, I do."

"A jerk," she said plainly.

"Yeah, well." He looked up, considering the roof of leafy branches above them. "My dad always says I'm not living up to my potential. Might could be that's what he means."

Edie noticed a spot of egg salad on his chin. She reached out and gently brushed it off. His face radiated appreciation, or maybe it was pleasure.

"I happen to like you this way," she said. "I bet most people do."

Did she mean most girls? Tucker wanted to ask but he was too busy savoring her first statement: *I happen to like you this way.* And how good her fingers had felt on his skin.

"I like you this way too," he said.

A faint blush bloomed on her cheeks. "Except when I'm *cussin'*, right?"

He grinned. "Nope," he admitted quietly. "Even then I like you."

The air between them grew soft with suggestion.

Did you tell Edie about Florence?

Tucker looked down, remorse flooding him. Maybe anger too, though he wasn't quite sure at whom it was directed. When he glanced back at

Edie, she was watching him expectantly. It seemed she wasn't sure what to say either. And yet, a flood of questions and wants waited at the back of his throat. If he let them loose, he and Edie might have been there for weeks.

They shared a brownie in the quiet, taking turns picking from the frosted block of cakey chocolate.

"My dad wants me and Jim to go with him to Boston next week for a few days," Tucker said. "But my mom's throwing one of her big parties when we get back. I'd love it if you'd come."

Edie gave Tucker a wary look. He knew what she was thinking; he'd thought the same too. Riding around in his convertible was one thing; stepping inside the cottage together in plain view was quite another.

Somehow he didn't care, and he didn't want her caring either.

He smiled, two perfect dimples creasing his jaw. "Say you'll think about it."

10

*E*die Wright steered the pickup past the old gatehouse shortly after three, her fingers clenched over the wheel, and she forced herself to loosen them. Was this a good idea? She didn't know. When Owen had balked at her acceptance of the job, she'd been so certain he was wrong to be concerned, to be angry. But as soon as she'd slid into her truck, notebook and smart phone beside her, doubt had crept in.

Now, as she pulled down into the driveway and saw the cottage appear through the trees, another cold panic climbed her limbs. What if she was wrong? What if she couldn't be back here after all?

She scolded herself. Enough. This was about her employees, her crew. She needed this job badly— and sure, it wasn't ideal that it would be here, but so be it.

She parked the truck beside the carriage house, grateful that Lexi was off-site today, not wanting to complicate her already frazzled state trying to hide her mood from her daughter. She climbed out of the cab, drew in a fortifying breath of soft evening air, and marched toward the house.

It was not James Masterson but Cooper Moss who met her at the door, recently showered and smelling of warm soap, and looking so much like Tucker that Edie's head nearly snapped back on her shoulders. It had never occurred to her that he might be the spitting image of his father. Never once. The same light brown eyes, the same narrow face.

"You must be Mrs. Wright." Cooper pressed the screen open with one hand and extended the other to Edie. She took it carefully, hesitant to step inside.

"I'm here to look at the guest house," she said, unable to resist a glance past Cooper into the kitchen, the space so unfamiliar to her now, what little of it she could see in the distance.

"Yes, ma'am. Jim told me you'd be coming." He stepped back to encourage her inside. "Can I offer you something to drink? Sweet tea? Coffee? A beer?"

"No," she said, politely but firmly. "I'd really just like to see the building."

Cooper smiled, the expression causing her another burst of startling recognition. Those were Tucker's dimples.

"Yes, ma'am," Cooper said, already on the move. "Just let me get my shoes."

Where *was* Jim then? Edie glanced around the property as she followed Cooper down the lawn. Hadn't he been the one to suggest the time?

"I should warn you," Cooper said, giving the

guest house door a shove to loosen it. "It's been badly damaged."

Edie winced as she stepped inside. The thick smell of mold clung to the back of her throat, strong enough to cause her eyes to water. There were gashes in the roof, revealing slivers of blue sky. Why had no one laid down a damn tarp? Ribbons of water stains curled down the walls. A startling swath of the once-polished wood floor was warped and dull, too swollen to maintain its snug joints—joints Hank had toiled over.

"I understand you and Alexandra's father helped build this," said Cooper. "I feel like I should apologize for the way it's fallen apart."

"Don't. With water, it doesn't take much to lose a lot of ground," said Edie, training her smart phone on several points in the room and snapping pictures for reference. She'd quote him high, she decided. Not out of malice, just survival. This could be the only job her crew would see all summer. And while that wasn't Cooper Moss's fault, Edie didn't see the harm in it.

"I'll need to see how bad it is up there," she said, pointing to the roof. "Do you have a ladder?"

Cooper nodded. "There's one in the garage. I'll be right back."

When he'd gone, Edie took a moment to scan the space in its entirety, the smell not so terrible now. All the years between its erection and this day, all the furnishings that had filled it in the interim, not to mention the laughter, the sleep, and, certainly, the lovemaking. And here she was, seeing it in its infancy of sorts again. The two of them equally aged, equally needing repairs, reunited after so long. An unexpected flush of nostalgia came over her, but on its heels came a rush of doubt as she recalled Owen's warning that she'd be biting off more than she and her crew could chew with this job. Pride reared up, swallowing everything else; she'd had a hand in building this place, hadn't she? Surely she could oversee its repair.

Yes, this was right, she decided firmly. She was meant to be here, to return this little house to what it had once been. Tears rose, clogging her throat. Hank would want that.

She wiped impatiently at her eyes, her gaze landing on the doorway that led to the cottage's small bedroom. She could still picture the framing underneath, the jagged words she'd found carved into the header that damp July dawn. How her heart had seized up with trepidation to see them. Surely time had softened those marks. She suspected they'd be indistinguishable now. Hoped, anyway.

She stepped back out into the sunlight to wait for Cooper, the brightness startling at first after the dankness of the guest house. She blinked to readjust her eyes.

"All you're missin' is the hat!"

Edie squinted into the glare to find Jim Masterson strolling down the lawn toward her, hands in his pockets, curly white hair caught in the breeze, tumbling like clouds. She smiled.

"And the braid, of course," he added, reaching her.

"I think I might still have the hat somewhere," she said. "But you're out of luck with the braid."

"So I am." He smiled. "Sorry to be late. I was upstairs on the phone with the firm. Looks like I've got to go to Boston and put out a few fires tomorrow. Cooper took care of you, I see."

"He did. He's getting me a ladder so I can find out just how grim it is up there."

"I did warn you, young lady."

She sighed. "Yes, you did."

"Funny thing, isn't it?" Jim tilted his head, considering the guest house. "It seems this place has sucked us all back to it."

Now you're both back down there.

Edie raised her chin defiantly, determined to shove aside Owen's concern.

Jim swept his gaze to her. "I take it this means you've decided to accept the job?"

"I wasn't aware I was the one who needed convincing." She gave him a wary look; wasn't he at all curious why she might have an available crew when none of the other Cape companies did?

"There are plenty of other crews around here if you're willing to wait till fall, James."

157

"Maybe. But none led by the woman who built the place."

"*Helped* build it," she clarified. "You were here. You know I spent most of that summer moving supplies and picking up lunch for those fools."

"There was no shortage of those then, was there?" He smiled sheepishly. "Present company wholeheartedly included."

"That was another lifetime ago," she said, turning back to the cottage.

"Several, possibly. Come have dinner with me and we'll do the math on a cocktail napkin. My treat."

"James. I don't think it's a good idea. . . ."

"Why not?" he demanded gently. "Two old friends breaking bread. What's the harm in it?"

None. Plenty. She squinted up at him, considering her answer.

"Before you say no," Jim continued, "let me assure you I won't have to remove any dentures, and I don't make unfortunate noises when I eat. . . ."

Edie laughed in spite of her determination to decline.

Jim smiled. "It's just that Cooper has been such a sport about me showing up here unannounced. I thought the poor boy might appreciate having the kitchen to himself tonight. And frankly, I've been craving a basket of fried clams ever since I got here. I remember the ones I got all those years ago, and I swear, not a day has gone by I haven't thought of 'em."

Edie gave him a dubious look. Oh, he was laying it on thick, all right. A flicker of possibility teased her thoughts. She'd been shameless herself in securing this opportunity; why not seal it up with a bow by accepting his invitation?

She folded her arms and drew in a resigned breath. "All right."

"Wonderful," said Jim, gleefully rubbing his hands together. "But you'd better pick the restaurant. I don't know my way around here."

"Flannigan's is good. Nothing fancy. It's just outside of the village. It shouldn't be too busy if we get there by six."

"And they have fried clams?"

"Some of the best on the Cape."

"Flannigan's it is," he said with a decisive nod. "I'll call us in a reservation."

"Oh, you don't need to do that. Bob knows me."

"Then I'll be dining with a celebrity."

"Not quite. His wife, Connie, and I have been friends forever. Trust me; they'll make room."

11

Despite their attempts to beat the evening crowd, Flannigan's was already packed when Edie and Jim stepped inside the brick restaurant that overlooked the harbor. Edie saw Connie at the bar and waved to her old friend as she steered Jim to a free table in the back. Within minutes, a waiter arrived with a pair of menus and two ice waters and left them to make their selections.

Edie glanced over the top of her menu and saw Jim studying her. "I still can't believe you cut it," he said.

She reached reflexively to the back of her neck, her fingers smoothing down the clipped hairs that hugged her scalp. "What is it with you men and long hair?" she chided, exasperated.

"The last time I saw you it was almost down to your waist. It was exquisite!"

"It was a *pain,*" she said, feeling a maddening flush heat her cheeks. She returned to her menu and squinted down at the blurry lines.

"Forget your glasses, did you?"

"I don't wear any," she said, squinting harder.

"Ah."

She saw the smile creeping at his mouth as he scanned his own menu.

Edie skimmed the entrées, wondering how it was she didn't recognize a single item. Had it really been so long since she'd been to Flannigan's?

After another blurry and useless search, she slapped the menu closed.

"Decided?" he asked.

"Cobb salad," she said, looking around the restaurant, seeing more evidence of time's passage. They'd changed the decor, the color of the walls. And had there always been those valances on the windows? They were so gaudy. What had Connie been thinking?

Jim set down his menu. "I was very sorry to hear about Hank."

"Thank you, James." Edie took a sip of her water, glad for the ice. "What about you? Did you ever marry?"

"Twice," he said. "Both divorces. Two-time loser is the official term, I think."

Edie looked at him tenderly. "That's an awful thing to say about yourself, James. Lots of marriages don't work out."

"Yours did."

"Yes, but I was lucky."

"As was Hank."

She smiled. "I remember there was that girl you were crazy about that summer. Ellen, was it?"

"Helen," corrected Jim. "Helen Willoughby."

"I don't suppose Helen was one of the two Mrs. Mastersons?"

"Sadly, no. Not for my lack of trying, of course."

Edie grinned. "Of course."

"That's enough about me. . . ." Jim leaned forward. "Tell me about your life now."

Their waiter arrived with their drinks, a gin and tonic for him, iced tea for her. Jim sat back and regarded Edie while she shared the news of her family, his study so outwardly admiring that she grew embarrassed after a while and finally demanded, "What?"

He grinned. "You haven't changed. Not one bit. It's remarkable."

"I could easily say the same for you." She shook a pair of sugar packets into her tea, stirring it briskly. It was true; time had been kind to him, she decided. He still had all his hair, curls now white as smoke. His eyes were a pleasant blue, not milky and filmy the way so many blue eyes seemed to turn in old age. His were crisp and playful. Attentive. Kind.

"So what keeps *you* busy now, James?"

Jim reached for his drink. "I turned over my law practice to my oldest son a few years ago, but I still pop in unannounced from time to time. Much to his delight."

"Then you have children?"

He nodded as he took a small sip. "Two boys. Four grandchildren."

"How nice for you."

"What about you?"

"I have a granddaughter, Meg."

"Alexandra's daughter?"

"No," said Edie. "My son Owen's. Meg lives most of the year with her mother in New York City. It's been terribly hard on him."

"I can imagine."

She scanned the restaurant, her thoughts swerving from wistful pleasure to concern. She'd been so eager to get there that she'd barely considered how it would look being out in public with Tucker's best friend. Was she imagining it, or were the other diners looking at them? On their way in, she'd waved at old neighbors across the restaurant—had they appeared suspicious when they'd waved back, or was she simply reading too much in their sun-weathered faces? Would the news of her shared meal be all over town the next morning? No, she was being ridiculous. It was the summer season. She herself barely knew half the diners in the restaurant. They couldn't have cared less about an old woman and her equally old companion. Sure, maybe a few familiar faces might look twice, might even inquire or make the connection over coffee at the market in the morning, but there was no great scandal in it. Who but she and maybe a handful of locals would even *remember* James Masterson?

"Everything all right, Edie?"

She looked back at Jim, seeing the concern in

his eyes, his gentle smile. She sat up straighter, forcing her features to soften. "Everything's fine," she said, taking up her iced tea. "I was just thinking how different it looks in here; that's all."

"It doesn't take long for things to change."

She shrugged. "Some things," she said. "Other things seem to take forever."

Jim leaned in, his voice dropping. "We don't have to stay, you know. If this is uncomfortable for you. Being here. With me, I mean. I can get the check and have them pack up our food to go. . . ."

"It's not uncomfortable," Edie said firmly, her earlier modesty shifting to petulance. Why shouldn't she have dinner with an old friend, dammit? Despite what her children knew, that had been a special summer, and she was enjoying revisiting her memories of it, more so than she ever would have expected. She had nothing to feel bad about.

"You're sure?" Jim asked.

Edie settled back in her seat, determined now. "I'm having a wonderful time," she said as she snapped open her napkin over her lap. "So wonderful, in fact, that I might just order dessert."

12

exi unloaded her gear from the car and set up in the great room by the bank of windows. She'd come with hot lights, not sure what natural light she'd be granted and knowing the cottage had been emptied of most of its artificial lighting. She'd focus her work on the first floor today, wanting to make the most of the sun while she had it for the home's most impressive rooms and historic features, most especially for the stained-glass panes that would truly sing backlit by strong sunlight. In the morning she kept her field of vision small, focusing on details: copper heat registers, leaded-glass panels in the great room's cabinets, the chair rail molding above the wainscoting, nickel-finished cabinet latches, hand-hammered escutcheons and finger loop pulls, finding just the right levels to make the textures come through.

She knew better than anyone that such careful composition was gratuitous for a straightforward registry application, but she didn't care. Photographing interiors like these was too rich an opportunity to rush through or document with blown-out lighting. Cooper had agreed to pay her fee, no matter how long she took to shape her shots, and so she lingered lovingly over every detail, spending a half hour getting the settings just right on a copper light fixture, another half hour on the fireplace mantel.

She was so immersed in her work that she didn't hear Cooper descend the great stairwell at three thirty, emerging for the first time all day from his "writer's cave," as he'd called it.

"Getting some good shots?" he asked.

"I think so," she said. "I just hope they're as good as I think they are."

Cooper ran a hand through his short hair. "I know that feeling. You pound out a couple thousand words and pray they sound as brilliant when you read them over again. In my case, they rarely do." He grinned. "I find rereading them after a few beers helps."

Lexi smiled. "I'll have to try that." She brushed a wave of loose hair behind her ear. "I take it your swim yesterday worked its magic?"

"I got a few good ideas," Cooper admitted. "Enough to get started. Sometimes that's the hardest part."

She nodded, wondering for a moment whether his comment was strictly about writing. In the days since she'd accepted his job offer, her curiosity about his memory of their night together had lingered. It seemed she saw opportunity for confirmation in all of their exchanges. Once or twice she'd nearly come right out and asked him whether he remembered. Now she felt the same temptation. And why not? She'd been here a few days and she felt comfortable in his company—maybe *too* comfortable. It shouldn't have made any difference whether he remembered or not, but it did to her, try as she did to pretend otherwise.

The clang of the kitchen screen rang out; Cooper glanced at the doorway. "That would be Jim back with a mess of lobsters," he said. "Why don't you stay for dinner? I'd love to hear more about your work."

"I can't," Lexi said. "My best friend's son has a Little League game tonight at six. Her husband's on the road this week and I promised I'd keep her company."

"Sure." Cooper smiled. "Maybe some other time."

An unexpected disappointment settled over her; she suddenly wished she had been free to accept his invitation. The hours of dusk had always been her favorite in the house, watching the evening sun slip lower through the windows, feathering the floors with shades of lilac and silver, bringing with it the gentle breeze of coming night and the luscious smells of earth and sea settling into sleep. It was a sexy time, full of secrets and promise. She'd always thought so. Now, here with Cooper, she felt the stirrings of that promise again. Somehow she suspected dinner with him, their table basking in the lavender glow of sunset, would be a deeply romantic experience.

Not that she had any business having a deeply romantic experience with Hudson's younger brother.

She smiled, as if to hide her thoughts.

"Maybe some other time," she said.

The smell of burned food was evident even before Lexi had stepped inside the house, assaulting her senses the moment she climbed the steps. Her mother, seemingly oblivious to the stench, sat at the kitchen table amid a sea of supply catalogs and receipts, fitfully tapping at a calculator.

Lexi walked to the stove and peered down into a pot, her nose wrinkling at the charred ropes of what was once pasta clumped at the bottom. "Please tell me that wasn't your dinner."

"That wasn't my dinner," Edie muttered absently as she continued to enter numbers.

Lexi wandered over to the table and took a seat. "Is that the quote for the guest house?"

Edie glanced up, wearing a guilty look. "Just say it already."

"Say what?"

"I'm a hypocrite."

"You're not a hypocrite," said Lexi.

"Of course I am. One day I'm chastising you for going back down there, and the next day"—Edie flung her hand at the chaos of paperwork—"I'm right on your heels." Edie set down her pen and cradled her face in her hands. Lexi had always loved her mother's hands; they were tiny but strong, with round nails that she would still catch her mother chewing on in times of stress. Tonight Lexi noticed several were unusually ragged and short. Lexi leaned in to survey the spread of papers. "So how bad is it?"

"Bad," said Edie, picking up her phone and showing Lexi the pictures she'd taken that afternoon. "Water's been everywhere. We'll have to tear down to the studs. All new wiring, plumbing. Nothing's up to code. And don't even get me started on the roof. . . ." Edie took a breath, the tension in her features softening suddenly, turning wistful. "He's grown into quite a handsome man, hasn't he?"

Lexi flushed instantly, knowing who her mother meant.

"I suppose," she said, keeping her eyes fixed on the small screen of the phone.

"He looks so much like his father I nearly fell over," Edie said, then added with a wry smile, "and not a damn thing like Hudson."

13

The home team's dugout reminded Lexi of the bleachers at her first middle school dance, where all the boys sat slumped, looking bored in their fathers' ties and too-shiny shoes.

At the top of the eighth inning the Harrisport Harriers were down fourteen runs to the Sandwich Seals.

Lexi caught the eye of Kim's eleven-year-old son at shortstop and waved.

"I see Miles found his lucky socks."

"They're lucky, all right," said Kim, gesturing to the scoreboard.

"Sandwich always had better teams," said Lexi.

"Yeah, but we have better popcorn." Kim grinned as she scooped up a handful out of the bucket on Lexi's lap. "So how's it going down at the house? Still no sign of Hudson?"

A curious question, Lexi thought, unsure of how to answer. What sort of sign did Kim mean? Hudson may not have yet appeared in the flesh, but there was no question there was evidence of him everywhere Lexi looked, memories of their romance catching her off guard when she'd focus her lens on a part of the house. She'd simply have to work harder to ignore them.

"No Hudson," Lexi answered finally.

"Thank God for that. How's your new boss?"

"Cooper's not my boss, Kim."

"He's paying you, isn't he?"

"That's the idea," said Lexi, watching a base hit.

"Then he's your boss," said Kim. "So, no girlfriend's come on the scene yet?"

"No girlfriend. Just an old friend of his father's."

"And Cooper doesn't wear a ring, right?"

"No." Lexi felt a keen sense of embarrassment that she knew the answer. "But that doesn't mean anything."

"It means plenty," said Kim. "It means he's either not married—or he's married and he's not happy about it."

"Will you stop?" Lexi whispered harshly. "Can we just watch the rest of the game, please?"

"You watch the game," said Kim, suddenly grinning. "I'll watch the hottie who just walked up."

Lexi looked toward the end of the bleachers where Kim's eyes had landed and drew in a quick breath to see Cooper climbing the steps, knowing she should say something before he reached them, but unable to find her voice.

"Hi." Cooper arrived and took a seat beside Lexi. "I hope you don't mind a last-inning crasher." He leaned forward, extending his hand to Kim. "I don't know if you remember me; we met out at the house a long time ago. Cooper Moss."

"Cooper, of course! I didn't recognize you," Kim said, shooting Lexi a knowing look, then turning her smile back to Cooper. "Welcome."

"I would have been here earlier," said Cooper, "but I stopped in at four other games before I found y'all. I had no idea there were so many Little League teams around here. Which one's your son?"

Kim pointed. "Shortstop in the red socks," she said. "Don't ask. It's all my husband's doing. He thinks Miles needs lucky socks."

"That must be why I've been having such a hard time with my novel," Cooper said to Lexi. "No socks."

"You're working on a new book?" Kim asked, leaning over. "What's it about?"

"You know, I'm still trying to figure that out myself," Cooper admitted.

"Does anyone fall in love?" asked Kim. "Because someone has to fall in love for me to read it. Oh, and they have to have lots of sex in the process."

Lexi sent Kim a disapproving look; Cooper laughed. "I'll keep that in mind." He turned to Lexi. "You missed a good dinner."

"I'm sure I did." Lexi could feel Kim's questioning eyes on her as the crowd cheered an out at home plate, and they all turned their attention to the field.

"I could really use a Coke," Cooper said, nodding to the shingled snack bar at the end of the bleachers. "Can I get either of you ladies anything?"

Lexi and Kim shook their heads.

"Well hello, handsome," Kim breathed when he'd left. "No wonder you took the job. And when were you going to tell me he asked you out?"

"He didn't ask me out," whispered Lexi,

glancing around. "He asked me to have dinner with him and his old friend Jim at the house. He was obviously just being polite because I was still there when the food arrived."

Kim looked unconvinced. "So which would you rather it was?"

"What do you mean?"

"Would you rather he was being polite, or would you rather he wanted to rip off all your clothes and feed you lobster in bed?"

"How can you even ask me that? He's Hudson's brother."

"So what?" Kim argued. "He's sexy as hell, and he's obviously hot for you. He drove around for God knows how long to find you tonight, didn't he?"

"He doesn't know anyone here. I'm sure he was probably desperate to get out."

"Why are you making excuses?"

Was she? Lexi scanned the snack bar for Cooper, finding him already at the counter.

She turned to Kim. "He kissed me."

"What?" Kim stared at her. "When? *Today?*"

"No, the night Hud and I broke up. He kissed me in the car in front of my apartment."

"Wait—like, *really* kissed you? Like on the lips?"

Lexi nodded, feeling utterly infantile having to describe it that way. How old were they, for God's sake?

"Why didn't you ever tell me?" demanded Kim.

"Why do you think? I was twenty-three; he was eighteen. It was probably against the law."

"Oh, please." Kim smiled wickedly. "You brat, I can't believe you never told me."

"Shh, he's coming back," Lexi said, her eyes fixed on Cooper as he slipped through the crowd with his drink.

"So was he a good kisser?"

"*Shh.*"

"He was, wasn't he?"

Cooper arrived and took his seat. "What did I miss?"

"Nothing," said Lexi, wanting to answer before Kim sneaked in a telling comment.

He pointed to the board, the Harriers' zero still unchanged. "Any chance the home team might score tonight?" he asked.

Kim gave Lexi's thigh a discreet but pointed nudge. "Hard to say," Kim replied. "The away team might be too hot for them to handle."

Lexi returned the nudge firmly, feeling her cheeks burn and hoping Cooper wasn't picking up on Kim's innuendo. Leave it to her best friend to reduce them to a pair of tittering twelve-year-olds.

"I'm an incurable optimist," said Cooper with a smile. "There's still plenty of time."

Kim grinned at Lexi but didn't say a word.

Harrisport, Massachusetts
July 1966

*H*ank watched Edie coast down the driveway on her bicycle just after eight thirty on
Monday morning. It was the third time in a week
that she'd arrived late to work. What was more,
she didn't even look particularly concerned as
she sailed through the rows of trucks and hopped
off her bike, setting it against her usual tree. A part
of him wanted to stand in the guest house
doorway so she couldn't slip into the crew
unnoticed this time, to force her to explain her
recent tardiness, not to mention her carefree
expression. She knew her father's rules—which
were his, Hank's, too. It confounded him: Here
she was, always complaining that the guys
didn't take her seriously, didn't let her take on the
challenging jobs, and yet she had no compunction
about gliding in to work a half hour late, not
bothering to give an explanation, clearly not
thinking he deserved one.

But who was he kidding? She didn't have to
give her reasons for being late getting to work
and for acting distracted the entire time she was
there; Hank knew. It was Moss.

It shouldn't have bothered him—it clearly didn't

bother the rest of the crew, who Hank often feared were relieved not to face Edie Worthington's fiery temper at eight o'clock in the morning because one of them might have implied she was too short/weak/small/slow/take your pick to handle something, and suffered a speech trimmed with more obscenities in one breath than a single man might use in a whole day.

No, it shouldn't have bothered him, but it did. Why? That was the part that Hank couldn't get a fix on. As her boss, it bothered him professionally. Who could argue with that? But there was another side to it, something far less logical, something closer to disappointment than frustration. As long as he'd known Edie Worthington—and he'd known her for years now—she'd never taken an interest in a summer guy. While Hank had watched plenty of local girls, sisters of some of his best friends, fall headlong for a wash-ashore, Edie had proudly declared that she would never date a boy from away.

Until this summer. Until Tucker Moss.

Hank didn't see what was so special about the guy, frankly. Sure, Moss had money, but so what? And okay, he dressed well and carried himself like his too-good-for-everybody old man—or at least tried to. But since when had Edie cared about all that?

He thought about Missy Murphy, how she'd arrived dressed like she was heading for a yachting party, and all he could think was what Edie must have been saying about those open-toed shoes of hers, or Missy's crisp white sailor shorts. There he was, getting a surprise visit from one of the most sought-after girls in Harrisport, and he was worrying about Edie Worthington's opinion. It hadn't been this way before. Until the beginning of this summer, until Edie had joined their crew, Hank had never much thought about Edie except as the daughter of his boss, the girl who was always underfoot or tooling up and down the Cape on her bike like a paperboy on a constant route. He'd never studied the shade of her hair or found himself counting the freckles that ran along her jawline like bonnet ribbons. Once or twice, when she'd been standing still (which wasn't often), he'd even tried to picture her body under her clothes. It didn't make a lick of sense. There was Missy Murphy strolling up to him, smooth shoulders and pearly stomach bared for him to see, and still he wondered about what lay under Edie Worthington's layers of denim and bunched-up cotton. He had to be out of his mind . . . didn't he?

Thinking it over, Hank felt his agitation growing, so much so that by the time Edie had reached the guest house, hitching up her tool belt as she walked, the slow burn of his frustration was nearly at a boil.

She kept her eyes down as she snaked around him to get through the door.

"You're late, Edie."

"A half hour," she said without stopping. "So dock me."

"Maybe I should."

Now she halted her march and spun to face him, her eyes flashing with shock that he had called her bluff.

"It's not fair to the other guys, Ede. They get here on time every day."

"It's just a few days, Hank."

"Four days. A half hour each day. That adds up."

"So then dock me already," she challenged. "What do you want me to say?"

Sonny and Don glanced over.

Hank frowned. "I just want you to say you'll get here on time from now on," he said, forcing a calmness to his voice to balance her rising volume. "And that you'll keep your mind on your work."

He knew as soon as he said it, as soon as he saw the flicker of indignation crackle in Edie's pale eyes, that he'd crossed the line and made this personal. He regretted it immediately.

"What the hell is that supposed to mean?" she demanded.

Hank glanced over to find Sonny and Don still listening in; he moved to the door and motioned for Edie to follow him out of the guest house. She did, hands on her hips as they stood in the dewy grass.

"I just don't know how your dad would feel about you going around with the son of our employer; that's all," Hank said low. "It's making the guys feel awkward."

"The guys—or *you?*"

Hank folded his arms, meeting her blazing eyes. "This isn't personal, Ede. I'm just thinking about the work."

"I think it *is* personal. I think you just don't like Tucker Moss, and you don't even know him."

"I know the type," said Hank. "I've grown up here, Edie."

"And I haven't?"

"I know how these rich kids think they own the Cape just because they have money."

"Tucker's not like that," Edie insisted.

"They're all like that."

"But not Missy Murphy, right?"

Hank bristled at the accusation. "Missy's local. It's different."

"How's it different? She might as well be from away, the way she looks down her nose at everyone. You know it's true."

"Missy's a nice girl. It's not the same thing."

"Well, I don't really see how it's any of your business who I'm friends with anyway, Hank Wright," Edie said.

"Maybe I don't want you getting hurt."

"Who said anything about me getting hurt?"

"I hear stories too, you know," Hank said. "I

know that it's nothing for some of these guys to come in and have some fun and not think twice about leaving a girl behind."

"Tucker would never do that. And I don't see what difference it should make to you anyway, so long as I quit being late and stop making you look like a lousy boss. That's really what you're worried about, isn't it?"

Hank turned to face her, startled and hurt at the force of her words. "Is that what you think?" he said quietly. "That I only care about you because your dad put me in charge of this crew?"

Edie stared at him for a long moment, her eyes seeming to search his face—for what, Hank wasn't sure.

He didn't wait to find out.

"Do what you want, Edie," he said firmly. "Just be on time from now on or I won't have any choice but to dock you."

He could see she wanted the last word, and he even gave her an extra moment to come up with it, but when she remained silent, Hank had no choice but to turn and walk back into the guest house.

14

*L*exi had been sixteen the first time she'd stepped into Fletcher's Camera Shop. She'd needed only a frame and had instead found herself, a half hour later, hunched over the counter learning everything there was to know about apertures and shutter speeds from the store's owner, Mo Fletcher. She left that day with a frame and the seed of a passion for photography firmly planted. It was Mo who lent her photography books and explained color theory and about shadows and highlights. He taught her how to use a light meter and would eventually help her set up a darkroom.

In the years since her first visit, there had been enormous change to the industry, thanks to the advent of digital photography, but somehow Fletcher's had managed to weather the slower business. Like all professional photographers, Lexi knew she could order her supplies online at a considerable discount, but it was important to her to support a local business—especially this one.

Stepping up to the shop's door, she was just relieved to see its Open sign still swinging in the window.

"How's the big graduate?"

Lexi smiled to find Mo behind the counter.

"We missed you here, kiddo. You didn't have to place orders from us over there, you know. The shipping must have broken you."

She shrugged. "What can I say? I don't trust anyone else to supply me."

It was a stretch, but Lexi could see from the flush on Mo's full cheeks that he appreciated it. She walked to the loupe display, chose one and brought it to the counter. Mo picked up the magnifying tool and frowned first at the tag, then over his glasses at her. "We have cheaper loupes, you know?"

She knew. "It's the one I want," she said firmly, setting down her credit card.

"How's the gig at the cottage?" he asked, ringing up her sale.

"News travels fast."

"Not really. Cooper Moss was in here yesterday."

Cooper had been to the camera shop? Lexi wondered why.

"It's going well," she said. "It's a photographer's dream."

"Good for you." Mo leaned forward on his elbows. "Bet they taught you a whole bunch of newfangled tricks over there, didn't they?"

"None as good as the ones you taught me," she said, slipping the loupe into her purse. "Give Juanita a hug for me."

Back outside, a soft rain had started. Lexi was almost to her car when she saw the sign for the

Salty Shelf Bookstore across the street and stopped.

She wandered the narrow aisles for several minutes before she found the book. There were several copies of Cooper's novels, two of his Tide McGill books. She pulled out one called *Sundown* and flipped it over, seeing Cooper's familiar face smiling up at her. He was posed in front of a seascape, his expression relaxed but thoughtful.

"You might want to start with *High Tide*," said Lynn Dodd as she tapped the cash register. "*Sundown*'s the third in the series. *Undertow* is the one in the middle. That's my favorite. You know, someone was telling me he's back in Harrisport, at the house. Have you heard that?"

Lexi shrugged as she handed Lynn a twenty, not about to indulge in—or start—town gossip.

"Well, if it's true," continued Lynn, handing Lexi her change and the book, "I hope he'll stop in and sign some stock. Who knows, maybe he'd even do a reading here. Imagine that."

At the suggestion, Lexi envisioned a cozy gathering at the back of the store, a table bearing bottles of wine, customers sitting in a semicircle, and Cooper on a stool, reading aloud, his warm laugh floating through the aisles while customers stood waiting for him to sign their books.

It was only when she pulled into the driveway and didn't see the Town Car that Lexi remembered Cooper saying Jim had business in Boston—news that at the time had seemed irrelevant to her. But now that she was back at the house, his absence was oddly palpable and bore a weight she couldn't shake as she parked. Though she and Cooper had been alone at the house that first morning—a condition that hadn't concerned her in the least then—now their lack of a third party left her feeling at turns nervous and excited. Her thoughts retreated to his company the night before, her pleasure at his unexpected arrival at Miles's game, Kim's insistence that he was interested in her.

In the kitchen, Lexi saw no evidence of activity except for a half-full coffeepot that was still warm and an opened bag of bagels. She helped herself to one and considered her day's shot list as she unpacked. At just ten o'clock, the air in the house was still cool, but she knew it would thicken as the day progressed. She'd want to start upstairs and work her way down as the heat collected. She remembered how hot it got in those upstairs rooms, the ones she and Hudson had sneaked away to so often, how stifling it could be under those eaves, how she'd press her face against the screens when they'd come up for air, hoping for the gift of a breeze.

She pushed the memories away as she walked through the downstairs and climbed the main stairwell, wanting to assess the area and decide which shots to take before bringing up her equipment. At the top of the stairs, she stopped and surveyed the corridor that ran on both sides of her, the square of landing dividing the main house from the servants' wing. To her left were what had always been the family's bedrooms, papered and plush, while to her right a narrowed corridor was flanked by smaller bedrooms that would have housed summer staff. All the times she'd stood in that very spot with Hudson. Nowhere in the house was the division between their worlds more acute than on that stretch of polished wood.

She looked down the hall to the door of the master suite, knowing Cooper was in there writing, able to discern a faint tapping on his keyboard. In all her summers with Hudson, she'd only ever been in that room once, and it had been in near darkness; Hudson's sexy idea during one of his parents' cocktail parties. She'd been briefly resistant, sure they'd be caught, but his powers of persuasion (in the form of a searching, searing kiss) had turned her quickly.

She would need to photograph its interior eventually. Maybe she'd wait until tomorrow.

By two, the heat had grown unbearable. Lexi had arrived in a long-sleeved tee when the damp morning air had carried a chill. Now she peeled off the sticky knit and let the air at her bare arms, glad she'd worn a tank underneath. She'd taken enough pictures of the upstairs for one day; now she would spend the rest of the afternoon photographing what remained of the first floor, starting with the kitchen. She glanced down the hall at the door to Cooper's room as she descended, wondering how he could bear it in there, filled with a strange hope that he might emerge eventually.

When he finally did, she was bent over her tripod, squinting into the viewer at the shot of the kitchen cabinets she'd been fighting to get right for nearly a half hour. She didn't even know he was there until she stood up to move for another reflector and sucked in a startled breath.

"You were concentrating so hard, I didn't want to disturb you," he said, smiling apologetically. He held up his glass. "I just came down to get a refill. Join me?"

"Um, sure." She wiped at her forehead, feeling a new thread of sweat travel down her neck. He was shirtless, a fact that shouldn't have mattered. It was his house. So why did she feel a flush of embarrassment as he drew down a tumbler from the cabinet and tugged open the freezer?

Reaching in, he blew out a weary breath. "I forgot how hot it gets up there this time of day."

Lexi watched him scoop up a handful of ice, the cubes shining through his fingers as he split the ice between two glasses. A sudden image of him sliding one of the wet, cold blocks across her skin pierced her thoughts.

He closed the freezer door and moved to the

sink to fill their glasses, sweat glistening in the hollow between his shoulder blades. She followed the trail down his spine.

He turned back to face her, catching her study.

"Thanks," she said, taking the water.

She smoothed back a moist lock of loose hair behind her ear as she watched him down the whole glass in one swig. "So why work up there if it gets so hot?" she asked.

"Because I'm superstitious," he admitted, refilling his glass again. "The writing's going well and I don't want to risk messing things up by moving my computer." Lexi smiled dubiously; Cooper grinned. "It's crazy, I know."

"It's not crazy," she said. "I think all artists have little superstitions."

"Do you?"

"Of course."

"So what are they?" He leaned against the counter, resting his sweating tumbler against his chest.

Lexi waved dismissively. "Forget it. You'll think I'm nuts."

"Come on. I just told you I'd sooner risk heatstroke than move my computer," he said. "I think I've already won this round."

She laughed. "Well, I pack up my camera a certain way," she confessed. "I always have to have my lenses pointed toward the front of the bag, not the back."

"That doesn't sound superstitious. That sounds like someone who takes good care of her equipment."

"Maybe." She looked at him. "So was that true what you told Kim about not being sure what your story's about, or is that another one of your superstitions—that you don't like to talk about a book before it's published?"

"A little of both," he admitted with a sheepish smile. "The thing with a story—at least for me—is that I never know if it's going to work or not, if it's going to go the distance essentially, until I'm deep into it. I may have to write a hundred pages before I know."

"And if it doesn't go where you want it to go?"

He shrugged. "Then I start over with something else."

"After all that work? That sounds heartbreaking."

"It is, in a way. But it's my process."

"And you don't feel like you've wasted your time when that happens? All those pages and you just throw them away?"

"It's no different from a relationship," he said. "You don't know from the outset if it's meant to run its course for a lifetime or a month. You always hope it's the one that lasts, but you never know for sure."

He rolled his glass a few times across his chest, the simple action so startlingly erotic, Lexi had to look away.

"I had a great time at the game last night," Cooper said. "Made me think of those summers here when Hud and I were kids. How we used to practice our swings out on the lawn."

She nodded, the mention of Hudson somehow shattering the comfortable exchange they were enjoying. She set down her water. "I should get back to work before I lose my light," she said, gesturing to the butler's pantry.

Cooper looked at her curiously. "What's to shoot in the pantry?"

She smiled. "See for yourself."

She motioned for him to follow her into the small, narrow space. The light from its single window was soft on the tall beadboard walls.

Cooper looked around wistfully, grinning. "I can't tell you how many dinner parties I used to hide out in here, Mrs. Dodd sneaking me root beers and lobster rolls."

Lexi recalled her own stolen moments there. Mrs. Dodd's discovery of her and Hudson in her pantry one summer afternoon hadn't been quite as warmly received.

"So what exactly do you see in here?" Cooper asked.

"Little things." Lexi pointed to the cabinets. "The leaded-glass panels, the pulls. Even this switch plate." She moved beside him to the wall and let her fingers dance over the rounded buttons, inlaid with mother-of-pearl.

Cooper leaned in to study where her hand had landed, close enough that Lexi could feel the heat coming off him, could smell the faint musk of sweat, sweetened slightly by his deodorant. She caught whiffs of her own skin, wishing she had that ice cube now.

"All the time I spent in here growing up," he said, moving back, brushing her arm when he did. "Funny the things you see every day and never really notice."

The connection of skin to skin sent a shiver down her bare limbs. For him too, Lexi thought, because in the next instant, their eyes met and held. She was aware suddenly of how thin her tank top was, how threadbare, the fabric sticking to her skin like wet paper. She'd never meant to be seen in it.

She folded her arms across her breasts as if he could see right through to her bra—and what if he could?—then slipped around him to the other side of the pantry, searching the counter for something—anything—to draw his eyes off of her, and hers off of him.

"Brackets," she practically blurted. "There used to be brackets under these cabinets."

He tilted his head. "I don't remember that."

"No?" She wiped at her cheek, her skin hot under her fingers. "Maybe I'm remembering it wrong." She pointed lamely to the doorway. "I really had better get these shots."

"And I'd better get back to work too."

Cooper gestured for Lexi to exit first and she did, feeling her body cool and calm as soon as they were back in the wide-open safety of the kitchen.

"Thanks for the tour," he said.

She smiled. "My pleasure."

He picked up his glass. "I was wondering if I could cash in that rain check tonight."

Lexi stared at him, needing a moment to understand the reference.

Dinner.

Cooper pointed to the fridge. "Jim left me with fresh scallops and I have honestly no idea what to do with them."

"How could you spend all those summers here and not know how to cook scallops?" she asked.

"I read comic books, not cookbooks, remember?" He grinned. "So what do you say? Join me for dinner? Keep a mess of scallops from dying in vain?"

Her thoughts raced. A moment ago she'd panicked at being alone with him, terrified at her attraction. Now all she wanted to do was say yes.

Cooper watched her expectantly, waiting for her answer.

It's just dinner, she told herself. *With a friend.*

(Who just happens to be the brother of the man who broke your heart.)

191

(Who kissed you passionately a million years ago and you still think about it.)

Dinner.

In a hot, empty old house.

Lexi drew in a deep breath, as if she were about to go underwater.

And maybe she was.

15

A little after four thirty, her light nearly gone, Lexi heard Cooper's footsteps landing on the servants' stairs as she packed up.

"Can I get you a glass of wine?" he asked.

"Please." She closed up her light cases and joined him at the counter while he uncorked a chilled bottle of white and poured them two generous glasses. Lexi took a short sip, the wine perfectly tangy and cold. She detected the warm smell of soap and noticed that his hair was wet. He'd showered.

Cooper reached past her to return the bottle to the fridge and pulled out the bag of scallops. Lexi took them, grateful for the activity.

"All right, wash-ashore," she said. "Watch and learn."

Cooper smiled. "I plan to."

She kept her recipe simple: pan-sear in white wine, garlic, butter, and parsley. Thanks to Jim, she'd been delighted to find a well-stocked fridge and an impressive collection of fresh herbs.

"We'll cook the scallops first, then take them out and reduce the wine sauce," Lexi explained as she lowered the plump ivory coins into the shallow puddle of melted butter. Cooper stood beside her at the stove, close enough that their elbows touched, but this time she didn't shift to force a gap between them. Maybe it was the smooth buzz of the wine, or maybe it was the music. He'd dug up an old clock radio in the closet and found them a local jazz station, the gentle beat lending a perfect pace to their movements at the range.

"How long do they cook?" he asked.

"Not long," she said, turning them gently with a small spoon. He'd diced a pair of garlic cloves a few minutes earlier, his fingers still fragrant when he lifted his glass. Lexi smiled reflexively. To her, the smell of garlic was one of the sexiest smells on earth. Garlic, newly mowed grass, and old wood. Somehow she'd always associated the three with this house.

"You realize your mother would have a fit if she saw us in here."

"She never liked to cook," said Cooper. "She just didn't like anyone in her kitchen."

"Including herself," said Lexi.

Cooper arrived with a plate. She carefully removed the scallops from the pan.

"Now we need the garlic and the wine," she

said. He added the diced cloves while she stirred, the strong scent rising immediately, heady and tangy. Then he drizzled wine over the top until she told him to stop, replenishing their glasses before he returned the bottle to the fridge.

They made a side salad of spinach and avocado, then took their plates and the wine out to the porch, settling into a pair of wicker chairs and pulling the small coffee table between them. The sun was low but the air was still warm, the tide out and lending a salty flavor to the breeze, just as Lexi had remembered.

Cooper raised his glass to hers. "To not ruining fresh scallops," he toasted.

She smiled, clinking her glass against his.

"So how much longer do you think you'll need here?" he asked.

"Two more days," she said. "Maybe three. I still have the master suite to shoot—and, of course, the guest house." She nodded toward the edge of the lawn where the cottage sat.

"I never knew your parents helped build it," Cooper said.

Lexi sipped her wine, not surprised. Surely Tucker hadn't spoken about that summer—or his romance with her mother—to his sons.

"They must have been young when they were here," said Cooper.

"They were. It was my mother's first construction job. She was just eighteen. My father was older. Twenty-two, twenty-three. She says they fought constantly. He never let her do what she wanted on the job site."

Cooper grinned. "They obviously made up."

"You could say that."

Cooper took a bite of scallop, moaning approvingly. Lexi tried one of hers. It was flavorful and slightly chewy, the seared edges boasting a slight crunch.

"I'm glad you agreed to this," Cooper admitted.

"I'm sure you are," Lexi said, nodding to the scallop he'd just cut into.

He chuckled. "I don't mean dinner—although I am glad about that too." He caught her gaze a moment and held it; Lexi could see the warm interest in his eyes. "I mean I'm glad you took the job. I wasn't sure you'd want to come back here after everything that happened. And I would have understood if you didn't."

Lexi took a slow sip of wine, wondering whether they might finally speak of the night he'd taken her home, the kiss that had lingered in her memory.

"Was that night the last time you ever talked to Hud?" he asked.

Lexi considered her glass, not sure how to answer. There had been the requisite pathetic middle-of-the-night phone calls to Hudson in the months after their breakup, some of which he'd picked up, others he'd let the machine take instead, none of which she would have categorized as "talking." She'd always been sure Laurel was there to screen his calls. It had made her stomach turn and yet she'd kept calling, wanting something from him: closure, peace. The chance to deposit the useless and cumbersome anger he'd left her with, like a closetful of clothes no one wanted. But of course he never did.

She set down her wine. "I can't remember."

Cooper pushed his fork through his salad. "I hated Hud for months after all that happened, after what he did. For all I know it's still why we don't talk much anymore."

Lexi studied Cooper's face as he speared a pile of spinach leaves, unexpectedly moved by his confession.

She smiled at him. "You saved my life that night, you know."

"I doubt that."

"It's true. I was ready to stumble down to the beach and throw myself into the surf, I was so upset. If you hadn't come along, I might have done it."

Cooper looked at her. His smile thinned; his brow knotted with genuine concern. "He wasn't worth it."

Lexi lowered her gaze, feeling contrite. "I thought so at the time."

They fell quiet, the only sound the tinkling of

their utensils shifting on their plates and the rustle and hums of the night insects coming out with dusk. Lexi searched the air, expecting fireflies. The lawn shimmered like a blanket of crushed velvet.

"If it makes you feel any better," said Cooper, "you saved *me* that night too."

She looked up at him.

"My dad and I had an awful fight." Cooper reached for his glass. He considered the wine as he swirled it. "He wanted me to apply to Duke, to follow Hud, who'd followed him—to keep the chain going, of course—and I didn't want to. I had my heart set on the creative writing program at NYU. Dad told me he'd never support my doing that, and I told him I didn't care, that I'd find a way to pay for it myself."

"And what did he say?"

"I'm sure you can guess. You remember my dad."

Though she'd rarely exchanged more than a dozen words with Tucker Moss in all the times she'd come to the cottage, Lexi would never forget the frosty looks he'd sent her way anytime they were in a room together, no matter the occasion. Even as a young woman it had galled her that this man who had jilted her mother couldn't reveal even an ounce of penitence in the presence of her daughter.

Cooper leaned back in his chair. "So I had this

idea I was going to steal his keys and drive his precious Porsche to New York that night."

"Not really?"

"Really. I was halfway across the driveway when I heard you and Hud fighting in the guest house."

"You really meant to leave that night?" she asked.

Cooper nodded. "Why do you think I already had the car keys to take you home?"

Lexi blinked at her plate, the thought having never occurred to her at the time. How quickly he'd offered her an escort, how she'd been far too despondent and drunk to find it curious that Tucker would give his eighteen-year-old son permission to take his beloved automobile for a joyride.

"What about after you dropped me off at my apartment?" she asked. "You could have just kept driving."

"I thought about it."

"So why didn't you?"

Cooper met her eyes. "Because I was a kid with a crush, and I thought maybe with Hud gone there was a chance for me."

Heat rushed across her scalp. Lexi stared expectantly at Cooper. Relief and fear collided. Here it was: the answer about that night that she'd been longing for since she'd seen Cooper, since hearing his voice on her phone.

"I wasn't sure if you remembered," she said.

"That I kissed you?" Cooper smiled, still holding her gaze. "You don't want to know how well I remember that kiss."

The warmth that had prickled her scalp now rushed down her throat. She reached for her wine.

"What about you?" he asked.

She took a quick sip, then lowered her glass, seeing the wine shudder as she did, proof of her nerves. "Most of that night was a blur," she confessed, "but I remember that kiss very clearly too."

He caught her gaze when she'd meant to keep it from him. In the silence, he searched her face, his features fraught with remorse.

"I shouldn't have kissed you that night," he said. "You were hurting and I took advantage of a moment."

She smiled. "No, you didn't."

"Yes, I did. . . ." He grinned sheepishly. "And if I had the chance to do it over, I'd do exactly the same thing."

Lexi studied him in the fading light, trying to balance her tilting thoughts: the pull of the past, the warm glow of the present. He'd been a teenager then; now he was a man. The dusty blue light of the sky matched the color of his jeans, one side of his face gilded by the slipping sun. And those dimples, deepening like crevices she wanted to sink into.

She dropped her eyes to her glass, nearly empty now. "Did you ever tell anyone about that kiss?" she asked carefully.

"No," he said. "Did you?"

Lexi shook her head, lifting her eyes to meet his. "Not even Hudson?"

"*Especially* not Hud," Cooper said, reaching for the bottle to replenish her glass.

"I'm not so sure he would have cared."

"It wasn't that," said Cooper. "I wanted it to be private; I wanted to protect it. I knew Hud would ruin it."

Warmth filled her at his confession.

"I'm sure there have been plenty of kisses since then," she said.

He smiled. "Oh, sure. But I'd like to think I've improved my skills since that night."

Show me, she wished to herself.

"What about you?" he asked.

She met his warm gaze, the urge to confess things to him as swift as the desire to have him show her how good a kisser he'd become in the years since that night.

"There have been a few special men, yes," she admitted quietly.

"Anyone recently?"

"A man in London. My professor . . ." Lexi glanced up to gauge Cooper's reaction, expecting to find evidence of his disapproval, but seeing none. "It wasn't a good fit."

"I'm sorry."

"And you?" she asked. "Is there anyone in Raleigh?"

"Not anymore. I was living with a woman up until a year ago. She managed a wine store. I learned a great deal about wine. Among other things . . ."

The air quieted between them, their shared stories settling on the growing breeze like a fragrance. Suddenly the years between this night and the one when Hudson left her seemed desperately long, a realization that left her both hopeful and melancholy.

She brushed back her hair. "Life seemed so complicated that night, didn't it?" she said.

"That's funny." Cooper smiled sadly. "I always thought it seemed terrifically simple."

Lexi looked up to find Cooper's gaze fixed on her, his eyes tender.

"I don't know why I said that," she whispered, feeling her skin grow warm again. "I don't know why I'm saying *any* of this."

"You don't have to stop."

But she did. Confessions were like bottles of wine; Lexi knew that. One glass always led to another and soon the bottle was drained. She glanced to the bottle between them on the table; they'd nearly emptied this one.

She set down her wine. "I should go."

16

The irony, of course, was that Lexi had been sure Hudson had brought the champagne that night to celebrate their engage-ment. After months of his promising "just a little while longer" before they could share their news with the world, she'd been certain that he'd asked her to meet him at the guest house to make the announcement official with his grandmother's ring. It was only years later, when she looked back on the scene, when she'd been strong enough to dissect the pieces without falling apart, that she realized he'd only brought champagne to soften the blow.

The slow pace of the evening had also been a trick of time. In the moment, it had seemed an eternity from the time he'd arrived to the time he walked back out the door without her, when in truth his dismissal had been brutally swift. But why not? She'd been let go, fired. There would be no fighting for her position, no trying to reason her way back into his heart. Only later did Lexi see that; then, she'd pleaded for one more minute, one more chance, one more explanation —even though he'd made his decision perfectly clear.

He'd chosen Laurel Babcock after all.

"But you told me you didn't want to be with her."

"I know I did. But it's complicated."

"Only if you let it be."

"No," Hudson said, his voice firm now. "It's complicated because it is. It has nothing to do with letting or not letting. You don't get it."

"You're not like your father," Lexi said. "You don't have to want what he wanted."

"How do you know what I want?" Hudson demanded. "Why does everyone think they know what I want? Maybe *I* don't even know what I want."

Hudson dropped into the love seat, his head in his hands. Lexi stared at him, outraged that he thought he got to be the one angry or sad or lost. But what had she expected? Was this scene any different than the one her mother had endured with his father?

Shame pooled in the pit of Lexi's stomach; still, a stubborn flicker of hope burned.

She moved toward him. "You said I wasn't like Laurel."

He answered without lifting his head. "You're not."

And that was the problem, wasn't it? All this time Lexi had seen her opposition as a victory, when it was actually an insurmountable flaw. Not immediately fatal, but eventually.

Tears rose up Lexi's throat, fast and choking.

She felt the panic of someone who'd had the wind knocked out of her, certain she'd never regain her breath.

That was when she saw Cooper. His form slipped into view just beyond Hudson's bent head. Cooper called out to her, asked her whether she was all right. Hudson spun to face his brother, said they were fine and to mind his own business, to which Cooper said, "I didn't ask you; I asked Lexi." But she couldn't answer for herself and she knew she didn't need to. It was clear she was nowhere close to all right.

What came next? Lexi stared at the milky cone of her headlights blooming into the night as she peeled back the layers of her memory.

She remembered the sky. The stars strung together like jewelry as she rolled her head against the Porsche's headrest. She remembered the sound of Cooper's voice, steady and unwavering. She remembered taking long swigs of champagne and the bubbles stinging her nose. She remembered staring at his hand on the stick shift, the auburn down below his knuckles catching the light of the radio, trying to focus on his fingers. He'd buckled her in. She'd been content to sit slumped in the seat, uncaring whether she was tossed from the car, because what difference did it make now? But he'd pulled the belt across her body and snapped it securely for her. Still, as he steered them down the dark, rutted road, she'd felt as loose as a sheet of paper, hoping the next rush of wind might just lift her out into the atmosphere.

When they'd arrived at her apartment she didn't get out, and Cooper didn't seem in any hurry to encourage her. She stared at her feet, aware for the first time that she was barefoot.

"Your shoes are in the back," he said, reaching behind her for the impossibly high pumps Hudson had bought for her months earlier, shoes she would never have worn in a million years on her own, shoes that made her whole body ache the day after she'd worn them, but for Hudson she'd suffered the pain gladly. Now she hurled them, one at a time, out into the empty street, the action thrilling.

"Feel better?" Cooper asked.

She nodded, sniffed. But the relief was fleeting. In his eyes she saw pity—or something close. Shame pushed its way through the soft clouds of her champagne fog. Lexi stared out at the street, wondering how this could be the same street she'd left three hours earlier. It looked the same but it wasn't. In three hours her whole world had crumbled, so where was the evidence here? She needed to see proof that the universe was as ruined as she was. But all around her, life went on untouched, uncaring.

Except for Cooper beside her.

She swung her gaze to his, needing to find the anchor of his eyes.

"I don't know what I'm supposed to do now," she whispered.

"We can keep driving," he said. "We can just *go*."

Go. Lexi loved the sound of that. Maybe that would be best: to just let him take her away. In the car, speeding along the water, she could pretend the night had never happened, that Hudson would still be waiting for her back at the guest house, wondering what was holding her up.

She nodded, the raw need in her voice startling to her as she answered, *"Yes."*

He drove them up and down the coast for almost two hours. She'd felt certain the whole ride that she'd fall into a deep sleep; her eyes were so swollen and aching from crying, and yet she'd remained awake, frighteningly so, wondering whether she might never fall asleep again. Everything reminded her of Hudson. Everywhere. There was nowhere safe to point her gaze that didn't hurt.

Except at Cooper.

At Nauset, he pulled them into the parking lot and turned off the car. Stars blinked in a sea of endless black. Lexi looked up and blinked back at them.

"Nights like this I always wish I knew the constellations," Cooper said. "Do you know any of them?"

She shook her head.

"We could always make some up," he said brightly, lifting his hand and pointing to her right. "That one there looks kind of like a can of motor oil, don't you think? And that one there . . ." His finger swerved to the left. "You can't tell me that doesn't look exactly like a slice of pizza."

She rolled her head toward him, giving in to a small laugh. Lexi knew what he was doing, and she was grateful to him. For a while longer she stared at the night sky, her amusement thinning, her ache returning. She looked at Cooper and found him watching the view, his eyes narrowed wistfully, where the dunes slipped into the darkness, the sound of the water just beyond.

"I came to this beach with my first surfboard," he said.

She sniffed. "I didn't know you were a surfer."

"I'm not," he said with a sigh. "I knocked myself out on the board within the first ten minutes I was in the water. Blood everywhere. Two lifeguards brought me in. It was utterly humiliating. I was twelve and my dad made me promise I'd never get back on a board again."

"So you didn't?"

"Of course I did." He grinned at her. "The day the stitches came out, I was right back here."

Lexi watched him as he spoke, thinking how much older he looked to her, how she had never noticed the way he'd been aging all these summers, how handsome he'd become. How remarkably different he looked from Hudson. Why had she never noticed?

"It's cold," Cooper said suddenly, reaching down to start the engine again. "I should get you home and warm."

They said little driving back, letting the sound of the radio fill the air between them until they were in front of her apartment again.

"Are you hungry?" he asked.

Lexi shook her head.

"Do you want me to take you somewhere *else?*"

Again, she shook her head.

Cooper looked pensive. Regret bubbled up inside her. What did she expect from him? He was only eighteen, and he'd drained his gas tank to make her feel better.

"I'm sorry," she said, crying again.

"Why are *you* sorry?" he asked. "Because you trusted someone and he turned out to be a creep?"

"He's your brother."

"He's a jerk."

She licked a fat tear off her lip. "I'm such a fool." She turned to look at him.

He reached out and wiped at a new tear with his thumb, the gesture so swift and certain that Lexi gasped, shocked at her body's response to his touch. Crazy as it was, she wanted his hands on her again, wanted the fingers that had gripped the gearshift moments earlier to possess her with the same conviction, the same sense of purpose.

"You're not a fool," he said. "You just fell in love with the wrong brother."

The wrong brother. She stared at him for a long moment, the champagne making it hard to hold on to his words, though she understood, even blurry with alcohol, that he meant them. Overcome suddenly with emotion, Lexi leaned over to kiss his cheek, to thank him for helping her home, to say good night, or maybe to feel him near. But at the last moment, he turned his face and caught her lips, landing his mouth squarely on hers and keeping it there until she pulled away, a slight and slow retreat.

Her mind spun; desire and sorrow knotted in one terrible tangle. She fumbled for the door handle, shivering now with chill. Cooper reached across to still her hand. "Wait." In the next instant, he was at her door, helping her out, walking her up her stairs and inside. When he'd settled her under a blanket on the couch, she felt her body finally quiet its tremors and slip into sleep.

A moment later, she opened her eyes to thank him, to wish him back, but Cooper was gone.

Harrisport, Massachusetts
July 1966

*P*arties at the Moss cottage were so frequent that Tucker knew better than to lounge around in anything less than a collared shirt and khakis after six. You never knew when a jazz quartet might be setting up on the terrace, or a champagne toast might be called on the back lawn. From seven until midnight, corks popped like gun salutes, so loud and so frequent you'd cease to notice them after a while.

No sooner would the sun start its slow drop than the preparations would begin. Dorrie would call her troops to order and delegate from the counter, sending the handful of sun-kissed local girls hired to help serve out into the party. The rich, buttery smell of crab tarts would begin its journey down the hall shortly before five, floating up the main stairs, too strong to be swallowed by the lingering smell of the tide it encountered on its way. Linen tablecloths, snapped open with all the efficiency of a rigger tending to a sail, were smoothed across tables and sideboards. There was rarely any occasion. Sometimes a party would be organized to celebrate a summer neighbor's return, or a surprise visit from family, but usually the reason, as far as Tucker could see, was simply that his mother and father couldn't bear to be alone together.

Tonight's party, however, had a very specific purpose: to celebrate Tucker's graduation (and Jim's too, of course). Though Lois and Garrison had produced a luxurious event in Charlotte at the beginning of the month to commemorate their son's successful tenure at law school, his parents were determined to have everyone on the Cape know their pride also.

Tucker swung into the bathroom doorway and grinned to find Jim leaning over the sink, inspecting his foamy jaw in the mirror as he shaved with the concentration of a surgeon.

"Jimbo, you've been at that cheek for ten minutes."

"This could well be the most important shave of my life," countered Jim, pausing in his meticulous strokes to give his friend a disparaging look.

"Yeah, well, shave any closer and you'll bleed to death before your first date. Relax, will ya?"

"How the heck am I supposed to relax?" demanded Jim. "I've been waiting to meet this girl for three months."

Tucker wasn't one to criticize; he'd been nervous all day thinking about Edie Worthington's possible attendance.

Would she or wouldn't she? The question had been banging around in his head for days now, a broken-record accompaniment throughout their drive to and from Boston, and there all through endless hours of meetings and feasts. To say he hoped so would give away his heart, make him a cheater, a wretched human being. And his father would have a fit.

So let him, Tucker thought. In his joy after his trip to the Grange Hall, Tucker had hoped that his father might have seen him coming up from the beach with Edie, might have gotten wind of their blossoming friendship, but Garrison hadn't spoken of it. Neither had his mother. It was a small rebellion—not that it was the reason for his interest in Edie Worthington—but Tucker wouldn't lie that it thrilled him just a bit to think his desire for a local girl might rile his father to the core.

Moments later, both of them feeling as shiny and bright as new pennies, he and Jim made their way down the hall and descended the main staircase, pausing for a moment at the landing to survey the crowded room.

"Look at them all." Jim took in a deep breath, staring out into the sea of guests. "It's like someone's wound them up and they're just begging to be let go."

"It's the sea air," Tucker said, waving to a bright-eyed blonde standing in the corner with a middle-aged man Tucker recognized as one of his father's associates from Boston. "It makes everyone crazy."

Jim's blue eyes grew big behind his glasses. "Oh, let's hope."

Deciding it was best to be as far away as possible from a clock, Edie biked to the town beach after dinner. It was a good crowd, she decided, scanning the familiar faces that were milling about, moving around the bonfire with sodas and beer. If she hadn't been so chilled in her thin sweater, she might have picked up one for herself from the overflowing coolers that were stuck into the sand. Instead she moved as close as possible to the fire's crackling flames and held out her hands to warm them, noticing the crescents of caked drywall mud that still lined her cuticles, try as she had to scrub them clean.

"Hi."

Edie glanced up to see Hank beside her. He looked dressed up, she thought. His hair tidier than usual. His shirt tucked in. She wasn't used to seeing him this way. They'd known each other since they were kids, and he'd worn his hair the exact same way the whole time: short, except in the front. For reasons she never could understand he insisted on keeping a puff of his coal-black curls at the front of his scalp, like a rooster. She'd always meant to ask him why he did it. Sometimes she wanted to tease him when he'd nag her because she'd wrapped the cords wrong or misplaced some tool, but she didn't. The truth was, when he sweated, which he did standing still most days, those black curls turned under themselves in a way that she found annoyingly darling. Sometimes she'd wanted to reach out and push her fingers through the tangle of them, just to see what it would feel like. Now was one of those times.

"You okay?" he asked.

"I'm fine," she said. "Why?"

"I'm just surprised to see you here; that's all. I thought you didn't like hanging out at bonfires."

She shrugged, pulling her sweater tighter around her front. "I figured it was a nice night." What else could she say? Certainly not the truth: that she'd made herself come because she'd been afraid that if she'd been home alone and unaccounted for, she'd have given in to temptation and raced down to the Moss cottage to accept Tucker's impossible invitation.

Hank sipped his beer. "You look really pretty tonight."

Edie looked up at him, startled by the compliment, even as a flush of pleasure warmed her skin. In all the years she'd known Hank Wright, he'd never once told her she was pretty. Suddenly it seemed desperately important that he had.

"Thanks," she said. "You look nice too."

Hank squinted into the blaze. "You think I keep you from doing big jobs on the site because you're a girl, don't you?" he asked.

Edie frowned, bewildered. "Well, don't you?"

He shook his head. "I do it because I worry about you. Because I don't want anything to happen to you."

"So you already told me."

"I don't mean like that," he said. "Not like someone worries about a little kid, Edie." He turned to her then, the glow of the fire catching the hard lines of his jaw. "I mean the way a man worries about a woman that he feels for. A woman he feels *very deeply* for."

Edie blinked at him, the words sinking in. She wanted him to repeat them, wanted to savor them one more time, but then on the other side of the fire, she saw Missy Murphy, foolishly underdressed and huddled with her girlfriends, the young woman's eyes fixed on Hank, her turquoise satin blouse shimmering under the firelight as she waved. Edie glanced to see whether Hank had noticed his admirer, and sure enough, he had. He waved back. A flicker of discomfort charged through Edie. She felt silly in her fat braid, immeasurably young in her polka-dotted skirt. She reached up and touched the elastic, fingering the knot enviously. Did Hank like Missy's hair that way, pulled up on one side like a foamy wave about to break? She wanted to ask him—it seemed desperately important to her now—but before she could he touched her on the shoulder and said, "I'll see you, Edie."

"See you," she answered dully, disappointment

filling her as she watched him make his way around the fire to where Missy waited for him, the feeling growing when he slid his arm around Missy's waist and Missy looked up at him with an expression that Edie could describe only as victorious.

At ten till nine, Tucker decided he would wait outside. The porch was teeming with guests, few of whom would spill over into the harsh exterior light above the side entrance. There he would be safe from their curious eyes, but in plain sight of Edie's when—*if*—she came.

It was a cloudless night; the stars blinked from one end of the sky to the other. He'd left Jim well-off; no sooner had Helen Willoughby slipped through the door between her parents, tanned legs stretching out from a skirt of petal-pink tulle that made her look like a long-stemmed carnation, than Jim was a goner. Though Tucker's escape hadn't been guaranteed: there were still obstacles to get through, several of his father's associates and their wives, a few neighbors. There were inquiries into school and future plans, but mostly it was talk of Florence, how she was doing and when they could all look forward to seeing her this summer. Tucker had answered every query pleasantly, patiently, even as his eyes had drifted over their shoulders toward the clock on the mantel. When he saw his mother coming out with

217

an unfamiliar couple, Tucker excused himself to the porch before she could arrive with introductions. He'd pushed through the clumps of guests, squinted through the clouds of cigarette smoke, and crossed the lawn, free at last.

Now he stood with his hands in his pockets, staring out into the blackness beyond the fence of pines like an expectant retriever. He told himself he wouldn't be crushed if she didn't show, but as the minutes ticked by, his heart thundered right along with them. Suddenly everything felt fleeting, fragile. Huge and tiny all at once. His thoughts raced with possibility—outrageous and reckless questions. What if he took them away tonight? What if he asked Edie to leave the Cape with him, and what if she said yes? But as the waiting continued, his hope faded. Maybe it was better she'd changed her mind. He'd been brash and thoughtless and just plain dumb thinking he could change the course of his life in one night.

Then, just when disappointment had finally settled over his heart, he caught a shimmer of metal and movement through the black, and he was wholly unprepared for the rush of excitement that tore through him, his doubts blowing away like ashes.

The click of bicycle spokes came seconds before she did. In his relief, he let go a laugh, then took a deep inhalation of air, a man coming to the surface to taste oxygen after nearly drowning.

17

*T*he beast awakens!"

Edie grinned as she approached the porch where Jim had arrived with a cup of coffee shortly after nine, his white hair and shirt collar gently askew.

"I wondered how much noise we'd have to make before you woke up," she teased.

"In my defense, I got home just after three a.m.," he said, coming down the steps to meet her at the edge of the lawn.

She smiled. "Then Boston was good?"

"As good as it ever is," Jim said. "The old gang still has a pulse; we take what we can get these days." He squinted out at the lawn, considering the scene. "Boy, you don't waste any time, do you, young lady?"

"Not when I've got weather like this," Edie said, gesturing to the swath of cloudless blue above them.

"So when does everyone else get here?" Jim asked.

Edie frowned up at him. "What do you mean, everyone else? This *is* everyone."

"But"—Jim slid his gaze back to her—"they're all . . ."

She smirked. "I think the word you're looking for is *women,* James."

"I might have known," Jim said, a smile spreading across his face.

"You're not sorry, are you?" she said. "Because if you are, too bad, James Masterson. A deal's a deal, and I'm not letting you out of this one."

"I wouldn't dream of any such thing. I would, however, dream of having dinner with you again."

Edie reached to her neck, smoothing the short hairs that curled behind her ears. "I can't tonight," she said. "I'm having my kids to the house for pizza."

"Speaking of kids . . ." Jim glanced back at the house. "Cooper and Alexandra seem to be getting along, don't they?"

Did they? Edie considered Jim's observation with a lump in her throat. As much as she wanted her daughter to move on with her love life and finally let someone in, Edie didn't imagine it would be Hudson's brother, Tucker's other son. Of course, what did she know? And what difference did it make? Love was never as neat and tidy as her daughter—or son—wanted to imagine it.

"Of course they would get along," she answered at last. "I'm sure Cooper barely remembers all that foolishness."

"Now, now," Jim scolded gently. "You didn't think it was foolishness when it was you and Tuck getting along so well."

"It was never a good match," she said softly, her eyes shifting to the guest house.

"Tuck was in love with you, Edie."

She shrugged. "He just thought he was."

"I was his best friend for fifty years." Jim's light tone dropped into a heavy register. "I *know* he was."

Edie turned back to Jim, searching his unusually serious expression for a moment, then forcing her gaze away. She tugged on her work gloves. "I should get back to my crew."

"Maybe you'd better," Jim said, nodding toward the guest house, where a crowd had formed around the doorway. "It looks as if something's happening in there."

Lexi wasn't at all surprised to see the hulking shape of the green Dumpster as soon as she came around the bend in the driveway the next morning. She knew how fast her mother worked when it came to securing permits and equipment delivery. The driveway, quiet for days, was suddenly crowded with unfamiliar cars and trucks, their owners already busy carting armloads of discarded material from the guest cottage across the lawn to the enormous trash bin. Lexi parked and carried her first load of equipment toward the house, seeing the crew as she neared the lawn. Her mother's all-woman crew had changed in the two years she'd been away, but Lexi still saw a few familiar faces as she scanned the group.

A part of her, too small to indulge, was sorry to

see them there. She wouldn't lie; it had been lovely having the house to herself—or rather, to her and Cooper. She'd enjoyed the privacy, and their time together, maybe more than she wanted to admit.

But now even Jim had returned; Lexi had spotted his Town Car in the mix of vehicles in the driveway.

Where was Cooper? she wondered as she let herself into the cottage, thinking as she did how easily she had resumed her circulation in the big house. For so long, it had been unimaginable that she would ever set foot in the Moss house again, let alone feel comfortable walking through its enormous rooms unannounced, and yet, here she was.

Cooper's confession swam through her mind, filling her with a palpable excitement and relief. She'd hoped he'd remembered their exchange all those years ago, hoped she hadn't fabricated her recollection of his interest, the way they'd been drawn to each other that night. Was that why she'd arrived early today? Why she'd taken the time to think through her wardrobe instead of throwing on the first clean shirt she saw?

"Good morning."

Cooper was in the kitchen when she stepped inside the house, leaning against the sink with a cup of coffee, dressed in a T-shirt and swim shorts.

"Good morning," she answered, settling her bag on one of the kitchen chairs.

"Coffee?" he asked.

"I'd love some." A second cup? Since when did she allow herself a second cup? she thought sheepishly as she took the mug he held out to her.

"So much for the peace and quiet, huh?" he said.

Lexi nodded as she blew across her coffee. She wanted to tell him that it was better this way; she wanted him to say it first. Didn't he feel it too? It was as if they had been unsupervised children the day before—dangerous hours when they might have chosen poorly in a weak moment: drawn on the walls, made forts with the sofa cushions.

"I really enjoyed last night," he said.

"So did I." She smiled at him. "I'm afraid I had too much to drink, though. I said things . . ."

"We both did. But I'm not blaming the wine."

Lexi dropped her gaze to her coffee.

"So are you sorry you never got to New York?" she asked.

"Oh, I got there," he said. "Moved into a closet in the Lower East Side, waited tables at night, and paid for the whole program myself."

Lexi considered him, impressed to know that he'd stood up to his father and gone his own way. Had Hudson been outraged, she wondered, at his little brother having the strength to do what he, Hudson, could never do?

"How's the novel coming?" she asked. "Getting any closer?"

"I must be," Cooper said. "I usually reread the previous day's pages and edit them on the spot but with this book I'm like a runaway train. I don't dare stop on the tracks."

"Maybe that's a good sign."

He smiled. "An optimist."

"Not always," Lexi said, returning the smile.

Maybe lately.

His eyes shifted to her bag, where she'd dumped it on the chair, unzipped and gaping.

"Is that what I think it is?" he asked, gesturing to the corner of his novel poking out.

"It is; I just got it," Lexi said, feeling a flush of embarrassment when she reached into her bag and pulled it free, as if he'd found her doing a search for him online. "I haven't had a chance to start it yet."

"Well, good," Cooper said, holding out his hand. "Then I can inscribe it for you before you do."

"You don't have to do that. . . ."

"Of course I do. Everyone knows it's bad luck to sign a book after the reader's already started it."

She laughed. "Bad luck for the reader or the author?" she asked.

"Probably both." He scanned the counter until he found a pen. Lexi watched as he spread the book open to the title page and began to write. Try as she did, she couldn't make out his words before he'd closed the book and handed it back to her. She slipped it into her purse without reading it, wanting to save it for later, and not sure why.

"No pressure," he said. "I can take criticism. If you don't like it, tell me the truth."

"I'm sure I will," she assured him. "How was the beach?"

"I haven't been yet. I was just on my way, actually." Cooper yanked his T-shirt over his head and tossed it over the back of the chair. All the times he'd loped around the property as a teen, shirtless and barefoot—now she had to drag her gaze away.

He picked up the towel he'd left on the table and swung it over his shoulder. "Want to join me this time?"

She smiled, gesturing to her clothes. "Still no suit," she said.

"So don't swim."

"But you just poured me coffee."

"So take it with you."

She might have surrendered if not for a knock on the screen door. A young woman with spiky blond hair stood on the porch, wide-eyed and winded. Lexi recognized her at once from her mother's crew: Hannah.

"Lexi! Girl, you've *gotta* see what we found," Hannah exclaimed. "Come see it before your mother covers it up. It's too awesome!"

Though Lexi didn't want to spoil the excitement

for her mother's giggling crew, she knew exactly what they had found under the layers of cracked wallboard as she followed Hannah down the lawn to the guest house: her father's declaration of love, the one he'd carved deeply into the framing to show Edie Worthington—and the world—how he really felt all those years ago. The testimonial that had buoyed her mother after Tucker Moss's heartbreak.

Lexi smiled as she began to move toward the open doorway to finally see the confession for herself, and as she did, she realized something.

She wasn't the only jilted woman to be both set adrift and rescued in the guest house.

Harrisport, Massachusetts
July 1966

I t wasn't too late to go back. That was Edie's thought—the strongest thought of the hundreds that rushed at her when she came sailing through the pines and saw Tucker Moss in the cone of the cottage's floodlight. She could still change her mind, still turn her bike around and race back up the road. The truth was, she hadn't expected him to be there. Not in any real way. She wasn't even sure she'd *wanted* to find him there. Then why had she come? Because it had thrilled her, scared her? Maybe for the same reason she'd been waiting for her father in the cab of his truck that damp April morning, the morning after he'd told her that a construction site was a hard place for a girl, that she'd probably be happier working at the ice-cream stand or at the Peppercorn, handing out paper baskets of fried clams?

Now she was here at the cottage, not in dungarees and work boots, as she'd been hours earlier, but in a skirt—a skirt! She felt decadent —even if her hair wasn't as glamorous as Missy Murphy's—and strange in her own skin, yet utterly excited. Until her gaze caught on the porch behind him, the banner stretched between the posts snapping gently in the evening breeze: CONGRATULATIONS, TUCKER!

Her skin turned cold.

She blinked at him and whispered harshly, "You didn't tell me this was *your* party."

"I was afraid you wouldn't come if you knew it was for me," he admitted. "And I wanted you to be here. I know this sounds crazy, but it makes more sense to have you here than ninety-nine percent of the people who are already in there."

It sounded *very* crazy, Edie thought, yet she smiled, helplessly delighted at his confession. Besides, wasn't she crazy too for being here?

"Are you hungry?" he asked.

She looked up at the cottage, bursting with activity and light and sound, laughter and music rolling out like smoke. Suddenly the thought of walking into that world with him didn't seem so unthinkable. She had as much right to be there as anyone. She wasn't a construction worker now. Tonight she was a guest. A friend.

She turned to him and smiled. "Starving."

The air inside the kitchen was hot and moist with the smell of dish soap and the lingering sweetness of baked goods and freshly brewed coffee. A pair of older girls Edie recognized from Hank's class rushed around the deep double sink in crisp light blue uniforms, their hair pulled back into shiny blond buns. Silver platters were lined up from one end of the stainless-steel countertop to the other, some bearing the remnants of dinner and the rest untouched with neatly stacked desserts. Edie stared dazedly at a platter of napoleons, cut as big as bricks, while Tucker slipped into the butler's pantry. Seeing those mountains of puff pastry and petit fours iced in flawless pastels, wedges of dense chocolate cake dusted with confectioner's sugar, made her dizzy. It was like something out of a child's picture book.

"Edie?"

Edie turned toward the sound of the voice, recognizing it seconds before its owner appeared. Doreen Packard. Edie flushed immediately. In her excitement, she'd forgotten that her mother's dear friend would be working this party.

The older woman squinted as she drew closer. "Edie, I hardly recognized you, hon."

"Hi, Mrs. Packard."

Edie saw confusion and then concern strain the woman's features as she no doubt figured out why Edie was there and, more important, with whom. Edie glanced away, feeling admonished. But before Doreen could inquire, their exchange was interrupted by the sound of clattering dishes. The older woman sighed wearily. "Who's in there making a mess of my pantry?" she called over her shoulder.

Tucker appeared in the doorway, wearing a

victor's grin and holding two cut-crystal flutes that looked exceptionally expensive.

"Those are your mother's very favorites, young man," said Doreen, hands on her hips. "She'll have your head mounted on a wall if you break 'em."

"Yes, ma'am, I'm sure she would." He winked at Edie and walked to the caravan of platters that sat on the counter, leaning in for a closer look. "Remind me again which ones have the custard inside them, Miss Dorrie?"

"Don't even think about messing up my trays," Doreen ordered, snapping her fingers at the girls who'd been stealing glances first at Tucker, then at Edie, then at Tucker again. "Those are about to go out."

Ignoring her command, Tucker scooped up a sampling on a small saucer and balanced it in the crook of his arm while he swung open the door to the second refrigerator and pulled out a chilled bottle of champagne, brandishing it toward Edie.

Edie felt hot color return to her cheeks. It didn't help that when she glanced over at Doreen, her mother's friend wore a reproachful look that plainly asked, *Do your parents know you're here about to make yourself sick on pastries and drunk on champagne, Edie Worthington?* So she was grateful when Tucker came at last to retrieve her, steering her and the plate of desserts through the kitchen and into the heart of the house.

"No," whispered Edie, resisting his lead. "Don't take me through there."

"Why not?"

He knew why not—she could see he did—so he turned them around and led her instead to the servants' stairwell, where she was relieved to disappear up the angled steps.

Though she could still hear the muffled sounds of the party below, the paneled walls of the servants' wing were a delicious cave they moved through before the ceiling lifted, opening into the main end of the house. They passed several guest rooms, some untouched, others in use, before Tucker pushed open a door nearly at the end of the hall. Edie's fierce determination halted briefly. This was altogether dangerous, she thought to herself as she followed him into the room. A decoratively turned bed, its canopy trimmed with icicles of lace, seemed almost terrifyingly imposing as she passed it, as if it might slide across the floor and demand a password from her before letting her by.

Tucker led them out onto a small terrace, the view of the back lawn and the water beyond it even more breathtaking under a roof of stars.

She walked to the railing and looked down; Tucker came beside her. She caught the scent of his cologne, a pleasant lime. She wasn't used to men who wore cologne, but she liked it.

"It's like they don't even know we're here," he said.

Edie considered Tucker's profile as he stared out at the lawn, wondering whether he'd already had champagne. He seemed unusually reckless to her. She'd never seen this side of him—not that she had known him long, but still she suspected this was a curious mood for him.

"How was Boston?" she asked.

"Torturous. Endless."

"What happened to your great plan to declare your independence?"

He sighed. "I'm building up to it."

She nodded.

"I thought of you the entire time," he said.

Edie glanced away reflexively, unprepared for his confession, less prepared for the flush of excitement that charged up the skin of her throat.

It seemed Tucker had even startled himself. "Sorry," he said quietly. "I shouldn't have said that. I just meant it was nice to have something to look forward to when I got back. Some*one*."

Edie looked up, searching his warm eyes, trying to understand what he meant by *something*. Did he have expectations of what she might say or do with him tonight, the hope of something intimate? Hank's disparaging comments echoed; she forced them quiet with a sip of champagne.

"You have James," she said.

Tucker leaned on the railing. "You know what I mean."

Of course she did. She looked down into her

champagne and took another sip to recover. This time the bubbles left a mark; when she looked up, the simple motion felt slower, like pulled taffy. It seemed all she wanted to do was let the rest of her slide away too.

"I wasn't going to come, you know," she said.

"I know. I'm glad you changed your mind."

She looked out at the lawn. "Where *is* James?"

"Probably seeing stars in the eyes of Helen Willoughby. She's a neighbor. I thought they might hit it off."

"That was awfully nice of you."

"I hope Helen thinks so."

"Tucker!"

They turned to look below. There on the lawn an older man in a seersucker blazer and a cherry red bow tie waved up at them.

"That's Dover Woodhouse," Tucker whispered. "He works with my father in Charlotte. He's here for the weekend." Tucker moved to the edge of the terrace and called down, "Evenin', Mr. Woodhouse, sir!"

"Son, your father's lookin' for you," the man yelled back. "I think he wants a word."

"Yes, sir. I'll be right down." Tucker returned to where Edie sat, his face drawn, that retiring smile, briefly gone, now returned. "Shoot. Isn't it just like my old man to ruin a perfect moment?"

She grinned. "'Shoot'?"

He wagged a finger at her. "Now, don't you go corrupting me, Edie Worthington."

"I couldn't if I tried," she said, playfully swatting his hand away. He caught it and held it to his chest, his eyes meeting hers.

"You could," he said, taking a step closer. "And I'm hoping you'll at least try."

The pleasant flutter in the pit of her stomach bloomed in an instant, spreading throughout her body. She looked up at his face, thinking he had beautiful lips. "Your father's waiting," she reminded him, not pulling her hand out of his.

"He's *always* waiting."

Maybe it was the champagne, or maybe it was that Tucker said it with just enough sadness that her heart swelled for him. Whatever the reason, Edie reared up on her tiptoes and pressed her lips to his, deciding she didn't want to wait another minute to find out what sort of kisser he was, or how those perfect lips would feel on hers. He tasted like champagne and walnuts.

Then, just as quickly as she'd kissed him, she pulled away and searched his face for his reaction. He looked dazed, she thought. Utterly dazed and deliriously delighted. She smiled.

"*Now* you can go," she said, reaching up to smooth his hair.

"Promise you'll be here when I get back."

"What if someone comes up?"

"No one will. No one's staying in this room tonight."

"Are you sure?"

He handed her the bottle of champagne, that curious heat in his eyes evident again. "This'll keep you warm until I come back."

She took the bottle with both hands, startled at its weight. For a moment she was sure he meant to kiss her. He took a short step forward, his head tilted just slightly. Uncertainty and excitement charged through her, a whiff of his citrus cologne feathering the air; then he shifted at the last minute, changing his mind—or maybe she'd just imagined it.

Either way, his face betrayed his affection.

"I'm glad you came," he said.

"You said that already," she whispered. "Go."

He grinned. "Yes, ma'am."

When he'd slipped through the terrace door and closed it behind him, she sat down in a wicker chair and sipped the champagne.

Above her the sky was warm and endless, the only break in it the sliver of crescent moon. It looked just like a smile, she thought suddenly, wondering how she'd never seen it that way before now.

18

*O*wen Wright stared at the text message as if he were under a hypnotist's control. For the life of him, he couldn't drag his eyes away. He knew he had to; any minute Meg would come out of Russo's with their pizzas and slide back into the truck, wearing the same carefree smile she'd left with a few minutes earlier, when she'd insisted she be the one to get the pizza this time, because she didn't trust him to order her veggie.

Now what? He juggled his choices in a hot panic, his eyes darting up to check the door, then snapping back down to the pink-trimmed screen of her smart phone, lying on the seat beside him. He had two options: one, say nothing and pretend he hadn't seen it; or two, accost his daughter the second she got back and demand to know who this sleazeball was who was sending her sex messages over her phone. But how could he do that? It wasn't as if he'd innocently glanced over and lo, there was her phone, faceup, the message right there. Hardly.

The truth was, he'd meant only to peek, to see once and for all what might have been the reason for his daughter's apparent discomfort as of late, the unshakable sense he'd had since she'd arrived that something was going on in New York with

Heather. He'd been certain that if he could just have seen a few text messages, he might have been able to calm the roiling nerves in his gut, quiet them without having to drag it out of Meg and spoil their precious time together.

But he'd never expected to find *this*.

And there were so many! All the times he heard those telltale chimes ringing out in the middle of dinner, in the middle of the night. He'd been so certain it was Heather nagging Meg about something. He'd never thought, not once, that it might be—

His jaw tightened. Bewilderment turned back to burning rage. Who was this guy propositioning his daughter? Did Heather know about this? And why hadn't she done something about it?

Owen shifted in the driver's seat until he could see the length of the take-out counter, and Meg, still waiting. Safe for the moment and too livid to wait, he scooped up his cell and dialed Heather.

He gripped the wheel while he waited, watching his knuckles turn white.

"Did you know about this creep?" Now it was his turn to rush past cursory greetings when Heather picked up.

Heather was, not surprisingly, unprepared. "Owen? What's going on? Do I know *what?*"

"You can't believe what this guy is writing, Heather. It's . . . it's disgusting."

"What are you talking about?"

"I'm talking about our daughter getting text messages sent to her by some kid—at least, I *think* he's a kid—hell, maybe he's not; maybe he's some—"

"Wait, are you talking about Ty?"

Ty. The calm in his ex-wife's voice stopped him cold. "You know him?"

"Of course I know him, Owen," she said evenly. "She's been dating him since the spring. She hasn't mentioned him?"

"No," he admitted quietly, hurt flooding him. How could Meg not have told him?

"So you know that this Ty kid has been sending her rude text messages, and you're okay with that?" he demanded.

"Owen, just calm down."

"I need to calm down? I think you need to get a little more worked up. Have you read these things?"

"Of course not. I don't read my daughter's texts, Owen. She has her privacy."

"*Our* daughter," he corrected. "And I'm glad one of us does, because clearly you're more concerned with being hip than caring that our daughter is over her head with some punk kid—"

"Don't you dare imply—"

"And she tells me you're letting her drink *wine?*"

"A glass here and there," Heather defended hotly. "What is this? Child services?"

Owen glanced back at the window, seeing that Meg still waited against the counter. "I want her to stay on another two weeks," he said firmly. "I think she needs more time here to get her head on straight."

"Oh, for God's sake, Owen . . ."

"I mean it, Heather."

"Owen, she can't. She has a prep course. I told you that at the beginning of the summer."

"She can skip it."

"No, she can't. She was the only person on the waiting list who got in, and she is not missing it. Besides, have you even asked her if she wants to stay?"

"Of course she would want to."

"Owen. She needs to come home."

He felt a sharp twinge of longing push past the anger and dread. "This is her home too."

"Don't make this about you and me, okay?"

"How am I doing that? I'm telling you she would want more time here."

"If she does, it's only because she's worried about you finding out about the wedding."

He stilled, his eyes locking on the dashboard. "What wedding?"

Heather blew out a shallow breath. "I've been debating how to tell you. Meg's known this whole time, which I know hasn't been easy for her, and I feel terrible for that; I do—"

"Tell me *what?*" Owen demanded.

"The show in LA . . . It's not really a show so much as a *ceremony.* . . ." A pause, as excruciating as the seconds between lightning and thunder. "Owen, George and I are getting married."

He looked up, dazed by the news. So that was it. Why Meg had been so nervous around him, why she kept avoiding calling Heather.

"Jesus." He swallowed. "How could you do this?"

"What kind of question is that, Owen? We're divorced."

"Christ, that's not what I mean. Did you know Meg's been trying to get me to go out on dates like I've got two weeks left to live? She's making it her mission to see me involved with someone, and now I know why."

"She worries about you," Heather said. "We all do."

Owen glared at the steering wheel. "It's not worry, Heather. It's guilt. You just don't want the guilt anymore of having me alone."

It had been a pathetic claim to make, but he didn't care. As he expected, Heather was indignant. "Why should I feel guilty? We're both adults. If you want to be alone, that's your decision. I found love again; you can too."

"You found love again, all right. Found it before I even knew ours had gone missing."

He heard her draw in a frustrated breath and expel it slowly. "I don't feel any responsibility for making you happy."

"No, you just passed that on to our daughter."

The line went quiet. Owen sighed. "I didn't mean that," he said.

"Of course you did."

More silence.

"Anyway," continued Heather, "the point is, Meg is sixteen years old and I trust her to make good decisions about this relationship. You need to do the same."

Owen stared at the restaurant door, feeling utterly deflated, all the indignation and determination seeping out of his body like smoke out an opened window. Five minutes ago he'd been a steam engine, ready to roll over every defense his ex-wife might have thrown up; now he felt like the one who'd been run over by the train.

"Owen? Are you still there?"

He looked up to see Meg pushing through the door, carrying two pizza boxes. The ache of loneliness fisted around his heart.

"I have to go," he said, hating the defeated sound of his voice but not having the energy to remedy it.

"Don't say anything to upset her, Owen. You'll only push her away."

He hung up, Heather's final words sinking in his stomach as he exited Meg's text messages and set the phone facedown on the dash where she'd left it. For a feverish moment when Meg first slipped back into the truck, he considered telling her what he'd found, but Heather's advice kept him quiet. Still, he must have worn his worry on his face. Meg watched him as she snapped her seat belt. "You okay, Dad?"

He turned to her, the concern in his daughter's eyes only making him feel worse. He pasted on a smile and said, "Yeah, I'm fine. Just hungry."

"Good," she said, his answer enough to return the delighted glow to her face as she proudly patted the top of the pizza boxes on her lap. "This veggie will fix that."

19

*F*or all her love of historic interiors, Lexi had never wanted a house of her own. She'd had plenty of chances over the years, always learning of listings before they'd been made public, and a few times had even met with a bank to discuss loans, but it had never gone very far. When her parents had pressed her on the subject, she'd explained—or tried to—that she didn't want the responsibility of a house, and that she had little interest in a renovation project of her own. "So you buy a *new* house," her father had suggested, but still Lexi had always demurred. With all the wonderful rentals on the Cape, many of which were a steal in the off-season and steps away from the beach, why would she sink her savings into a house that might cease to please her after a while? With rentals, she could change her mind every few years: live one year by the water, another year move to the village, then back to the water again if she wished.

Yet now, as Lexi stood in the middle of the empty one-bedroom cottage that had unexpectedly—and miraculously—come up for rent in Truro, she didn't feel the same familiar sense of possibility, of excitement, of freedom. What she felt instead was strangely unsettled, a weariness she hadn't expected. Why? It was a charming place—cozy, and steps from the beach. The kitchen had been updated: new appliances, a sleek splash guard in frosted seafoam green tiles. Shutters with heavy wooden louvers. Mexican tiles in the living room. And at this very moment, an evening breeze was sailing through the screens, promising perfect crosswinds for a comfortable sleep on even the hottest of summer nights. What wasn't to love?

The rental agent stepped up her pitch. "As you know, a place coming up for rent at the height of peak season is unheard of, but the tenant had a family emergency and frankly the owners would rather just move in someone for the year now than try to fill it for another month. Understand, the rest of July and August would be considered in-season, so you'd be looking at a higher rent for the first two months—but then the off-season price would kick in for September."

Lexi asked the woman for a few more minutes to look it over; the agent excused herself to the deck to make a call.

She wandered through the space, thinking this was usually about the time she'd start to lay out her new home, when she'd start to imagine her prints on the walls, her rugs on the floor, her brightly colored collection of Fiestaware on the kitchen shelves. So why wasn't she? Why did she feel exhausted at the thought of starting over, of putting all her energy into a space that wasn't hers, that would never be hers, no matter how much of her stuff she put inside it?

She needed a place to live again—that much was certain. So why hadn't she written a check for the deposit that instant, instead of staving off a decision by asking for more time to look around?

The rental agent returned. "I've got five more showings for this place tonight. If you want it, hon, I wouldn't wait."

Funny thing was, Lexi thought as she tugged out her checkbook and laid it on the counter, she had been doing exactly that for nearly her whole adult life: waiting. She'd waited for Hudson to return to her every summer, then waited for him to want her back, then waited more for someone to fill the space he'd left behind. It was startlingly clear to her now. It didn't matter the season; her whole life she'd been waiting for someone to move her forward.

Thoughts of Cooper standing close to her in the butler's pantry tore through her, the currents of electricity she'd felt when he'd grazed her breast. Heat flared in her core, the unmistakable warmth of wanting.

Maybe she'd waited long enough.

She signed her name on the check, tore it out, and handed it to the agent.

"Then let's not wait," she said.

It had been forty-six years since Edie had seen that inscription carved into the guest house timber, but as she'd looked on it today, it might have been forty-six days. Just as she had the first time she laid eyes on that stretch of wood, her heart shuddered with a feverish tangle of emotions: excitement, embarrassment, dread.

I LOVE EDIE WORTHINGTON

Had it not occurred to her when she took the job that those four words would be revealed as soon as demolition began and the damaged wallboard was pulled off? Of course it had; she wasn't dim. And it wasn't as if Lexi and Owen didn't know the carving was there, either. Its existence had long been a favorite story in their house—the family lore of their father's creative and spontaneous declaration. Edie had indulged the legend too, but somehow its history was easier to endure when it

246

was safely hidden behind plaster and paneling.

The sound of crunching gravel drew her out of her thoughts; she turned to see Lexi's car through the kitchen window, her daughter climbing out with a bottle of wine and looking more relaxed than Edie had seen her since before she'd left for London. Was that Cooper Moss's doing? Edie smiled, uncaring of the reason as she greeted her daughter at the door.

"I splurged," Lexi announced, twisting the bottle to show the label as she stepped inside.

"What's the occasion?" asked Edie.

"I took that place in Truro tonight—the one I told you about. It's adorable, and I can move in this weekend."

"So soon?"

"I've been back almost three weeks now," Lexi reminded her mother as she set the bottle down on the counter and tugged open the utensil drawer.

"I know. But we haven't even had a chance to get into a really good fight yet. We always get in at least one or two before you move out."

"You mean like the kind we have after I tell you this kitchen is a disaster because I can't find the corkscrew?" Lexi said, still rummaging through the drawer.

"Exactly," said Edie, walking over to the counter and calmly pulling the corkscrew out of the pencil tin she kept by the sink. Lexi gave her mother an even look as she took the tool. "It isn't a disaster just because you don't know where anything is, Miss Smarty-pants." Edie grinned. "So is that the *only* reason we're celebrating?"

"The shoot's going well," Lexi said, pouring them each a glass. "I'm happy about that."

"The shoot." Edie smiled. "Okay."

Lexi searched her mother's inquisitive eyes.

"There's nothing to tell, Mom."

"Well, if there is, you'd better do it now, before your brother gets here," Edie advised, taking her wine.

Lexi frowned. "Owe needs to get over it."

"He's every bit your father that way. Everything's black or white, good or bad."

"No wonder Meg can't talk to him," Lexi said, sighing into her glass before taking a sip.

"Meggie said something to you?" Edie asked.

"She didn't have to. It's obvious he doesn't want to see her grow up."

Edie had suspected that; she'd watched Hank face the same challenge with Lexi once, ached at how they'd fought, father and daughter, to break those comfortable routines when puberty had set in. It had been so hard for Hank to let go of the little girl he'd grown so attached to. It was hard for a mother too, but in a different way. Maybe it was having gone through it herself and knowing the challenges Lexi would face, the work she had ahead of her to get what she wanted.

Hank had taught their daughter to build walls, while Edie had tried to teach Lexi to knock them down. It was a painful realization to Edie now; for a woman who had little interest in constructing, Lexi had become an expert at building walls around her heart.

"It's not an easy thing to do," Edie said diplomatically, not wanting to fuel her daughter's ire. "Watching your kids need you less and less. It's what you know is right, but it's still painful."

"Owe's too judgmental, Mom. He always has been. Daddy was the same way. He always bashed the Mosses."

"*Bashed* is a strong word," Edie argued.

Lexi raised her eyebrows dubiously; Edie consented with a shrug and another sip of wine, swallowing it with a bubble of guilt, knowing she'd done nothing in those crucial years to temper Hank's visible distrust of the Moss family. Why hadn't she? She knew better than anyone what had really happened that summer, yet she'd let her family—no, a whole town, really—hold firmly to a grudge and stood by silent.

Owen's truck rumbled into view. Edie turned to Lexi. Regardless of her regrets, Edie wasn't ready to air this debate quite yet. "Just let it lie tonight, okay?" she pleaded. "I want us all to have a nice, quiet dinner. No drama."

"Sorry we're late," Owen said as he and Meg stepped inside with the pizzas, the sweet smell of

249

baked onions and sautéed mushrooms floating in with them.

"You're right on time," Edie assured him.

Lexi glanced over at her brother as he shrugged out of his sweatshirt, thinking he looked particularly cantankerous tonight. Surely he wasn't going to carry on this sulking forever?

"Want a beer, Owe?" she offered, moving to the fridge.

"No, thanks," he muttered, tossing his sweatshirt on the bench by the door.

Lexi gave her mother a pointed look across the table as they all took their seats, as if to say, *See? I'm trying.*

Edie handed out plates. "I hear you and Lexi had a great day at the beach, Meggie."

"The best," said Meg, pulling at a spiderweb of cheese as she freed a slice from the pie. "You should come with us next time, Grandma."

"Grandma doesn't go to the beach," said Lexi. "Believe me; we tried for years to get her to come with us."

Eddie tossed up her hands. "I burn," she said, as if that explained everything.

"Grandma, I was thinking maybe I could come see that house you're working on one day next week," said Meg. "Aunt Lex was telling me all about it. It sounds supercool."

Owen glanced up as if waking from a trance, his eyes fixing accusingly on Lexi. She met his gaze.

"We can talk about it, honey," Edie consented quickly. "Pizza's better this week, don't you all think? They were so skimpy with the cheese last week."

It was an obvious attempt to shift the subject, but Meg wasn't yet ready to move on. "Hey, maybe you can even show me how to do some construction stuff," she suggested cheerily. "How cool would that be?"

"I think you've got your hands full at Scoop's," Owen said.

Meg plucked a mushroom off her slice and snorted. "As if."

"Your father's right," said Edie with a wink. "One career at a time."

Meg glanced pleadingly at Lexi; Lexi complied.

"I think it's a great idea," she said, feeling the daggers of her mother's glare almost immediately.

"Well, I don't," said Owen. "She's too young."

"How am I too young?" demanded Meg. "Grandma, didn't you say you were my age when you first started working for your dad?"

Edie glanced at Owen, feeling ambushed. "I can't remember exactly," she lied.

"You need to let her grow up, Owe," Lexi said.

"Alexandra, please," said Edie, her voice more wary than warning, but Lexi wasn't budging.

"We're dropping this," said Owen. *Now.*

"Why can't you just be supportive of us working down there?" Lexi demanded.

Owen set his forearms on the table, his fists flanking his plate, his eyes hard. "Support you *how,* exactly? By telling you that I think it's just great that you're helping the same jerks who didn't think you were good enough to marry their son, but you're certainly good enough to take pictures of their bathrooms?"

Edie closed her eyes and sighed. Meg reached for her Coke, taking a hard sip.

"This is different," Lexi said evenly. "Cooper isn't like Hudson."

Owen threw down his napkin. "Oh, come on, Lex—wake up. Every Moss is like every other Moss. You can't trust them—you of all people should know that, and yet the second they whistle, back down you go."

"Whistle?" Lexi repeated, leaning forward, wide-eyed. "Tell me you did not just compare me to a *dog,* Owen."

"Stop it, you two," ordered Edie.

"I don't have to defend my reasons to you," Lexi said. "And Mom doesn't either."

"Oh, God, please don't bring me into this."

Meg sat back in her chair, frowning at her father. "I think it's lousy too."

"Young lady, this is none of your business."

"Then why are you talking about it in front of me?"

"Ask your aunt," said Owen, glaring at Lexi. "She was the one who brought it up. Thanks, by the way."

"What did you expect me to do?" said Lexi, exasperated. "It's like this big elephant in the room, Owen. And your sitting there scowling about it only makes it worse."

"How do you know I'm scowling about that? Did it never occur to you I might have other things on my mind besides that damn house?"

Lexi took up her wine, feeling repentant. Her mother's chastising glance didn't help.

The table fell silent and remained so for the rest of the meal.

"And you were worried you wouldn't get your fight," whispered Lexi to her mother as they cleared the table ten minutes later.

Try as he did to let Lexi's comment slip from his thoughts, Owen chewed on it all the way home. What did she know about raising kids? He knew his daughter better than any father knew his child. If anyone needed illumination on Meg, it was her mother. Owen felt certain of that: putting wine in front of her all the time, placing her in schools with girls who thought they were thirty instead of sixteen—and parents who treated them that way. Was it any wonder she had some kid sending her those texts? No wonder Meg had never said anything to him—she'd been too embarrassed, obviously. That wasn't Meg; that wasn't his daughter—didn't Heather understand that?

"Mom told you about the wedding, didn't she?"

Owen glanced over at Meg. "You knew?"

"She sent me a text when we were at Grandma's." Meg looked at her lap. "Are you mad at me?"

"Mad at you?" Owen blinked at her. "Why would I be mad at *you?*"

"Because I knew and I didn't tell you."

"Meg . . . *sweetheart.*" He turned them into the driveway and killed the engine. "The person I'm mad as hell at is your mother for putting you through all this, for making you feel like you had to hide it from me. And if you don't want to go, you don't have to go. She can't force you to go."

"She's not forcing me, Dad." Meg swallowed. "I want to go."

"You do?" He stared at her, startled by her answer. "Really?"

Tears filled her eyes. "I like George. And I feel like I'm supposed to pretend I hate him to make you feel better, but I don't hate him, Dad. He's a good guy. And he doesn't treat me like I'm ten years old. He doesn't freak out because I want a glass of wine or if I stay out late with my friends." Her tears spilled over; she wiped them harshly with the sleeve of her sweatshirt.

Owen shifted his gaze to his lap, her complaint scalding, her disloyalty crushing.

Heather's words of advice to keep quiet evaporated in an instant. "Well, sure. He can do that because he isn't really a father, Meg. Because a real father wouldn't let some jerk send his sixteen-year-old daughter text messages like that."

Meg's face drained of color, then filled scarlet. "You looked at my phone?" she whispered, horrified.

"I don't want you seeing him anymore. In fact, I'm calling the headmaster first thing Monday and telling him I want that kid suspended for harassment."

"Dad," Meg started, "Ty hasn't been harassing me. He's my boyfriend and"—her voice turned shrill—"oh, my God, I can't believe you read my *texts!*"

Her eyes darted all over the dashboard in a panic; he imagined her cataloging all the things he'd read, and shame came over him.

"I'm sorry, Meggie; I know I shouldn't have read them—"

"No," she shrieked. "You shouldn't have!"

"Why didn't you tell me you had a boyfriend?"

"Why?" She stared at him, her face shiny with tears. "Dad, you buy me Nilla wafers like I'm still five years old! I can't even wear the bathing suit I want to the beach because you'll freak out. How could I tell you I have a boyfriend?"

She bent her head and covered her face with her

hands, her slight shoulders trembling with her sobs.

"Meggie . . ." Owen lifted his hand to reach for her, but she shoved open her door and rushed out into the night, dashing up the front steps and disappearing into the house with a slam of the screen, leaving Owen in the driver's seat, headlights glowing, his seat belt still buckled, heartbroken.

Cooper's call came in when Lexi was already dressed for bed and shutting down her laptop for the night.

"I know it's late," he said. "But I was just out on the porch. And you can't believe how clear the sky is right now."

Lexi moved to her window and drew back the lace curtain, seeing the street below, quiet and dark.

"I thought if you weren't busy, maybe you'd like to come over for a drink and a little stargazing."

Nights like this I always wish I knew the constellations. . . .

Her eyes swerved to the pile of clothes she'd just peeled off and tossed into the corner of her room, when she'd imagined this night over and done. She reached for her shorts, already pulling them back on before she'd answered, Cooper's words sailing back to her.

You fell in love with the wrong brother.

20

The first time Lexi had visited the Moss house at night, it had been a full moon—an event that Kim had assured her was a good sign, even though she couldn't explain why. Lexi hadn't argued. She herself had decided the ripeness of that yellow moon was proof of her and Hudson's enduring love even before he'd sneaked her into the guest house where he was staying that summer. It had been a risky act. She was still living at home and it had required her to lie to her parents as if she were fourteen and not eighteen, not newly graduated from high school, not about to start classes at a local college that fall.

She'd felt utterly childish and deliciously reckless steering her car down the unlit dirt road. Now she was making the same pilgrimage sixteen years later, her heart racing just as fast. Only this time she knew just where to park her car. This time she didn't worry about being caught. This time she knew just what she would find when the pines yielded and the coppery tint of the house lights came into view.

But she wasn't prepared for the rush of heat that scalded her body when she saw Cooper's silhouette at the end of the porch.

Or the sense of urgency that hastened her steps

across the driveway, the fear that she might begin to run to reach him, or what she hoped he might do when she got there.

There was already a bottle of red wine sitting open on the porch. Cooper poured her a glass and held it out. Lexi savored a long sip as she wandered to the edge of the steps, looking up at the quilt of stars.

"I still don't know a single one," he confessed, joining her with his own glass.

She smiled. "Not even the constellation Pizza Slice?"

He laughed at the reference. "I'd forgotten about that one," he said, looking where she looked. "Yeah, I see it now. Pepperoni, right?"

"Right."

In the soft quiet, Lexi had to remind herself they weren't alone. She glanced back at the house, unaware of the telling concern in her expression until Cooper said, "He's already asleep."

She met his gaze.

"There's something I want to show you," he said.

"Something beside all these?" she said, gesturing to the sky.

He nodded.

Lexi followed him wordlessly back into the house, through the great room down the hallway toward the study. Just shy of the last doorway,

Cooper pointed them to a smaller room and stepped inside.

It took Lexi a moment to understand what it was she was seeing as her eyes traveled the space. The room's two windows had been boarded up cleanly. A table hugged one wall; empty processing trays lined up on one side of an enlarger, a pair of printing tongs, a row of bottles.

"What is this?" she whispered.

Cooper grinned. "Wow, you really *haven't* been in a darkroom for a while, have you?"

She looked around, overcome.

"Your friend Mo set it all up," Cooper explained as she toured the room. "He told me what to get and what went where."

Lexi scanned the supplies, the chemicals she hadn't seen for years: developer, stop bath. She wanted to open the bottle of fixer and take a whiff, suddenly craving the vinegary smell. A fresh swell of gratitude filled her; she knew how much a setup like this would mean to Mo's summer sales.

Now she knew why Cooper had visited the shop.

She turned to him. "You didn't have to do this."

"I know I didn't," said Cooper. "I wanted to. It's a gift."

I know; that's why it's a gift.

The memory of Hudson's present and her similar refutations shoved its way into her thoughts.

She met Cooper's eyes, seeing the unmistakable darkening of suggestion in them.

I'm sure I'm not the first guy to leave college thinking darkrooms are sexy as hell. . . .

Her eyes fell to his mouth, imagining those lips on hers again, imagining how much deeper and longer their kiss could be now. She'd be ready this time.

The floor creaked with movement above them. Lexi looked up.

Cooper smiled. "It's a big house."

She remembered just how big—and how small. Did he hope to make love to her in this room? She glanced around, thinking how ironic it was that he'd brought her here, that he'd set up a darkroom for her, a place where pictures were revealed from blank paper.

"What if it's too soon?" she asked.

Too soon for what? She regretted the question as soon as she said it, but Cooper didn't need clarification for whatever "it" she meant.

"I think eleven years is the opposite of *soon*." Cooper took a step toward her, filling the safe space they'd left between them. Lexi searched his face, drawing in a quick breath when he reached out to slide his palm under her cheek, his thumb grazing her bottom lip.

"That night," she said. "You told me that I fell in love with the wrong brother."

"I remember." He moved his thumb back to her mouth, tracing the edge.

This time when he leaned in to kiss her, there was no hesitation, no question of her desire. Lexi could feel her own eyes pooling with it as Cooper took her mouth under his. She sank, like someone slipping naked under flannel sheets. Whatever this was, wherever it went, she wanted to wrap herself inside it, to leave it swimming on her tongue so that she could taste it, over and over, before she had to swallow it. He searched and she revealed. When he slid his hands up to the top of her head and released the knot of her hair, loosening the thick coil, the sensation of his fingers against her scalp pushed the air out of her in a sound that was unquestionably craving, and forced gooseflesh to bud along her bare thighs. When he held handfuls of her waves, she closed her eyes and let her head fall back into his palms, baring her throat. He dipped down and delivered a trail of hard kisses, an electric path paved from the hollow to her ear, drawing the flesh of her earlobe gently between his teeth and sucking hard enough that her eyes shot open.

She searched the ceiling, the places where the weathered beadboard planks held fast to their joints, her mind trying to see the unfamiliar in every tongue-and-groove seam but how could she? She knew these rooms too well. And they knew her.

She shut her eyes and the reminders faded.

There was nothing but Cooper's kiss, deep and warm, and her own aching need.

This time it was Cooper who pulled away first.

Lexi's eyes opened slowly, as if she were afraid she might find herself having been kissed by the wrong brother, but there he was, Cooper, smiling down at her, his dark eyes sincere. How long had it been since she'd felt that feverish speeding of desire, that pressure of lust building deep within her core like air bubbles, combustible and dangerous?

"I want you," he whispered. "I've wanted you for a long time."

Lexi searched his eyes, reminded of how he had been her anchor that night, how the only thing that had kept her mind from spinning away from her was to watch Cooper as he drove her deep into the dark. Now the same need for escape filled her; she didn't care about what lived beyond this room. Let the wine bottle be drained; let the fixer reveal the true picture.

"I've wanted you too," she confessed. "I wanted you even then, but I didn't understand how I could. I felt so guilty."

He reached out to the collar of her cardigan, fingering the top button, rolling the pad of his thumb over the smooth, pearl-inlaid surface.

He grinned. "You planned this, didn't you?"

She arched her body against his hands, aching for him to undress her. "Planned what?"

"These buttons," he said, slowly freeing each one. "They're just like the ones on the switch plate in the pantry."

She smiled up at him, immeasurably impressed that he would remember that.

"So turn me on," she whispered as she shifted her arms to let her sweater slide down to the floor.

Part
Two

21

$\mathcal{S}$un was everywhere when Lexi woke. The master suite, dark when she'd come into it with Cooper the night before, was now drenched in light. Everything was so clear: the sloped ceilings, the papered walls, the dormered nooks.

And Cooper. She rolled over to find him still asleep, his face calm, one hand over his shoulder, the other reaching out to her.

She could leave, she thought, surveying the room. Her clothes were within reach, mostly in one place. She could slip out and dress in the hall. She'd take the back stairs, and even if Jim was already up and in the kitchen, there was no way he'd see her coming down the steps. He'd hear the car start, but so what? She'd be gone by then.

But she didn't *want* to leave. The smell of him was killing her. That warm, musky scent of sleep, a mix of used sheets and sweat and skin—her whole body softened like butter left out.

Cooper shifted, stretched. His eyes opened, fixing on her right away. "Morning."

She reached out and ran her fingers through his short hair. "Morning," she whispered back.

As much as she knew they'd pushed their luck sleeping so late, she couldn't bear to think of leaving this bed, this room. They were safe in here.

Beyond this door, all that would change. There was the world of Jim, of her mother, of Owen, and Kim. Her best friend would surely do a dance on the hood of her car in celebration; somehow Lexi didn't see her family doing the same.

She scanned Cooper's face, searching his eyes for a clue to his thoughts.

"Are you sorry we did this?" she asked.

He smiled. "Trust me; you don't want to know how *not* sorry I am."

Relief bloomed in her, faster and fuller than she would have imagined. He tugged away the sheet that she'd been so careful to tuck into all the right places; off it came, kicking up dust in the ribbon of sunlight she'd been trying to hide her body from. Skin to skin, mouth to mouth. Her moment of lucidity had come and gone.

Then a terrible noise: the familiar whine of a power tool, the cacophony of the crew below on the lawn. She slipped out from under him, panicked. Surely her mother had seen her car there, had known she hadn't come home the night before. Lexi chastised herself, reminding herself she was thirty-four and not eighteen. Still, she wasn't crazy about emerging from the house to an audience.

"I should go," she said. "Everyone's here."

Cooper weaved his arm around her waist, slowing her departure. "Everyone's *out there*," he corrected.

She smiled back at him. The balloon of panic

that had expanded in her chest popped, deflated. But only a bit. There was still Jim to consider, her car sitting in plain sight. Probably blocking the driveway. She'd been so eager to get to Cooper last night, to get close to him, like a love-struck teenager. Had she even turned off the engine? Applied the parking brake?

"I need to move my car," she declared.

"What for?" He traced the curve of her hip. "Are you expecting someone?"

"No, but it's right in front of the house."

"It's a big driveway."

It was. Why was she acting as if this were the first time she'd ever been in this house? She looked over her shoulder at him, a smile trying to play at her lips, a natural response to his grin that refused to go away, no matter what let's-get-real excuses she threw at him. And she had plenty more.

Cooper climbed off the other side of the bed, plucked his boxers from the floor, and pulled them on. "Stay put," he said. "I'll go make us some breakfast."

Stay put. All right, she could do that. She reached for her shirt; Cooper sent her a wary look from the doorway.

"Don't bother with all of it," he said, pointing to where her shorts and undergarments dangled off a nearby chair. "I'm not done with you."

Desire flared under her skin. She felt idiotic. She felt sensational.

She hurled a pillow at him. "Go," she said. "I get the worst headaches if I don't have coffee before eight."

When he'd gone, quietly closing the door behind him, Lexi glanced around the master suite, surveying it freshly. It was strange to see it in daylight, this room that had always stood at the end of the hall. She still had yet to photograph it. Now she wandered its spaces, taking a slow inventory of the room and its details in preparation for where she would begin when she returned later today with her camera.

He'd set up his desk by the room's oversize dormer—not surprisingly—though it could hardly be called a desk, just a rough table nestled in front of the window seat, his laptop and a printer, a stack of papers, and a cell phone charger the only things on it. Coming closer, she saw the pages more clearly. They were manuscript pages. Trepidation skittered down her arms; it was like finding a diary—she knew that. Something deeply personal she hadn't been given license to read.

For a moment she considered walking by the stack, but something changed her mind. It was the names that caught her eye. Too familiar to be chance. A knot of something, not yet dread but alarmingly close, began to form even before she sat down and began to make her way through the pages.

Harrisport, Massachusetts
July 1966

*I*f she squinted from where she stood on the guest room balcony, Edie Worthington imagined she could see the glow of the bonfire below the town pier, but she couldn't really. She might as well have been on the other side of the country, not just the other side of the beach, for how removed she felt from that world. The dream she had stepped into a few hours earlier had now taken over. She'd fought it at first, too afraid she'd be somehow betraying her family by enjoying herself. But thanks to the magic of the night—and maybe the magic of the champagne too—she'd surrendered fully. What was the harm in savoring this perfect evening, this rare celebration? Here she wasn't Edie Worthington, freckled and fraught carpenter's apprentice. Tucker Moss had made her feel remarkable, a woman capable of doing anything. She wouldn't apologize for that—wouldn't feel bad for it, either.

"Well, hello, over there!"

The cheery voice startled her from her thoughts and she glanced around to locate its source. Finding no one behind her, she leaned forward and saw Jim Masterson peeking out from the neighboring balcony.

"Hi, yourself," she said. "Why are you over there?"

He grinned. "You know, I was just askin' myself the same thing." He pulled one foot up onto the railing.

Edie blinked at him. "What are you doing?" she demanded.

"What's it look like?" He'd now climbed up onto the railing and managed to get himself to the other side, where she could plainly see he intended to cross the roof to her.

She reared back. "It's too dangerous!"

"Not for me," he crowed, his long legs stretching across the divide between the two dormers. Nearly there, the sole of his oxford slid on a shingle and he lost his footing. Edie lurched forward to help him, panicked, but he managed to throw his weight with enough force that he crashed down onto her balcony instead of skidding all the way down the roof and off the end. He lay on the balcony floor, holding his stomach and laughing like a fool.

She stood above him, furious. "What were you thinking?"

He sat up at last and Edie reached down to help him to his feet. He was only too happy to throw his arm over her shoulder. She could smell the alcohol on his breath, hot and sweet.

"You're crazy! You could have fallen and broken your damn neck," she said.

Her scolding had no effect on his merriment. He merely smiled wider, the lanterns from the lawn below flickering in the lenses of his crooked glasses like fireflies as she helped him into the empty chair. "I'm crazy in love is what I am," he slurred. "Y'all had better lock me up and throw away the key. I'm certifiable."

Edie smiled, remembering Tucker's mention of Helen Willoughby. "That was quick."

"I'm a hopeless romantic. I've been known to fall in love in less time than it takes to iron a shirt." He winked at her. "Lucky for you I was already destined for Helen or you might have been in trouble."

"Lucky for me, all right." She glanced around. "So where *is* your beloved?"

"Powdering her nose or her chin or whatever it is y'all powder when you say that. Do you know her well?"

"I don't know her at all," said Edie. "She's summer people."

"She's perfection," corrected James, staring moonily up at the sky. "A man could be a good fifteen minutes just deciding if her eyes were blue or green."

He spied the plate of pastries and downed one whole with a groan of pleasure, a curl of cream spilling out the side of his mouth. "Do you suppose she'd marry a man with glasses?"

"I'm sure," said Edie. "So long as you took them off when you went to sleep."

He laughed loudly, his eyes growing huge behind the lenses. "You are a hoot; you know that, Edie Worthington? No wonder Tuck likes you. Speaking of Tuck . . ." Jim craned his neck to peer through the French doors. "Where's our boy at, anyway?"

"Talking with his father," said Edie. "He promised he wouldn't be long."

Jim sat up and smiled. "You're good for him, you know that?"

"What do you mean?"

"All these fellas you see," Jim said, rising to meet her at the edge of the balcony and gesturing down to the guests who spotted the lawn. "All puffed up in their bow ties and their shiny noses—Tuck's not like that. He doesn't want any part of that."

She glanced down at her hands, folded over the railing. "Then maybe he should stand up for what he wants."

"I wish he would. *You,* Edie Worthington," Jim said, landing a finger gently on the tip of her nose, "are a girl worth standing up for. No offense to dear Florence, of course."

Edie frowned at him. "Who's Florence?"

Jim didn't have to answer; she could see at once from the rueful look on his face that Florence was Tucker Moss's girl.

Jim winced. "Oh, crap."

Edie turned from him, feeling her stomach clench, then chastising herself for it. What right did she have to be hurt or even angry? She and Tucker had become friends—nothing more. After all, it was she who'd kissed him—not the other way around, right? So why was her heart thundering with disappointment to know someone had already claimed him?

Jim moved closer to her, his hand hovering tenderly over her shoulder a moment before he changed his mind and lowered it to his side. "He doesn't love her, Edie. Not the way you should love someone you're gonna marry."

Marry? Edie closed her eyes and swallowed hard, the shock of the news dizzying.

She shook her head. "It's none of my business. It doesn't matter."

"Yes, it does," said Jim. "He's making a mistake."

She spun to face him. "How can you say that? You're supposed to be his best friend."

"That's exactly *why* I'm saying it."

"Maybe he doesn't think he's making a mistake."

"He does," said Jim. "I know he does. But he won't go against the old man."

She looked up at him, his bleary eyes suddenly focused behind his tilted glasses. "Why are you telling me this?"

"Because I think Tucker knows you're someone worth fighting for. Because he hasn't stopped grinning since he met you."

"I barely know him." As soon as she said it, Edie felt false. She *did* know Tucker Moss—maybe not as well as she knew other friends, but she felt a deep connection to him that the calendar had no part in affirming. She knew what it was like to have to prove yourself to someone who didn't believe in you, who pushed you down a path you wanted desperately to veer off of.

"Don't give up on him, Edie," Jim said softly.

"I'm not the one with a fiancée," she whispered, too low for Jim to hear as he stepped back, wobbling a moment before he regained his balance.

"Now if you'll excuse me," he declared, "I have to go find my future wife and her powdered nose."

"Better wipe your damn mouth before you propose," teased Edie, gesturing to his cheek.

Jim grinned as he wiped at the remaining streak of cream with his sleeve.

"For being the guest of honor, you're sure making yourself scarce, son."

Tucker had expected the admonishment from the moment he stepped into his father's study, closing the door behind him at Garrison's order, the heavy oak swallowing the music and voices that celebrated on the other side. He suspected too that there would be some mention of his company tonight; surely someone had seen him arrive with Edie Worthington. A part of Tucker hoped it very much. Being with Edie did that to him; she made him feel bold and reckless, carefree in a way he had never felt before. This was his party, after all; why should he pretend to feel otherwise?

His father sipped his drink and said, "It was good of you to find a date for your friend tonight."

Tucker nodded. There was little his father missed that happened under his roof; surely he'd seen Jim fawning over Helen Willoughby. Had his best friend made a true fool of himself? Tucker grinned, hoping so.

"Although," said Garrison, "with all the proper young ladies around here to choose from, I don't see why you felt the need to pair him up with someone so beneath his class."

"But Helen's not—" Tucker stopped, a chill prickling his skin. He met his father's narrowed gaze, seeing the quiet ultimatum behind his pale eyes and knowing there was no confusion as to whom Edie had come to be with. The confusion lay with Tucker, in thinking he would succeed with his declaration of independence—this night, or ever.

In the silence while Garrison Moss awaited his son's surrender, the room crackled with tension. Fear and excitement raced through Tucker. This was it and he knew it. His best, maybe his *only* chance to say no, to stand up to his father once and for all, to tell him that he didn't want Florence and he didn't want the firm. He wanted Edie Worthington, and whatever came with her. He gripped the rounded ends of the chair, rolling his palms over the turned wood, rehearsing the words in his head, clear and crisp and unwavering. He swallowed.

Then, just as swiftly, the moment passed. It was as if when Garrison Moss drew deeply on his cigarette, he inhaled all of Tucker's resolve and any evidence of his strength, then expelled it back out at him, used, in one even stream of smoke.

Tucker bent his head to avoid breathing it in.

"I'll be making a toast to you boys in an hour," said Garrison, moving to the window to signal that their meeting was over. "Tell James so that he might make sure his date sees her way home before then."

Tucker exited his father's study and took the stairs without meeting a single eye, wanting only to get upstairs, back to Edie and the dream he'd started. Below him, he heard his name called but he pretended not to hear, the simple rebellion almost as thrilling as the relief when he reached the top of the steps and saw Edie at the end of the hall.

An hour, he thought as he came toward her. A person could certainly change his life in an hour. In a minute, really, if he so desired.

• • •

Something had happened; Edie could see it the minute Tucker's eyes met hers. Or maybe it was a reflection of her own expression that she saw, the regret in his face a reaction to hers. Try as she did to hide her feelings of disappointment, of hurt, Edie could feel the truth of her heart pulling down the smile she was working to keep aloft.

"I'm sorry I left you alone so long."

"It's all right," she said. "Your friend James kept me company for a while."

"Jimbo? Was he with Helen?"

"No, she'd gone to powder her nose. He's head over heels for her."

"Good. It seems everyone's falling in love tonight."

Edie smiled in spite of the lump in her throat, wishing they could just go back to the day before, even the hour before, when she'd not known about Florence.

"It's late," she said. "I should really go."

Tucker's eyes widened with panic. "No," he pleaded. "Don't go. I won't have to leave again; I promise. I'm all yours."

But he wasn't, Edie thought, looking up at him, the disappointment she'd been trying to hide since he'd returned finally shining through. His smile dimmed the longer he searched her face.

What is it? his eyes seemed to say. *What's happened?*

"He said something, didn't he?"

Edie shrugged. "It's fine."

"He told you about Florence, didn't he?"

She nodded.

"Let me explain."

"There's nothing to explain," she said.

"Yes, there is."

"I shouldn't have kissed you."

"You can't know how glad I am that you did."

She looked up at him, tremors of excitement coursing through her. She grabbed at her arms, chilled.

"Here." Tucker shook off his sport coat and swept it over her shoulders, the linen warm and deliciously heavy. "Let's go somewhere," he said. "Anywhere."

"It's your party. You can't go."

"It's my party so I can do anything I want. And I want to be alone with you. I'll go as far as I need to. How about Paris?"

Edie smiled. "I can think of somewhere closer."

The smell of fresh lumber was still strong. Edie drew in a deep breath of it as she and Tucker stepped into the framed house, as if the scent might fortify her—though for what, she wasn't sure. Hank had recently finished framing up the kitchenette. He'd even agreed to let her help build the cabinets the following week.

She turned on a pair of work lights.

"It looks great in here," Tucker said, scanning the space.

But Edie didn't want to talk about the guest house. When she didn't respond, Tucker turned to find her eyes on him, his own expression fraught.

"I'll break it off with her," he said. "I should have done it a long time ago."

"I can't be the reason."

"You're not. I don't love her."

"But you're *marrying* her."

"Because my father wants me to."

Edie frowned down at her hands, twisting the fabric of her skirt. This was madness, and they both knew it.

Tucker reached for her hand. Edie watched him weave his fingers with hers, knowing she should pull free but not wanting to.

"You'll hurt her," she whispered.

"I don't want to hurt anyone."

"Then don't." She searched his eyes. "We haven't done anything yet. Well, *you* haven't done anything yet," she clarified.

But even as Tucker brought her hand to his lips and kissed her fingertips, Edie knew that was a lie.

Her mind whirled. She thought of Jim's plea to not give up on Tucker. She thought of Hank moving around the bonfire to join Missy Murphy, and how the sight of him sliding his arm around Missy's back had filled her, Edie, with an unwelcome and confusing envy. She thought of Hank's startling confession just before that moment—*a woman he feels very deeply for*—and how it had thrilled her to hear him say she had looked pretty. Then she thought of how good it had felt to sit in the shade of the Grange Hall with Tucker and to turn to find him smiling at her. The night's earlier euphoria, once so pure and simple, was now a knot of emotions she couldn't untangle. But looking up at Tucker, she saw his eyes were clear with purpose; for him, there was no confusion. Only longing. She wanted to feel that certain too, wanted it desperately.

"Spending time with you has been the bright spot in my life, Edie Worthington," he admitted. "I don't want that to go away."

"Then we'll just be friends," she said.

"I don't want to just be friends."

She sighed; they were going around in circles, getting nowhere.

"Give me a chance to end it," Tucker pleaded. "Be with me and I promise I'll stop it. I'll stop *everything*."

Edie searched his eyes in the faint light that crept in from the cottage, thinking how they shone with hope. *Everything*. Could he really mean it? She smiled, reminded of the unintentional pact they had made under the shade of the Grange Hall. *Looks like we're both going to have to fight to get what we want, doesn't it?*

"I'll wait," she said.

Relief shuddered across his face.

"Promise?" he asked.

"I promise."

22

*T*he last time she and Hudson had made love,
Lexi knew it was the last time. The same
way a person spots a lilac bush in late June and
thinks to herself, *Yes, those lavender blooms are
perfect but they have turned. You'd never know
it to look at them, and if you bury your nose in
their tiny blossoms and inhale that sweet scent,
you'd swear they might live on that branch
forever. But take my word for it and soak them up
as best you can, because tomorrow, the edges of
those tiny petals will have browned, and then
they are as good as gone.*

They'd agreed to meet for the weekend at their
favorite inn on the Vineyard and had sex on the
beach, something they'd done only a handful of
times in their five years together. Her skin had
itched incessantly afterward, a condition she'd
blamed on the sand and the flies, when the culprit
had been her own fear. Hudson had most likely
meant to leave her that visit, and might have done
it, had Lexi not surprised him with the gift of a
photograph, a framed picture of the guest house in
the mist. She'd captured it one morning the year
before, at dawn, when the fog was so thick that the
tiny cottage appeared to float inside it, like a
magical kingdom in the clouds, and that was

how she would always choose to remember the guest house, and their love. When she'd handed him the photograph, Hudson had considered it a long while before he'd thanked her and tucked it into his suitcase. She'd studied him the whole ferry ride back, looking for his promise in every gesture, every glance, every word.

In the days after Hudson had left her, Lexi had sworn she would never again be blindsided by desire. Now as she steered her car down the sun-dappled dirt of Birch Drive, she felt a sickening mix of outrage and shame, Owen's recent condemnation returning to her.

Every Moss is like every other Moss, Lex. You can't trust them—you of all people should know that.

She'd left through the main door, knowing that Cooper wouldn't see her go and that he'd never hear her engine over the din of the construction noises on the lawn. What else could she have done? Stayed and confronted him? Heard his weak excuses for why he'd never told her he'd been mining her mother's heartbreak for his next bestseller?

Her heart thundered as she swung the car onto the main road. All the times she'd asked him about his novel—all the chances he'd had to tell her the truth—and he'd remained vague. Her thoughts flashed back to their night together, his gift of the darkroom. Had that been given to her out of his guilt; had he hoped to buy her forgiveness when the book finally came out?

She sent the driver's window down all the way, taking in deep breaths of air as she sped toward town. She didn't want to burden her best friend at the store, but Lexi didn't know where else to go.

Kim was with a customer when Lexi pushed through the front door. She suspected the distressed look on her face was apparent, because almost immediately Kim excused herself and steered Lexi into the storeroom, motioning for one of the staff to take over the register.

"What's wrong?" Kim led Lexi to a sofa by her desk and sat down next to her.

"Cooper's book. It's about my mom and Tucker. It's about that summer."

"What? How do you know?"

"I found the pages of his manuscript," Lexi explained.

"When?"

"This morning."

Sure her guilt was all over her face, Lexi looked up to find her friend's eyes shining with understanding—and delight.

"Oh, my God, you slept with him, didn't you?" Kim breathed. "Finally!"

"No, not *finally*," said Lexi crossly. "Haven't you heard a word I've said?"

"So he thinks their story was romantic enough to be a real novel, okay," Kim said with a shrug.

"I knew you were going to sleep with him. I had this weird feeling last night; maybe it was the moon or something, but—"

"Kim!" Lexi rose, stunned. "You're not listening to me."

"Of course I'm listening to you," Kim insisted. "I just don't see what the big deal is that he's writing about your mom and his dad."

"The big deal," said Lexi, "is that it isn't his story to tell. The big deal is that I gave him plenty of chances to tell me what his book was about and he told me—he even told you!—that he wasn't sure. He lied to me, Kim."

"*Hudson* lied to you, Lex."

Lexi frowned. "This isn't about Hudson."

"Since when?" Kim demanded.

Lexi stared hotly at her friend, waiting for Kim to back down, to act like a best friend was supposed to act and to share in her indignation, her hurt. The way Kim had done when Hudson had broken her heart.

"Why are you defending him?" Lexi said.

"I'm not defending him. I just don't understand why you're blowing this out of proportion."

"*I'm* blowing this out of proportion?"

"Sweetie, look," Kim began gently. "All I know is that when you and Cooper were at the game, you seemed . . ."

Lexi stared expectantly at her friend. "I seemed *what?*"

"Happy," blurted Kim. "Okay? You seemed happy. Like really happy. Like I haven't seen you since—"

Hudson. Kim didn't have to say it. And maybe that was the problem.

Lexi moved for the door; Kim followed her. They walked out of the store and back to Lexi's car.

"I should never have taken this job in the first place," Lexi said as she tugged open the driver's door. "I should have known better."

"That's Owen talking," said Kim. "You know it is."

Kim waited while Lexi climbed in and rolled down her window. "Where are you going now?"

"To pack," said Lexi. "The agent said I can start moving some things in tonight."

"Do you need help? Jay's home today. And you know he loves any excuse to tool around in that truck."

"Thanks, I'll let you know."

Kim leaned in, her voice soft with worry. "I love you, Lex. And I know you well enough to know when you're falling for someone. I just don't want to see you give up on something special."

Lexi slipped on her sunglasses, suddenly needing to hide her eyes from her best friend.

"I'm not the one giving up, Kim."

Kim's gaze remained leveled but unconvinced,

289

even as she stood up and stepped back. Lexi started the car and with a halfhearted wave pulled out into the street.

Edie was at the sink when the yellow Jeep turned into her driveway shortly before six. Recognizing the car at once, she hurried to wipe her hands and meet her visitor.

"Cooper." She pressed the screen door open fully. "This is a surprise."

"I'm sorry to show up like this, ma'am. I was hoping Lexi might be here."

"She's not," said Edie. "She's moving into a house in Truro. She's been taking little loads over all day." Edie considered Cooper's fraught expression as he absorbed the news, a blade of late-day sun making hard shadows on his knotted forehead. Surely he knew that Edie was aware of what had transpired between him and Lexi; that Edie had seen her daughter's car in the driveway that morning and not seen it in her own driveway the night before. And yet she'd also seen Lexi flee the Moss cottage, peeling out without even a wave. Then Lexi had announced that she would start moving out her things.

Now Edie knew why.

Cooper offered a strained smile. "I think I may have screwed up, but I'm not exactly sure how. I'd just like to talk to her."

Maybe it was his eyes, kind and warm and

reminding her once again of Tucker, that made her go to the fridge and pull down the Post-it note that Lexi had left with her new address. Whatever the reason, relief flooded his features when Edie handed it to him. As she closed the door and watched Cooper pull back out onto the road, Edie told herself some people, even those who thought they knew better, needed a little push now and then.

23

*I*t would make a good home, Lexi decided as she surveyed the view from her back deck, her third—and last—carload of the day stacked in the bedroom. Since the power and water wouldn't be turned on until tomorrow, she wouldn't be able to spend the night, but she was still determined to christen her first sunset in her new home. She unwrapped a goblet from a box on the counter and poured herself a generous glass of a red she'd brought, then carried both glass and bottle back out to the deck, settling into one of the plastic chairs the previous tenant had left behind. A sultry evening breeze feathered her face as she sipped her wine, watching the horizon bruise with shades of violet and pink.

It was her first moment of real quiet since the morning, and she'd been dreading it. As perfect as the scene was, no amount of wine or pastel streaks in the sky would mask the overriding disappointment she'd been shoving into the back of her mind all afternoon. Not unlike that last box no one wanted to unpack, its contents having no real destination; better to just stuff it into a closet and deal with it after the next move.

Cooper had called three times, and each time Lexi had stared at her chiming phone, her heart racing with an impossible mix of relief and hurt that forced her to simply continue to stare at the screen until the phone fell silent again. She'd waited a whole ten minutes before listening to the first voice mail, her pulse quickening at the sound of his voice, the one she'd woken to that morning. When the next message came, she managed to wait an hour. When no more calls came, she grew even more hurt, feeling foolish. It hadn't helped that Kim had derailed what had been a clear course for sympathy, then gave her, Lexi, a disparaging look as she'd waved her off.

Cooper had lied to her; there was no getting around that. She'd let her guard down, hoping things could be different this time—let herself have feelings for him. Feelings that she only hoped would drain with the glass of wine she was well on her way to emptying.

The sound of a car pulling into the driveway made her set down her glass and walk to the edge of the deck to see around the house. Her breath caught to glimpse a yellow sliver of Cooper's Jeep and Cooper himself climbing out. How had he known where she . . . ? Her mother. It had to be. Who else knew the location of her new home?

Butterflies took flight in her stomach. She moved back to her wine, trying to compose herself in the few moments it took for Cooper to follow the narrow path of uneven pavers around the house. Hearing his footsteps near, she turned and found him standing at the deck steps, looking far too good in an olive green T-shirt and khakis, and holding a bouquet of gerbera daisies, her favorite. Had she told him that? She was sure she hadn't. *Kim.* He'd obviously gone to Tides for the flowers.

Great, she thought sourly. Now there were *two* traitors in her camp.

"This is quite a spot," he said, gesturing to the view.

She met him at the steps. "You should take them back," she said flatly, gesturing to the flowers. "I can't keep them here."

"No vase?"

"No water. They aren't turning it on until tomorrow."

Cooper considered the bouquet a moment, then turned to the neighboring house, a beach cottage like hers. "Hang on a second."

She started to dissuade him, but he had already made his way to the neighbor's door. Though

Lexi couldn't hear their exchange, he carried a plastic cup when he returned.

"Do you have a vase, or should I go back and ask for that too?"

God, he was determined. Exasperated, she reached down and took the flowers. Cooper followed her up the steps and through the sliding patio doors into the house. Saying nothing, she rummaged through one of her opened boxes for something suitable and found a porcelain pitcher, emptying his borrowed water into it and tearing off the bouquet's cellophane sleeve.

"You missed one heck of an omelet," he said. "Cheddar and tomato. One of the best I've ever made."

She stuffed the stems down into the vase.

Cooper folded his arms. "This is about the book, isn't it?"

She gave him a frosty look as her answer.

"I didn't tell you I was writing it," Cooper explained, "because I wasn't going to publish it."

"You honestly expect me to believe that? You said yourself you were desperate for a new book. Why would you bother writing a story you didn't plan to sell?"

"Look, I'll admit I wasn't so cavalier when I started it," Cooper said, watching her set the flower arrangement on the sink, then wipe her hands testily on her hips. "But the deeper I got into the writing, the more I knew I could never submit it."

"That doesn't change the fact that you could have told me the book was about my family. Instead you used me for research."

"What research?"

"That night," she reminded him. "When we were eating on the porch and you wanted to know about my parents building the guest house."

"I was just making conversation," Cooper said. "I was curious."

"Obviously."

She spun away from him and faced the sink. Cooper came beside her.

"It's not just the story," Lexi said, drawing in a shaky breath. "It's . . . it's everything." She turned to him. "Why did you have to set up that darkroom for me? Why did you have to try to compete with him?"

Cooper stared at her, stunned. "Is that why you think I did it? To compete with Hudson?"

"Isn't it?" she asked carefully.

"Why would I want to do that? From what I remember, my brother set the bar pretty low."

She dragged her gaze back to the window, tears of frustration pushing up her throat.

"It's just a story, Lexi. Something that happened almost fifty years ago. It doesn't have anything to do with us."

"It has *everything* to do with us," she said.

"You're writing about the man who broke my mother's heart wide open. You'll humiliate her."

"Is that what she told you? That my dad broke her heart?"

"It's the truth," Lexi said firmly. "Everybody knows that."

"Not according to Jim."

"And how would he know?"

"He was here that summer; he saw it all—and what he didn't see, my father told him."

"I'll bet."

Lexi felt Cooper's gaze still fixed on her, searching her profile a moment before he said, "I don't think it's me you're really mad at."

She swallowed. "I want you to leave."

Cooper stepped closer, his voice tender but firm. "I'm not Hudson, Lexi. I can't help that he's my brother, or that he came first and screwed it all up, but he's not me. And whatever still hurts, or whatever you feel you didn't get to say to him, I'm sorry, but I'm not interested in being his stand-in."

"Please go," she whispered again.

This time he did, the rumble of his Jeep backing out over the gravel coming through the screens a few moments later.

When he'd gone, she moved to her purse, reaching in for her phone to call Kim, not even sure what she was going to say, but her hand landed instead on Cooper's book and she stopped, remembering his inscription. She hadn't read it yet.

She pulled out the paperback and slowly opened it, her heartbeat hastening with anticipation as her fingers found the title page.

For Lexi,
To new chapters and new stories.
Cooper

24

*C*ooper saw the black Range Rover with rental plates as soon as he pulled down into the driveway of the cottage and a flash of dread bloomed in his stomach. If it had been any other style of car, he might have wondered whom it belonged to, but he knew too well of his brother's fondness for the model. He was just grateful for the walk from the driveway to the front of the house, precious time to settle his shock before he arrived at the porch to find Hudson seated with Jim.

"We've been wondering when you'd get home." Since Hudson's back was to the driveway, it was Jim who spotted Cooper first, and rose to announce him. "Look who dropped in while you were gone, son!"

"So I see," Cooper said stiffly, taking his time to

climb the steps to the porch. As Cooper might have expected, Hudson didn't rise, just turned slightly in his chair to watch his younger brother approach. He rested a sweating tumbler on the edge of the chair, a wedge of lime glinting behind ice cubes.

"Get you another?" Jim asked, pointing to Hudson's nearly drained glass.

"Yes, sir. That'd be great."

"How about you, Cooper?"

"No, thanks, Uncle Jim."

"Suit yourself," said Jim with a pleasant wave as he slipped back inside.

"And here I thought all you great writers drank your way through the day," said Hudson, raising his glass.

Cooper kept his eyes level with Hudson's, refusing to volley back the ball of his brother's jab.

"What are you doing here, Hud?"

"What do you think?" Hudson rose and ambled past Cooper down the porch, gesturing to the guest house with his drink, its exterior surrounded now by scaffolding, a bright blue tarp covering its ridge. "Mom heard about you hiring those women and she's worried you and Uncle Jim are being taken for a ride. She's sure a male crew could get it done sooner. She's impatient."

"She's delusional," said Cooper. "We're lucky to have a crew here at all. Every other crew was booked until the fall. Those women are good at what they do, Hud. As good as any male crew."

"Yeah, well, you try and tell her that." Hudson's smart phone rang out an alert on the coffee table; he walked over to pick it up and studied the screen.

"So why didn't Mom come herself if she's so concerned?" Cooper asked.

"You know she hates to fly," Hudson muttered as he read the incoming text message.

"You didn't have to come," said Cooper. "Jim and I have everything under control."

"Yeah. I hear you've been a busy boy." Hudson set down the phone and returned to his seat.

Cooper folded his arms. "What is that supposed to mean?"

"Don't get me wrong; I think it's great you hired Lexi. I'm happy for you." Hudson grinned suggestively. "Little Coop finally gets his shot."

Cooper stewed silently, glimpsing Jim's advance through the screen.

"Here we are!" Jim stepped onto the porch, carrying a fresh gin and tonic.

Hudson leaned forward to take it. "Where's yours, Uncle J?"

"Oh, no, I won't stay," Jim demurred, patting Cooper on the shoulder. "I've got some paperwork that needs my attention, and you two have some catching up to do, I'm sure. We'll talk more over dinner. Seven o'clock sound good?"

"Sounds good to me," said Hudson.

Cooper caught Jim's gaze and sent him a wary look; Jim smiled apologetically before he disappeared inside.

"You heard the man," said Hudson, pointing to the other chair. "Sit."

Cooper did so begrudgingly. He considered his older brother a moment as Hudson scanned his phone again. He looked tired, Cooper thought, heavier than he'd ever seen him. He thought of the last time he and Hudson had shared this porch, these chairs. The last day of summer, ten years earlier. They'd been waiting for their mother to finish her annual tour of the house with the caretaker while their father sat in the car. Even then, they'd struggled to carry on a conversation and finally given up, filling the quiet with the sounds of their footsteps as they'd paced the porch.

Hudson tilted his glass and shook out a piece of ice, crunching down on it. "So what's she like now?"

"Still talented," said Cooper. "Still beautiful."

"Married?"

"No."

"Kids?"

Cooper shook his head. Hudson squinted up at the house.

"We're selling it, Coop. Like it or not, Mom wants it gone." Hudson sighed. "What she'd *really* like is to see it burned to the ground."

"I get that she wants it gone," said Cooper, "but what's the rush?"

"The rush is that summer is prime market. You wait until fall, you might as well wait till spring." Another chime from the phone; Hudson leaned over to inspect the caller and decided to ignore it.

"The repairs will take what they take," Cooper insisted. "She's not being reasonable."

Hudson cocked his head wearily. "And this is news to you?"

"So you're saying she wants us to cut bait right now; is that it?"

"She doesn't think it's worth it to pay for the work on the guest house."

Did his mother really? Cooper wondered. Or was she merely still stewing in her own overcooked juices, knowing that Edie Worthington, the woman who had held her husband's heart for longer than anyone was aware, was overseeing the repairs? Knowing what he knew now, Cooper couldn't help but suspect that was the reason for his mother's renewed determination to sell quickly.

"You could talk to her, Hud. I don't have to be back in Raleigh until the end of August. I'll stay and supervise the work myself until then."

"Wow, famous author *and* expert contractor. I never knew you had so many talents, little brother."

"Just talk to her, Hud."

"Forget it. I'm not wasting my breath. Mom'll never go for it." Hudson drained his drink and rose, his gaze catching on the guest house again and holding there long enough that Cooper wondered what his older brother might be thinking. His mind turned quickly to the memory of his argument with Lexi. He'd convinced himself that they could start fresh, a new book in more ways than one. Seeing his brother here now, Cooper knew that might not be possible after all.

"Why are you fighting me so hard on this, anyway?" Hudson asked. "The house is gone, Coop. Our family's done with it. We have been for years now. Let it go. I have."

His phone rang again. This time Hudson took the call.

Cooper descended the steps for the grass, stopping halfway down the lawn to turn and look back up at the cottage. As much as he hated to admit it, maybe Hudson was right. If all the house did was hold memories of regret in its walls, what was he trying to hold on to? The irony struck him: He'd come to a place mired in the past, hoping to find inspiration for his writing future.

Now who was the fool?

25

*E*die glanced at the clock on her stove, hoping Lexi wouldn't try for another run tonight. It was nearly eight. Selfishly, Edie wanted her daughter home for one more evening —one more chance for them to connect in the midst of all this change, all this drama. She hadn't spoken to Owen since their tense pizza dinner; nor had she heard from Meg—surely her son and granddaughter were letting their own stews simmer. It was as it should be. Contrary to what she'd done earlier by giving Cooper the address to Lexi's new house, Edie didn't like to interfere with her children's lives. It had been a source of disagreement between her and Hank for years—why else had Hank insisted that his distaste for the Moss family be drilled into his kids from the time they were able to sit up on their own? A lot of good it had done, of course. For all of Hank's warnings, Lexi had fallen for Hudson and stayed there, stuck.

Guilt washed over Edie with fresh strength as she was reminded of the way she and Hank had reconstructed the story of that summer and all its pieces: the guest house, the carving, the moment when everything between her and Hank had changed.

• • •

How long had Hank been standing there watching her that crisp morning? Edie would never know. She'd been so startled to see the words on the header—I LOVE EDIE WORTHINGTON—that everything else had fallen away. Tucker must have dug them into the wood in the night, in the dark, long after everyone on the crew had gone. She'd turned to find Hank standing in the doorway, his tool belt slung over his shoulder; she might have known he'd arrive first to the job site; he always did. She'd hoped for only a few precious moments to absorb the carving on her own, to try to understand why the sight of those four words filled her with such confusion.

It had been three weeks since the night of Tucker's graduation party, three weeks since his vow to end things with Florence, and there was still talk of Florence's arrival at summer's end. Had Tucker known that they were scheduled to close up the walls in the next few days? Was this as close as he would ever get to making his feelings for her known? A part of Edie had wanted to feel something so much greater than she did to see those words, but in the days that had passed between that first day on her bike and this moment, the fierce curiosity she'd once had about Tucker Moss had shifted.

Hank cleared his throat. "Strange place to put a love note, don't you think?"

"I think it's romantic," she defended, keeping her eyes fixed on the crooked letters, suddenly afraid that if she turned to face Hank she might burst into tears on the spot, and not even sure why.

"It's easy to carve something into a piece of wood, Ede."

"Then why don't you go ahead and carve Missy's name in one too, if it's so easy?" she demanded, so incensed, so overwrought that she marched to their tool supply and rummaged furiously through the buckets until she found a chisel. "Here," she said, returning with the tool and shoving it at him. "Go on then, if you think there's nothing to it. Tell the world how damn much you love Missy Murphy and just get on with it!"

She wasn't even aware she was crying until she'd felt the tears slip between her lips.

Hank reached out, took the chisel from her trembling hand, and set it down on a nearby sawhorse. Edie dragged her sleeve across her eyes.

"Do you know what you want, Edie?" he asked gently.

She sniffled. Why did he have to ask her that?

"Because I do," he said.

She looked up at him. "Missy Murphy, right?"

He shook his head. She blinked at him through her tears.

"You don't?" she asked.

"Do you want Tucker Moss? Because it's pretty obvious he wants you."

Was it? Edie wasn't so sure anymore. He'd promised to stand up to his father, and still Florence's name remained a fixture in conversation like a bird that had nested permanently in a nearby tree.

Looks like we're both going to have to fight to get what we want, doesn't it?

She closed her eyes.

"I'm so confused," she whispered, but even as the words came out, she knew they were a lie. She knew exactly what—*whom*—she wanted; she'd known it that night at the bonfire, or maybe even before that. She opened her eyes slowly. The light in the unfinished cottage was watery with dawn's blue mist, but she could see the darkening of longing in Hank's brown eyes.

Her stomach dropped.

He came beside her.

"I don't want to be with Missy, Ede. I'm not in love with her."

"Liar." She swallowed. "Every guy in Harrisport is in love with Missy."

Hank grinned. "Seems to me every guy in Harrisport is in love with *you*."

Edie would have disputed his claim had he not quieted her at that moment with a deep kiss. She reached up and threw her arms around his shoulders. He released her lips slowly.

"You listen to me, Hank Wright," she said, still clinging to his neck. "You asked me if I know what I want. You really want to know? I want to *work*. I want to be a part of this crew, dammit. A *real* part. Not just your delivery girl. I want to nail boards and put up trim and measure studs and build forms and pour foundations and sheet roofs." She stopped, needing to catch her breath; her heart was racing. "Bet you're sorry you ever asked, huh?"

He smiled down at her. "The only thing I'm sorry about is that I waited so damn long."

"Me too." She reached up and finally touched the dark waves above his forehead, coaxing a wild curl back into place.

And it was then that they saw Sonny in the doorway, a smile splitting his sunburned lips before he began to clap.

Headlights swung through the kitchen, shaking Edie from the memory; Lexi had returned.

Edie drew in a fortifying breath, moved to the door, and held it open. "Done for the night?"

"I think so," said Lexi, looking decidedly wearier than during her entrance the night before.

"Great." Edie moved to the freezer and pulled out a box. "Now you can help me figure out how to make dinner."

Lexi smiled. "Mom, it's frozen lasagna. It's not rocket science."

"You'd be surprised." Edie rinsed her hands and watched her daughter tear open the flap. "So how is it over there?"

"Good . . ." Lexi slid out the sealed dish. "I've already had my first visitor."

Edie looked over to find Lexi delivering her a pointed look; she shrugged sheepishly. "He said he needed to see you."

"Did he tell you why?"

"I didn't want to pry."

"Of course not." Lexi put the lasagna into the microwave and set the timer. Slowly she turned back to Edie, considering her mother a moment before she said, "What really happened with you and Tucker Moss?"

Edie blinked, startled at the question coming so quickly after she'd just lost herself in the memory of it. Had Cooper said something? Had *Jim?*

"You know what happened," Edie said. "It was never a secret."

But Lexi wasn't satisfied; Edie could see that at once.

"Who really carved those words into the guest house, Mom?"

"Your father. You know that story."

"He didn't, did he?" Lexi smiled, and Edie saw tears fill her daughter's eyes. "It was Tucker Moss, wasn't it?"

Edie turned away, unprepared for the rush of emotion that came with the question. The days of being back at the cottage, the hours in Jim's company, had all been building to this moment. What a fool she was, thinking she could cover that carving twice in one lifetime. It had been revealed again for a reason; she understood that now.

Who was she to blame her daughter for never letting go of her hurt when she herself had gripped so tightly to her own lie for far too long?

Edie patted the table and the two of them sat down.

Her own eyes brimming now, Edie took in a deep breath and let it out slowly.

"It all happened so fast," she explained. "It was just your father and me in the guest house when the crew arrived, and of course they saw the carving as plain as day and they just assumed your father had done it—why wouldn't they? I mean, there we were, kissing. So he went along with it. And so did I."

"Even though Daddy knew Tucker had carved it?"

Edie nodded.

"So what happened?"

"I think you know by now."

"No, I mean what happened with Tucker?"

Edie's smile fell, a wash of regret straining her features. "He'd just come back from taking his friend James to the bus station, and I saw him across the lawn later that same morning. I didn't know, but he must have heard the guys in the driveway teasing Hank, congratulating him. The way Tucker looked at me, the hurt in his face . . ." Edie's voice broke. "I wanted to reach him to explain, but he wouldn't see me. He never spoke to me again. Not once."

Lexi stared at the table. "All this time we thought he broke your heart. But you broke *his*."

"It was your father I was really in love with all that time," Edie said. "I was so confused, so terrified to let myself feel that strongly for him, that I ran to Tucker, probably because I knew in my heart that it wouldn't have worked between Tuck and me. He would never have been strong enough to stand up to his father."

Lexi studied her hand in her mother's. "Then why did you and Daddy lie to us?"

"Stories have a way of getting comfortable quickly in a small town; you know that. Especially when everyone thinks they know what happened. It was easier, I guess, for everyone to believe Tucker had wounded me. And I felt so guilty for hurting him the way I did," Edie admitted softly. "His father fired us soon after that and brought in another crew to finish the guest house. Your granddad was furious. Your father was too—I don't think he ever got over that. He blamed Tucker, but I didn't. I knew Tucker would never do anything to hurt me. He wasn't cruel, just weak." She smiled. "It was Tucker who donated the money to restore the Grange Hall."

"It was?" said Lexi. "I thought it was an anonymous donation."

Edie nodded. "It was supposed to be but someone on the board spilled the beans. I'm only sorry I never got the chance to thank him. I suppose I didn't know how. But I know it was his gift to me."

Edie squeezed Lexi's hands in hers. "We all make our choices, sweetheart. Good and bad. But you can't let Hudson keep you from trusting your heart again, or making up excuses for why you can't love someone else."

Lexi wiped her eyes. "Is that what you think I've been doing?"

"I think you fell in love with the wrong person," said Edie gently. "I think both of my children did. Now it's time to open your hearts to the *right* one."

"It can't work, Mom. There's too much the same. Too many ghosts, too much history."

"That's all it is: history. Cooper's not the same man, and you're not the same woman. Believe me, sweetheart," said Edie with a peaceful smile. "It couldn't be the same even if you wanted it to be."

It had been Lexi's idea to paint the nursery rhymes in Meg's room. While Heather had pushed for detailed renderings of English gardens for their daughter's fifth-birthday surprise, Lexi had reminded them all of Meg's fondness for the well-worn Wright family copy of *Mother Goose*. And though Heather had voiced her displeasure

("This is ridiculous—she can't even read yet"), Owen felt certain the familiar poems would provide comfort to his daughter as she grew up around them.

Now as he stood looking at the faded lines of sweeping lavender script, he felt a swift surge of regret. In the months after Heather and Meg had moved to the city, he'd made excuses to come up here, storing things in his daughter's closet that he could easily have stashed in other parts of the house, but he'd wanted reasons to visit these walls, these words. Coming into this room had kept her there. Now he saw the sad irony of his fatherly intentions. He'd hoped the words might help her to grow; all the while he'd done everything to keep her a child.

"Dad?" He turned to see Meg in the doorway. She surveyed the cans of paint he'd brought up from the garage while she'd been out at the coffee shop with friends. "What's going on?"

"I had all these leftover cans from a job. They're great colors, pretty colors. I thought you could pick, you know. Change it up in here. Get rid of the nursery rhymes—"

"I like the nursery rhymes."

He looked at her. "You do?"

"Don't you dare touch them, Dad."

He smiled. "I won't touch them."

She walked to her bed and sat down on the edge. "It's not about my room, Dad."

"I know it's not." He walked across the floor and sat down beside her, feeling the tears at the back of his throat. "I'm sorry I snooped through your phone. I had no right to do that."

"I should have told you about Ty. I wanted to, but I thought you'd—"

"Freak out?" Owen finished for her.

Meg smiled, nodded.

"It's hard, Meggie." Owen reached for her hand and squeezed it, his eyes watering. "It's like I have to lose both of you. And I'm not ready for that. Your old man's just not ready to say good-bye to you too."

"You're not losing me."

"Yeah, I am," he said, sweeping her bangs to the side of her face. "In a way, I am. But it's okay. It's supposed to work that way. It just scares the hell out of me; that's all."

"What about me?" she said, her own eyes filling. "You don't think I'm scared too?"

"What are you scared about?"

"You," she said. "I'm scared that you won't find someone else. That you'll be alone."

"You worry about that, huh?"

"Tons."

"Tell me what I can do."

"You can stop acting like I'm still a kid, like I can't handle stuff."

"I do that?" he asked.

She gave him the same impatient look she had

313

given him when he forgot to eat his salad. "It's like you don't want to talk to me about what's real. Because you think I can't handle it or something." The earnestness in her face was heartbreaking. "I can handle it, Dad."

He didn't doubt it.

He put his arm around her and drew her close. She held on to his sleeve.

"You need to start going out," she added. "Like on real dates."

He smiled. "I know you want me to."

"Don't *you* want to?"

"Sometimes, sure."

"Then why don't you?"

He shrugged, sighed.

"Trust is a hard thing to get back, kiddo. I just need time."

Meg pointed to the wall above her dresser and recited the words that ran underneath the crown molding: " 'Birds of a feather flock together, and so will pigs and swine. Rats and mice will have their choice, and so will I have mine.' "

"Yeesh." Owen grinned. "Which one am I?" he teased.

"We're the birds," said Meg. "And we flock together."

"We do, don't we?"

"No matter what."

He laid a kiss on her temple. "No matter what."

26

*I*n honor of her last morning waking up at the house, Lexi indulged her mother's frantic wish to suddenly play the Great Domestic and let Edie make her a plate of toaster waffles, which she drowned in a puddle of imitation maple syrup. It would be another warm day. Lexi told herself that was why she'd changed her clothes again after breakfast—that she'd dressed in haste before knowing the weather—but she and her mother both knew her nerves had nothing to do with climbing temperatures outside.

There was a chance Cooper wouldn't be at the Moss house. Lexi knew that. She knew too that if she called first maybe he'd make sure to be there, but a part of her was afraid that would only guarantee his absence. As tender as her mother's words had been, as heavily as Lexi had pondered them before finally slipping into sleep, she still wasn't certain her feelings for Cooper could overcome the damage Hudson had done, any more than had her feelings for any of the other men she'd hoped to get close to in the years since.

She'd been certain of so many things when she'd left the big house the day before. Now as she steered down the crooked dirt road, everything seemed to have been tossed into the air and allowed to fall to the ground in a heap—not just her feelings for Cooper, but everything she'd believed about the history between her parents and the Mosses. It shouldn't have mattered, but it did in some small way. Lexi had needed to believe her mother's heartbreak was the model of her own. But maybe that was the problem: Instead of moving on, she, Lexi, had carried her heartache like some kind of legacy, a proud tradition among Wright women. Whatever she'd done, it was time to stop. The chain of heartbreak, and the beads of anger strung on either side of it, wasn't an heirloom to be passed down. If she ever got the chance, she'd tell Cooper that too.

The driveway was empty when she pulled in, the crew not yet arrived. Cooper's Jeep was gone, as was Jim's car. Not yet ready to admit defeat, she parked and crossed the lawn for the path to the beach, telling herself there was a chance Cooper was down there, maybe taking a quick swim.

She found the old path easily, her feet moving without thinking, the trail still fixed in her memory. At the edge of the rise, she slipped off her sandals and descended the dunes, greeting the expanse of empty beach, with the lone pier to her left, for the first time in eleven years. It had always seemed so decadent to her, the contrast between the crowded town beaches she'd grown up on and the Mosses' private stretch of sand. Not that she hadn't spent time on private beaches before Hudson. Growing up a year-rounder, she and Kim, like so many local kids, always picnicked on private beaches off-season, when the mighty homes that loomed territorially above them were temporarily vacant and without threat. But it was never the same as being invited in the heat of summer. Somehow the bonfires never blazed as high or as hot in autumn or spring as they did in August; walking through the dune grass never felt as freeing.

Now Lexi scanned the beach, memories of days and nights flooding her—tidal, like everything else in a life by the water. The driftwood log where she and Hudson had rested and fooled around through so many sunsets was gone. It had been a beast of a timber; she remembered that well. A fixture for several summers, rolled up to the edge of how many bonfires? She wondered what tide—or whose hands—had finally removed it, and how long ago.

It was then that she spotted a figure way down the beach. She tented her hand above her eyes and squinted to discern the man who walked along the sand, head bent and on the phone. It wasn't Cooper; she could tell at once. She moved slowly toward the stranger, realizing within a few steps who it was. Her pulse quickened as she stared, riveted.

Despite all of Cooper's assurances, Hudson had come.

• • •

Lexi had imagined this moment a thousand times. In the years after they'd broken up, she had played out this very scene a hundred ways, perfecting it, savoring it. Now it was here.

As she neared him, she wondered how long before he would look up and see her approach. She could hear his voice over the gentle breaking of the surf, his conversation tense, his body rigid as he walked. Finally, his head snapped up and his eyes fixed on her.

She slowed her advance, wanting to gauge his reaction.

At first, she wondered whether he might not have recognized her; that was how still his expression was. Then, in the next moment, he raised a hand and waved.

By the time she reached him, he had hung up his call and slid his phone into the pocket of his pants. She offered him a cautious smile. "Hello, Hudson."

"Lexi." He stepped forward to give her a brief hug, using only one arm, as if she were a teammate, or a guest in the receiving line at his wedding. She caught the smell of sandalwood, thinking it was an unfamiliar scent. He'd switched colognes.

"I didn't know you were coming," she said.

"No one did. It was sort of a spontaneous visit."

He looked older, she thought. Softer. A stupid observation—of course he did (didn't she?)—but somehow she was deeply grateful for those lines around his eyes, the creases near his ears, the faint dusting of gray at his blond temples. His face was fuller, his gray eyes not nearly as translucent as she remembered all those times she'd stared into them, seeing stars, seeing her whole life spread out before her, a never-ending galaxy of certainty.

"I hear you went back to school. Good for you. You always were talented."

"Thanks. It was a good opportunity." It was all she needed to say; she knew he'd only been filling the impossible hollow between them. "How are *you?*"

He gave an affable shrug. "Great. Work's busy. Kids are healthy. Can't complain."

Lexi waited for him to say more, to ask her to elaborate on the details of her life in the years since they'd parted, but he didn't. Instead, he turned his gaze toward the house. "I never in a million years thought I'd be back here," he said, his voice so wistful she wondered whether he'd not meant to say it aloud, or even been aware that he had.

"Me neither," she said. "It's been hard sometimes."

His phone rang; he pulled it out. "I have to take this," he said. "Give me just a second."

This was it, Lexi thought as she watched him on the phone. The opportunity she'd craved for so long to say all the things he'd never let her say, to unload all the hurt and anger that he'd left behind. She stared at his profile, waiting for the words to come, for the outrage to rush from her throat. God knew she'd rehearsed her speech plenty of times; it should have been easy. Yet all she could feel was emptiness, and maybe even pity.

It should have saddened her, this reunion that she'd envisioned over and over, limping along when she'd always imagined it fraught with longing and remorse. But standing there in front of him, she felt little disappointment. The heat she'd felt for him, the ache that had never seemed to subside, was gone. Maybe not gone, but nearly so. An ember. Like those faint coals at the end of a bonfire, slowly cooling, no longer hot enough to burn.

Cooper was right. Her mother and Kim were right. She had been waiting for eleven years for Hudson to close the door of his unexpected departure out of her life, her heart. She'd felt abandoned yet it had been her choice to leave that door open, waiting for something to close it. Some*one*.

What had she been doing all these years?

"Sorry about that." He returned his phone to his pocket. "What were you sayin'?"

She smiled, a sense of peace washing over her, the edges of her anger suddenly as smooth as shards of well-worn sea glass.

"I don't remember," she said.

"Oh." He gave her a curious look, as if he were considering their history for the first time, but then his features relaxed, whatever thought he might have had blown off his face like dust. For years, Lexi had believed him to be a man capable of great independence and spirit, someone bold enough to be his own person yet unafraid to be tender. It was clear to her now; she hadn't really known him at all.

Her mother's observation returned, its truth confirmed: Cooper may have inherited his father's looks and warmth, but Hudson had inherited Tucker's lack of personal strength.

"If you're looking for Coop, he's in town with our uncle Jim talking to a Realtor."

Lexi nodded, the knot of disappointment that she'd felt at first hearing the news of the cottage's sale now faded.

"Then it's going on the market soon?" she asked.

"I wouldn't be surprised if there's a sign up there by tomorrow," Hudson said. "It's time."

"Yes, it is," she said, already moving away from him.

"It's good to see you, Lexi. You want me to leave a message for Coop?"

She considered his offer as she began to walk up the beach.

"Tell him he was right," she said with a smile. Then she turned toward the dunes, and the house that climbed out of the grass, pale as a ghost.

27

The pastry box sat on the Civic's passenger seat, filling the car with the sticky-sweet smell of toffee.

There was no family battle—no harsh words, no broken promises—that wouldn't be forgiven with a dozen of Roy's pecan toffee rolls. In the Wright house, the pale pink box with the telltale blooms of butter stains on its sides was always a cause for celebration, and a common sight on the breakfast table every Sunday morning, well earned after a half-hour wait in shoulder-to-shoulder crowds at the Bread Basket. Years later, Lexi still felt the same relief in reaching across the counter to take the box, to feel that sugary weight land in her hands. It was a timeless signal of family. She'd been wrong to think nothing had changed in her hometown in the two years she'd been gone. It seemed in just the weeks since she'd returned from London, everything was different.

She pulled behind Owen's truck in the cape's driveway and climbed out, carefully balancing the warm box in her hands. She could already see him in the yard, pushing the lawn mower in shorts and a ratty sports jersey that she was certain he'd had since high school.

He looked tired, not surprisingly. The past few

days had worn them all out, each in different ways. She drew close, her heart aching with love for him. She'd heard the news from her mother, who'd learned it from Meg. As much as she'd prayed Heather would never come back to Owen, Lexi knew it was that singular hope that gave her brother purpose in the years since his divorce. Now that hope was gone.

When she slipped into his field of vision, Owen killed the mower's engine. He saw the box in her hands and grinned. "The ol' pecan toffee truce, huh?"

She smiled. "My favorite kind."

Inside the house, he made them coffee while she pulled a pair of plates from the dish drainer and set their places on the deck, noticing the remnants of Heather still in plain view: garden sculptures and painted clay pots. Maybe now her brother would begin to purge his home of his marriage in earnest. She hoped he would. But then, didn't she have some cleaning out of her own to do?

"Is Meggie here?" Lexi asked as they sat down.

"She's at the beach with one of the girls from Scoop's. They wanted to get an early start."

Owen popped open the box top, releasing the buttery scent of warm dough. Lexi reached in and dragged her index finger through a thread of toffee. She waited until they'd each served themselves a gooey knot before she confessed tenderly, "Mom told me about Heather and

George. Why didn't you say something at dinner?"

Owen shrugged. "I didn't want to upset Meg."

"You upset her more when you keep things from her, Owe. She's not a kid."

"I know," he said with a sigh. "Believe me, I know."

Lexi watched her brother as he unrolled a strip of pecan-laden dough and folded it into his mouth, reminded of how loudly he used to chew his food when they were little, how it drove her nuts at the table, and how she'd always insist that he was doing it on purpose to get under her skin. Her eyes watered.

She reached over and hugged him without warning. Even with a mouthful of food, Owen accepted her embrace, patting her head protectively the way he always did, no matter how old she was.

Lexi sat back, seeing his eyes reveal a shimmer of tears. "Love wasn't supposed to be this hard, was it?" she asked.

"Maybe that's the problem," Owen said, sniffing. "Maybe we thought it was supposed to be easy."

"Mom and Dad made it seem easy."

"Not always. We forget. There were hard times for them too."

She wiped her eyes with a napkin. "Mom thinks you and I can't let go of the past."

Owen shrugged. What could he say? Lexi knew

the accusation was true. Now, what were they going to do about it?

Owen smiled at her, his eyes, for days so harsh, now soft again. "I'm glad you're home."

She smiled too, dropping her cheek against his shoulder. "So am I."

Edie stared at the sea of produce in front of her, trying to muster up something close to enthusiasm. She'd promised Lexi that she'd do better about cooking for herself now that she was living alone again. ("And I mean real food, Mom. Nothing boxed. Nothing frozen. Real food.")

"Real food," Edie muttered to herself, picking up a green pepper and turning it as if it were a grenade without its pin. Oh, hell, she'd start on real food tomorrow, she decided, setting the bell pepper back with the basket of red peppers and pushing her cart farther down the vegetable display.

"I saw that, young lady."

She spun, startled.

"James!"

He arrived with his own cart, giving her a playfully scolding look as he plucked up the green pepper and returned it to its proper basket.

"I think those are my little rebellions, honestly," she confessed, low. "It's utterly reprehensible of me, I know, because the people who work here are my dear friends, but I swear I can't help myself. It's what comes from living with a man who had a twelve-step process for cleaning a damn trim brush. You should see my house," she said, raising her chin proudly. "It's a *shrine* to disorder."

Jim laughed, the sound calming her at once. He had that lovely effect on a person; she was growing to see that.

"Well, I suppose that explains why you're not an easy woman to find, then," he said.

"You were looking for me? How in the world did you find me here?"

"I did what any sensible man would do: I drove in random circles through town for over an hour until I saw your truck."

She gave him the very same disparaging look she'd worn that night on the balcony when he'd nearly fallen to his death. "You could have tried the phone, you know. It uses far less gas."

"True. But I wanted to speak with you face-to-face. I have news. Well—" He stopped, started again. "I should say I *may* have news."

Edie frowned. "Florence is firing us, isn't she?"

"Not exactly," said Jim. "She *has* sent Hudson up to tighten the screws, though. I've just been with Cooper to see our Realtor."

Dread skittered down her spine. "Hudson's *here?*"

"I'm afraid he and Florence want us to cease

work on the guest house and just throw up the For Sale sign. As is."

Edie bit at her lip, wrestling with competing worries: on one hand, what this all meant for her crew; on the other hand, a concern for Lexi, knowing Hudson had come back to the cottage. Unable to manage the weight of either one and feeling tears of frustration and disappointment well, she left her cart and marched for the door, not thinking of anything but getting out into the open air.

"Edie, wait."

Jim followed her outside. She slowed her pace, feeling foolish now as she stood in the path of customers entering and exiting the store. She scooted out of the way to an empty bench beside the cart station and plopped down.

Jim joined her. "You'll be paid for the full cost of the job," he assured her. "I'll make sure of it."

Edie shook her head. "It's not just the money, James—I mean, it *is* the money," she corrected herself quickly before adding, "but it's the work, too. The women want to work. The same way I did." She smiled up at him, leaking tears. "I know that fever better than anyone."

"I know you do, Edie. And I promise you Cooper and I are still working on Florence."

She rolled her eyes, then wiped them impatiently with her fingers.

Jim paused to draw in a fortifying breath. "I told Cooper, Edie."

She sniffled. "Told him what?"

"About that summer. About what really happened."

"Oh." She looked out at the parking lot for a long moment, then looked back at him. "Oh," she said again.

Jim searched her face in the silence that followed; Edie could see the trepidation in his eyes. Surely he worried that she'd be angry or hurt. Somehow seeing the carving again—having everyone else see it too—had freed her. What did it matter who knew what had happened that summer? She'd confessed to Lexi; soon she'd confess to Owen.

She smiled, seeing relief fix on Jim's face immediately.

"I thought you'd be furious with me," he said.

"No. I'm glad you told him, James. He should know what kind of man his father was. What kind of man he *tried* to be. You were the only person who knew Tucker the way I knew him." She sighed. "I never meant to hurt him, James. I didn't know what I wanted. We were all so young."

A couple with an infant arrived and took a cart. Jim and Edie regarded them as they passed.

"Do you ever wonder what it could have been like if things had been different?" he asked.

Edie shook her head firmly. "Never," she said. "We all did well, James."

"And we're not done yet, you know," he said with a wink. "Why do you think I spilled the beans about Florence that night at the party?"

Edie snorted. "Because you were drunk."

"I wasn't *that* drunk." Jim laughed. "Maybe I did it because I wanted you for myself."

"James." She set her hand on his knee; he closed one of his own over it, the warmth of his palm settling her again. He'd go back to Charleston soon, and it startled her to think how hard it would be to say good-bye to him. She'd grown attached to his company. Forty-six years later, they had so much more to talk about than they ever did those salty summer nights on rooftops under the stars. She'd miss him.

As if reading her thoughts, he said, "Come to Charleston, Edie. Say you'll come see me."

"And just how am I supposed to do that?"

"It's called a plane. They fly them quite often between here and there, I'm told."

She smiled, feeling a foolish flush creep up her cheeks. "What am I going to do in Charleston?"

"Same thing you do here. Eat, sleep. Look criminally radiant."

"Oh, God." She groaned. "You're *still* a terrible flirt; you know that?"

"Sad, isn't it? You'd think I'd have improved somewhat in all these years."

"Did you tell Cooper that part too?"

"Young lady, I'm afraid I told Cooper everything. Well . . ." He paused to clear his throat. "*Almost* everything. But then, it's something I've been keeping to myself for nearly fifty years, so I figured why quit now?"

It was the edge of tenderness that made Edie look up at him, the confessional tone to his voice that made her search his eyes expectantly.

"Tuck didn't carve that in the guest house, Edie." Jim smiled. "I did."

She stared at him.

"I sneaked in the night before I left the Cape," he explained. "No one saw me do it."

Edie blinked at his hand covering hers, trying to regroup the puzzle pieces that he had just exploded. No wonder Tucker had never approached her to argue Hank's claim. He had assumed Hank had carved it, like she and Hank had assumed it was Tucker, when it was really—

"James?" she whispered. "Oh, *James.*"

He took her hand, sandwiching it gently between both of his and stroking her knuckles with his thumb. "I never imagined in a million years that I'd be in front of you admitting it. But then, I suppose it has been close to a million years, hasn't it?"

"You should have said something."

"I just did."

"*Then.*"

"What would have been the point?" he asked gently. "I was on the bottom shelf of a *very* tall bookcase of suitors, Edie. I knew better than to throw my hat into that crowded ring."

"But still you carved it."

"And I had the blisters the whole way home to prove it."

She gently turned his hand in hers, searching the deep grooves of his palms, as if those blisters might still be there years later. She ran her fingers tenderly over the places they had surely been, as if to soothe their memory.

Her eyes pooled with tears. Jim took her hand to his cheek and pressed it there.

"I don't know what to say," she whispered.

He smiled. "Say you'll come visit me, Edie."

"I'll come visit you, Edie." She stroked his brow.

"Cooper wants to write the story of that summer. He wants to write it as his next novel. But he doesn't want anyone to be hurt."

"He *should* write it," she said firmly, and without hesitation. "Our story. Tuck's and mine and yours and Hank's. It's a beautiful story."

His eyes narrowed. "You're sure?"

"Positive," said Edie. "And you can tell him I said so."

"I think he'd rather hear it from you."

"Then he will," she said, rising purposefully to her feet. "I'll go tell him this instant."

Jim chuckled, still holding her hand.

She stared down at him, confused. "What?"

"Oh, nothing. Just that you might want to rescue your groceries first."

Part
Three

28

Lexi made a knot of her hair, set it snugly with a clip, and stepped out of the car into the damp morning air. The great house was quiet, just as she'd expected. It had been more than a week since the For Sale sign had arrived at the end of Birch Drive, a few less days since she'd learned that Jim and Hudson and Cooper had returned to their Southern homes, leaving the property empty and awaiting a new owner.

In all the confusion, Lexi had neglected to get the last of her photos. Today she would complete her shot list and compile the images to send to the historian in Raleigh.

She unpacked her camera bag and tripod from the trunk and carried them down the grass toward the small cottage on the edge of the lawn. The scaffolding had been taken down, and the grass around the foundation cleaned of loose sanding pads and dropped nails, but the blue tarp still remained over the roof, at her mother's urging. Lexi turned the knob and felt the door resist a moment before it gave way to reveal the interior of the guest house.

With a deep breath, she stepped inside.

What a shame, she thought as she wandered through the space, seeing the half-finished repairs everywhere as she drew down the boards her mother's crew had put up to protect the windows. They had made such progress, and now all their work might be for nothing. Lexi knew there was a good chance whoever bought the property wouldn't bother to finish what they had started. "Teardown" was the term used, a term she hated when it was so often code for developers who wanted an excuse to demolish instead of repair, to build new instead of restore old.

She reached out and touched a patch of fresh drywall, its seams not yet taped and floated, and ran her fingers lovingly over the smooth wallboard, imagining the old timbers beneath it, timbers her parents had helped cut and carry and finish.

This was her way of preservation, she thought as she snapped the cover off the lens of her Hasselblad and centered her first shot. *Your history will never be forgotten now.*

"I'm really going to miss this place."

Startled, she lowered her camera. Cooper stood in the doorway.

"Cooper." She swallowed. "I thought you left. I thought everyone left."

He came into the room. "We did. Jim and Hud drove back together a few days ago," he said, "and I moved into a place in Wellfleet."

Wellfleet? Excitement coursed through her. "You're staying on the Cape?" she asked.

"I thought I would. I got someone to sublet my apartment for another month, so there's no rush for me to get back to Raleigh. Especially since you aren't finished with your work here yet."

"It's the one place I hadn't photographed," she said, motioning to the interior. "Seems fitting I should leave it for last, I suppose." She looked at Cooper, sure he would make the connection, but his expression remained doubtful. "It was the last place I was that night too."

"If you don't mind, I'd rather not talk about that night anymore," he said.

Lexi nodded, regret washing over her. She'd accused him of trying to match Hudson's gift, of using the past to reach her, when she'd been the one to keep them bound to Hudson's memory, not Cooper. She was the one always making comparisons between the two brothers, the one who refused to detach herself from the ghosts of this house, this property. It was Cooper who'd tried to push them forward, to build something outside of the past. The roadblocks keeping her and Cooper apart had been of her own construction.

Now maybe she had a chance to fix it. Could she?

Would he let her try?

"I'm sorry about your darkroom," Cooper said. "All the equipment's still up there. The Realtor insisted we move it, so I packed it all up in one of the closets. I hope you'll take everything."

"I'll have to," she said, holding up her camera with a small smile, "if I ever want to see these shots."

"How's the new house?" he asked.

"It's getting there."

"Your mom said you have a few more jobs lined up. A lighthouse—and something else in Brewster, was it?"

"The Nickerson mansion," Lexi said, giving him a quizzical look. "You went to see my mother?"

"She came to see me, actually." Cooper met Lexi's expectant gaze. "She wants me to finish the story. She wants me to publish it."

"She does?"

He nodded. "What about you?"

"It's not up to me."

"It's your story too," he said.

Was it? She wasn't sure anymore. Maybe it was; maybe it wasn't. Or maybe that was all it was: a story in the past. It was the stories of the future that moved her now.

"I thought you didn't like to change your work space in the middle of a book," she said.

Cooper shrugged, circling a stack of boxed tiles. "I thought a new setting might do me some good," he said, catching her gaze and holding it. "Might do a lot of things some good."

She lowered her eyes to her camera. "I saw Hudson," she said.

"He told me."

"Did he also tell you what I said about you being right?"

Cooper came toward her, near enough that Lexi could smell the warmth of his skin, the piney scent that brought back memories of him in bed, above her, inside her, with startling speed.

"I don't want to lose this," she said. "I don't want to lose *you*."

"Then don't." Cooper took the camera from her hands and set it down on the tiles. He searched her face. "I'm not saying it won't be complicated. All I know is that my father and my brother were too weak to fight for what they wanted. . . ." He lifted his hand to the silver teardrop of her earring and rolled it suggestively between his index finger and thumb. "I'm not."

Lexi closed her eyes, exhaling as his knuckles drifted down her throat.

"This must be the part where you say we have to start writing the story to find out how far it will go, isn't it?" she whispered.

"No," Cooper said, reaching back to close the guest house door. "This is the part where we don't have to say anything at all."

Acknowledgments

With this book, my third, I understand more than ever how much of a collaborative effort publishing a novel truly is—and I am so fortunate to have the talents and kindness of so many people to partner with on this journey. My wonderful editor at New American Library, Danielle Perez, who always sees the best route on my characters' maps even when I feel lost on the road; thanks as well to Heidi Richter, Jessica Butler, Kayleigh Clark, Christina Brower, and Tiffany Yates Martin. To Fletcher and Company, and my phenomenal agent, Rebecca Gradinger, whose guidance remains a gift to me, and to Sylvie Greenberg for all of her help. My thanks to dear friend, gifted photographer and Cape resident, Roe Osborn, for answering all of my photography questions as well as giving me wonderful insight into Cape life. Any errors describing either subject are entirely my own.

To James Schroeder and his beautiful family, who brought me to the Vineyard and his aunt's "cottage" that summer—and inadvertently brought me to this novel. Thank you, Jimmy.

To talented authors and treasured friends, Marybeth Whalen and Kim Wright, who invited me to be a part of their writing circle when I first moved to North Carolina. Here's to sharing many more Eureka moments together, ladies—in writing and in life.

To the readers who have given their precious time to my books and buoyed me with their kind words. It means the world. I can't wait to share more stories with you.

To Ian, Evie and Murray, who are my everything, and who write the story of my heart every minute of every day. Who would have thought a writer could say there aren't words to express how much I love you?

The Architecture of Love: Writing *The Guest House*

After my freshman year at Hampshire College in my native New England, I had the chance to spend my summer at a classic shingle-style "cottage" on Martha's Vineyard. It was old and rambling, yet still steeped in a rustic elegance, and I was smitten with the home from the first moment I came down the driveway and saw it rise up behind a wall of pines. With its shingled mountain range of gables and dormers, it was everything I had imagined a traditional cottage of that era to be. It had been in my friend's family for generations, though it had seen fewer and fewer summer guests in the past few years. And although my time there was far from languishing (I worked six days a week at the town bakery), the romance of the house's past was never lost on me. I loved to walk its halls and imagine the socializing that had gone on there in its heyday, the various dramas that had played out in its many rooms or in even more secretive spots outdoors. And it was that summer—and subsequent visits to Cape Cod in the years after—that inspired me to write *The Guest House*.

As in my first novel, *Little Gale Gumbo*, and even in my second, *The Mermaid Collector*, I am constantly fascinated by the things that unite us as people, no matter our cultural differences. For the characters in *The Guest House*, the differences are immediately apparent. One family is local; the other family is from away ("wash-ashores"). One family is Northerners; the other is Southerners. And yet, for all of their differences, the cottage enchants them equally. They walk its halls, its lawn, marvel at its rooms and its scale, savor its beaches and expansive piazza—all of them drawn by the magic of its decadent setting.

Yet even though its decor and design are decidedly modest in comparison to the more ostentatious summer cottages elsewhere on the coast (e.g., the Breakers in Newport, Rhode Island), the house still manages to reinforce the class distinctions among its visitors. Several times in the novel, even when the main house is virtually empty, Lexi Wright can't help but be reminded of the struggle she felt to be truly included in the Mosses' social sphere. Just standing at the top of the stairs at the juncture of the servants' wing and the family wing reminds her of the times Hudson Moss might have led her physically (and symbolically) into his world, but chose to steer her away from his family's space and to the rooms of the servants' side instead. Even though the rooms are no longer used to house a summer staff, their function remains clear.

The Moss guest house is an extension of that simultaneous unification and division of the two families' social standing—albeit on a smaller scale. Like the main house, the guest house is built to host visitors, yet nearly all of the story's main characters face a defining moment in the smaller cottage—and it is, of course, the guest house that brings everyone back together again in the present story, as Jim points out to Edie.

I also wanted to use the house to explore how we process moving forward in our lives. At the novel's end, it is clear that the cottage (and the guest house) will be put up for sale, and doing so will finally cut the ties that have joined the two families for several generations. While it is a sad possibility, it will bring about an opportunity for everyone to move on from the tumultuous past they experienced on the property, signaling a chance for change—most specifically for budding lovers Lexi and Cooper to start fresh and give their attraction the new beginning they need to see whether—as Cooper says about writing—"it's going to go the distance."

Like the main house in *The Guest House*, the shingle-style "cottage" of my summer memory was eventually sold and torn down to make room for new construction, and the news of its demise—though many years after my time there—crushed me. I can only imagine how the family who'd grown up there felt, men and women whose hopes and dreams, loves and losses may have lingered in the walls like fireplace smoke, or clung to the sheets of unmade beds like the scent of sea air, full of secrets, and the promise of summers to come.

Questions for Discussion

1. For both families, the Mosses and the Wrights, the cottage holds many memories and great personal significance. In your life, has there been a place—be it one you visited only occasionally or maybe one you lived in year-round—that you remain deeply connected to? Does it still exist? If so, do you revisit it? Do you get the same sort of feelings there that you did years ago?

2. Even though she is reeling from Hudson's breakup, Lexi finds herself drawn to Cooper in the hours after she and Hudson part, and the memory of their time together that night lingers in her mind, even though she remains conflicted about her feelings for Cooper. It is only when she and Cooper meet again eleven years later that Lexi has the opportunity to better understand her feelings of attraction, even if she is hesitant to act on them. Have you ever felt yourself drawn to someone at a time of emotional strain and struggled to understand whether your feelings were real or just the result of a vulnerable moment?

3. When Lexi finds Cooper's manuscript, she accuses him of using her and insists his actions are

reason enough for why they can't further their romantic relationship. As a result, Cooper tells Lexi that she is only using the manuscript as an excuse to stop their romance because she still has unresolved anger toward Hudson and is afraid of being hurt again. Do you think Lexi is right to make such a big deal about Cooper's writing, or do you think Cooper has a point in his assessment of Lexi's behavior? Have you known people who put up barriers to love?

4. The summer of 1966, when the guest house is being built, is a pivotal one for many of the characters in the novel. For Edie, she is developing feelings for Tucker while trying to understand her changing feelings for Hank. For Tucker, falling in love with Edie is the chance he has always wanted to break away from family responsibility and expectation. For Hank, the introduction of Tucker into Edie's life has him feeling threatened and forces him to reevaluate the leanings of his own heart. Did you identify with any particular character's evolution and personal conflicts during that time? If so, which one, and why?

5. Owen is struggling to come to terms with his divorce and can't fathom that his daughter, Meg, might not be the same little girl who grew up in the house he now inhabits alone. Do you think

Meg shares his struggle, or do you think she has a clear understanding of her own changes? By the novel's end, do you believe that Owen will finally move forward and accept the changes in his world?

6. There's no question Lexi could have found a strong photography program closer to the Cape, but she chose to leave the country for two years. Do you think those closest to her—her mom, her brother, her best friend, Kim—think she picked the Royal Academy because she was running away? What do you think she hoped to gain by leaving for a fixed period of time? Even though many years had passed since her breakup with Hudson, do you think she was still looking to hide from her heartache by going away?

7. At eighteen, Edie has two men vying for her affections, but by the end of the summer it becomes clear in her mind and heart which man she belongs with. Did you agree with her decision, or did you wish to see her with the other man?

8. The novel features many parent/child relationships. Which of the relationships did you most identify with? If you are a parent, did you see yourself in one of the parents? As a child, do you see yourself in one of the daughters or sons? Why?

9. The title of the novel suggests the smaller building that initially brings the Wrights into the Moss world—but one could argue that the main house is also a guest house in that it hosts visitors too as the summer residence of the wash-ashore Moss family. Which structure do you think the title refers to? Who do you think are the "guests" in the novel, and why?

10. One of the novel's main themes is letting go of the past. By the story's end, do you believe the characters will manage to do that in order to move on? Which characters do you think will be most successful and embrace their chances at new love and starting over? Which ones do you fear will struggle to succeed, and why?

A native New Englander who was raised in Maine, **Erika Marks** has worked as an illustrator, an art director, a cake decorator, and a carpenter. She currently lives in Charlotte, North Carolina, with her husband and their two daughters. This is her third novel.

Center Point Large Print
600 Brooks Road / PO Box 1
Thorndike ME 04986-0001 USA

(207) 568-3717

US & Canada:
1 800 929-9108
www.centerpointlargeprint.com